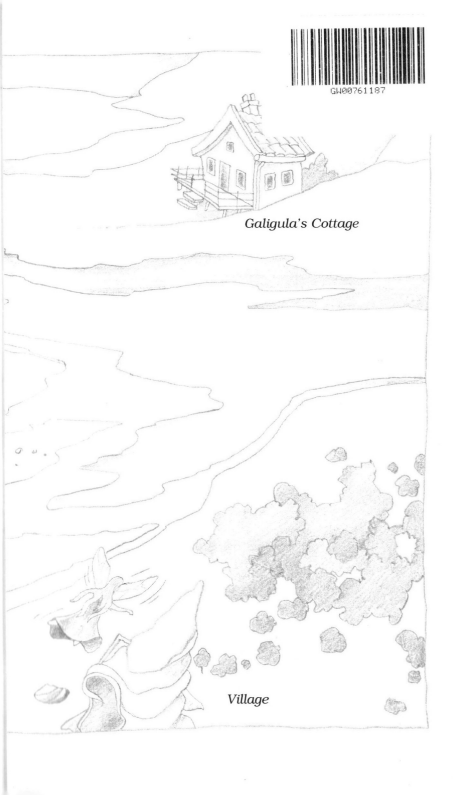

Galigula's Cottage

Village

Brave Hunter
and the Witches

By the same author:

Brave Hunter and the Giants
Brave Hunter and the Dragons
Brave Hunter and the Sea Snakes
Brave Hunter and the Pirates

For more information please visit our website on:

www.Brave-Hunter.co.uk

www.Brave-Hunter.com

Brave Hunter and the Witches

José Hofstede

Illustrations by
Ton Derks

First print 2006

ISBN-10: 90-78346-01-9

ISBN-13: 978-90-78346-01-2

Contents

THE LETTER

Brave Hunter was sitting on a wooden bench on the veranda in front of his log cabin, smoking his pipe. He was a big hairy man with large hands and feet. His muscles were as solid as coconuts and his blond curly hair bounced in all directions. His clear blue eyes seemed to look right through you, as if he knew all your secrets. Brave Hunter was a relaxed and friendly man who was always willing to help people. He got his name from being so courageous and fearless. Nothing fazed him; he would wrestle with bears, defeat crocodiles and even take on dangerous villains.

Brave Hunter wasn't just extremely strong but also tremendously smart! He could conquer danger with both brain and brawn. His cabin was situated on top of the hill on the out-skirts of the village of Oak-trunk. His garden always smelt delightful because of the various fruit trees and bushes, which grew there.

Brave Hunter was enjoying watching two birds arguing over a blackberry when he heard someone shouting:

"Brave Hunter, Brave Hunter, I have a letter for you!" It was Neston, the fourteen year old son of the village blacksmith. He was a cheerful boy with brown curly hair and brown eyes that twinkled like little stars. Neston always knew everybody's business so when the postman arrived with a letter for Brave Hunter, Neston was very quick to find him. He knew that, wherever Brave Hunter was, adventure was not far away!

Neston ran towards the bench where Brave Hunter was sitting.

"The letter looks very important", he shouted, gasping for breath. "It has just arrived with the postman from down south. I ran straight up the hill, Brave Hunter, to bring it to you", Neston panted. He handed the letter to Brave Hunter who looked at it very closely. Brave Hunter gave the letter back to Neston.

"Please read it to me Neston", he said in a friendly manner. Neston studied the letter. There were strange stamps on it, so the letter must have come from far away! Neston loved adventures and was desperate to see more of the world. This letter smelt of adventure. What would it reveal...?

"Come on, what are you waiting for? Open up the letter and read it to me", said Brave Hunter impatiently while taking a puff of his pipe. "Ok, ok", replied Neston, who, with trembling hands, opened the letter and began reading.

Corsica, 5 May 1825

Dear Brave Hunter,

Here is a letter from your old uncle in Corsica. We are all in good health, although your aunt is suffering with rheumatism but I suppose that's just part of old age.

At the moment we are living in the mountains and not at our farm on the coast because we have been attacked several times by pirates. We had to escape; we are much safer here as it is much harder to find our hideout.

Our men from the village have been trying to catch the pirates but they have not been successful at all. The pirates keep coming back so we are still stuck in these mountains.

We would so much like to go back to our houses near the coast. As you know, in five months the winter will start and then it will be far too cold to be in the mountains. We are completely desperate and that is why I have decided to contact you.

Brave Hunter, please help us to rid our island of these pirates. You are our last hope! When you arrive on the island, please let us know, using the secret family smoke sign. That way

one of our men can pick you up and bring you to
our secret hideaway.
Kindest regards,
Your Uncle Antonio.

"Pirates?", whispered Neston, looking at Brave Hunter wide-eyed. "Fighting against pirates?", he sighed. His eyes were sparkling with excitement at the thought of fighting pirates. He was imagining himself swinging his sword around and chasing the defeated pirates into the sea.

Brave Hunter put his pipe down and took the letter from Neston's hands. He had a worried look on his face. His uncle and aunt in Corsica were his favourite relatives. He began to fear for their safety; being out there in the mountains was not good for them at all. Who was to harvest their corn and wheat? And aunty with her rheumatism, she would be so much better off in her comfortable cosy cottage at the coast. Besides, what would the pirates do when they discovered their hideaway in the mountains? No, he had to go there as soon as possible and catch those pirates!

"Neston, go back to the village and ask Annie from the inn to prepare a large basket with food", ordered Brave Hunter.
"I will go right away Brave Hunter!", replied

Neston as he jumped up from the rock he was sitting on.

He then hesitated for a moment and turned around,

"Brave Hunter, can't I come along with you to fight against these pirates? I really am very strong and a very good fighter", said Neston enthusiastically, displaying his muscles. Brave Hunter shook his head.

"You are far too young to fight. Pirates are very bloodthirsty. If they are in a bad mood they cut off your hands just like that", he made a gesture as if cutting off Neston's hands. "They drink a lot of rum and they smell like the rats in the stables. You have to believe me; really you don't want to fight them! Now, off you go to Annie and ask her to prepare a large food basket." Brave Hunter waved his hands for Neston to go and then walked into his cabin. He wanted to pack his belongings as he had an early start in the morning.

Neston walked down the hill pondering:
"There has to be a way to join Brave Hunter. I am not in the least bit afraid of pirates!" He smiled and hopped down the hill singing a song to himself about pirates and rum.

ALICE THE LITTLE FAIRY

Brave Hunter was walking along the track, humming a song and kicking away some little stones. The two horses, which he'd taken along, were fully packed. He had left the cottage at sunrise and had already been walking for four hours.

"Time for a cup of tea and some of those delicious biscuits Annie has put in the bag", he thought to himself.

He noticed a nice flat spot near a brook so he tied the horses to the trunk of a tree and took out a blanket, the flask of tea and chocolate chip biscuits from his travel bag. He felt very content in the sun, nibbling on his biscuit.

"Hmm, hmm, Annie's biscuits really are the best in the whole wide world", he mumbled as he took a delicious bite of the biscuit.

"I sure do agree with you on that one!" He heard a voice behind him.

"Who is there?", Brave Hunter asked as he turned around.

"It is me!" Neston jumped out of the bushes where he had been hiding.

"What on earth are you doing here? You should be at home with your mother!", shouted Brave Hunter in both surprise and outrage.

"I have been following you because I want to

fight the pirates", said Neston, trying to grab a biscuit.

"You are not going to have a biscuit." Brave Hunter snatched the bag away.

"You are going straight back. And you make sure that you are home before dark." Neston looked at Brave Hunter with huge eyes:

"But I don't want to go home. Please, why can't I come with you?" Brave Hunter shook his head.

"That is out of the question, you should never have followed me. It is far too dangerous! Besides, I have enough things to worry about without having to watch over you."

Brave Hunter frowned as he looked at Neston. Neston bowed his head and nodded.

"Well, if you put it that way, I will go back but...........can't I have a biscuit and a slurp of tea before I go back?" Brave Hunter smiled and said:

"Of course, come and sit here with me on the blanket." He pointed at the blanket. "And here you are, have a cup." Brave Hunter poured the delicious steaming tea into the large cup and gave Neston one of Annie's biscuits.

Neston was just about to take a big bite of the biscuit when he heard a very tiny voice:

"Help me, please, help me!" Neston looked around but couldn't see anybody.

"Did you hear that, Brave Hunter?", asked Neston. Brave Hunter nodded.

"Yes, but I can't see anybody. It sounds as if it is coming from the other side of the brook."

Brave Hunter was looking over at the meadow on the other side of the brook.

"Please help me; I am over here near the large rocks in the water." They both turned their heads towards the rocks in the water and couldn't believe what they saw.

Above the rocks a little fairy was hanging on to the branch of a tree. Her wings were caught up in the branches of the tree. She was a very beautiful little fairy in a long blue dress with long curly brown hair and big brown eyes with long black lashes. A small case made of mother-of-pearl was hanging around her neck on a fine gold necklace and there were little golden shoes on her tiny feet.

"Please stop staring at me and help me get my wings out of these branches before they break." Although she was speaking, her little voice sounded sweeter than any song. Brave Hunter and Neston rushed over to the rocks and freed the little fairy from the branches. When they had put her safely on the grass she said:

"My name is Alice and I am on my way to

Brave Hunter to ask him for help." Brave Hunter looked surprised and exclaimed:

"I am Brave Hunter!" Alice jumped into the air in surprise.

"Oh, I am so glad that I have found you", she said. Her wings were fluttering with excitement. They sounded like hundreds of tiny bells as they whisked through the air. She then put on a serious face.

"I have such a terrible thing to tell you Brave Hunter! I am from Jingleland, it lies over there behind the hill." Alice was pointing towards the mountains to the right of the path.

"It is a very beautiful and peaceful country. It has all kinds of multi-coloured butterflies and so many colourful birds and lovely scented flowers! We fairies lived so happily and peacefully in Jingleland. It was so remote that nobody could find our paradise."

Alice shook her brown curls and sighed deeply.

"Until the witch Caligula found our Jingleland hideaway. Ever since, fairies have been disappearing. The witch catches the fairies and puts them in a glass jar." Alice shivered at the thought.

"And at night when there is a full moon, she puts the jars outside in a circle. She sits in the middle of the circle with her legs crossed and chants all kinds of spells. Apparently, she believes that this will give her greater magic powers. Then, when she has finished her chants, she starts to dance around the jars and sings a song about evil witches capturing fairies, who will be made into soup."

Alice's wings fluttered up and down with anger.

"The fairies in the jars are terrified, Brave Hunter! They don't laugh or sing anymore. Some of them have lost all their hair from worry. We are at our wits' end. We have tried everything to capture the witch and free our fairies, but every time a group of our bravest fairies set off to beat the wicked witch, they fail to come back. They too end up in a glass jar. We have no idea how to chase the mean witch away and free our fairies. That is why our fairy king has assigned me to ask you, Brave Hunter, to catch the wicked witch and free our fairies from those horrible glass jars."

Alice looked at Brave Hunter with huge eyes. He frowned and shook his head.

"This witch Caligula is really mean and she has to be stopped. But I am on my way to Corsica to help my uncle and aunt. They too desperately need my help." Alice flapped her wings and said in a high-pitched voice:

"But if you go via Jingleland, you will cut out a huge part of the journey, so you will get to

Corsica far quicker. Oh, please Brave Hunter, you have got to help us!"

Brave Hunter nodded.

"Ok, show me where Jingleland is, so I can talk to your king and queen. I am sure that together we can come up with a plan to get rid of this witch, once and for all." Brave Hunter clenched his fingers into a fist, to emphasize his words.

"Oh, I am so glad that you want to help us", said Alice with a smile as her wings fluttered in the wind and her bells rang softly.

"Please, follow me. I will fly ahead of you."

Alice flew off in the direction of the mountains.

"Come on Neston, get the horses, we are going to Jingleland with Alice." Brave Hunter gestured to Neston who quickly walked over to the horses.

"Wow, this trip becomes more and more exciting by the minute!", Neston mused.

"And in all the excitement, Brave Hunter has forgotten all about sending me home!", Neston chuckled to himself as he led the horses towards the mountains.

JINGLELAND

After walking for almost two hours, they reached the top of the mountain. Alice was standing in front of them, just as they reached the summit.

"First I have to sprinkle you with Jingleland powder, to make you the same size as the fairies. Otherwise you can't even see Jingleland!"

She took the case of mother-of-pearls from her neck and unscrewed the lid. She took a little of the magic powder out of the case and put it in the palm of her hand. She then flew towards Brave Hunter and blew the powder in his hair. Immediately Brave Hunter started to shrink.

"You're getting bigger and bigger Alice!", Brave Hunter looked around with surprise.

"Neston, you seem like a giant!"

"But not for long", said Alice, as she blew a bit of the magic powder in Neston's hair. The horses were then treated with the magic powder.

"You are a bit bigger than us fairies, but small enough to enter Jingleland." Alice gestured to them to walk to the very top of the mountain. Open mouthed, Brave Hunter and

Neston stared at the valley below them. The view from the mountaintop was magnificent. It was the loveliest valley they had ever seen. It was a lush green valley with little rippling streams and waterfalls. The whole field was covered with a variety of flowers in so many different colours and the air was filled with their scent. There were many colourful butterflies, fluttering from flower to flower. Flocks of brightly coloured birds were flying around in the blue sky. Horses, foals and ponies gambolled cheerfully in the meadow, while cows and sheep grazed peacefully.

Brave Hunter and Neston stared at the landscape, speechless.

"It is ......beautiful", Neston whispered finally. Alice laughed, made a bow and said:

"In the name of our king and queen I bid you a warm welcome to Jingleland. The land of fairies, dwarves, dreams and fairytales." Alice fluttered around and somersaulted in the air then started singing accompanied by tinkling bells:

> *"We are the fairies of Jingleland,*
> *Where joy and laughter go hand in hand.*
> *We love to flutter around all day,*
> *come join us now as we play."*

Suddenly Brave Hunter and Neston started

to laugh. They laughed so hard they were rolling on the ground.

"Oh, what a funny sight, I haven't laughed this much in years!", howled Brave Hunter as he rubbed the tears from his eyes. Neston lay on the ground holding his tummy as he roared with laughter.

"Ha, ha! What a show! And those funny bells on top of it all, oh I just can't stop laughing!"

"It is something in the air that makes you laugh", Alice explained.

"It makes all living creatures happy; birds, spiders, horses, dwarves, fairies and humans like you. Once you get used to the air the roaring laughter will stop and you will just feel happy.

Look, can you see the smoke coming from behind that rock? That is where we live."

"Yes I can see it", Brave Hunter nodded as he blinked a tear away and stood up to walk to the horses. Neston also got up and together they walked down the path. Not everybody walked.... Alice flew.

When they entered the village they were greeted by a large number of singing and dancing fairies. A couple of fairies took the horses from Neston to unharness them and put them in the meadow. There was delightful lush grass and a babbling brook. Jingleland was a lovely village. The walls of the houses were made of shiny silk, the windows and doors made of colourful seashells and the roof of diamantes. When the moon or the sun, drop their beams on the roof, the diamantes shine as bright stars in the sky. The whole air was suffused with a smell of biscuits, popcorn and cakes.

Neston sniffed the air.

"Hmm those biscuits really do smell good", he mumbled as he walked towards the smell of the biscuits. It seemed that the smell was coming from the kitchen of a fat fairy with pink blushing cheeks, who was just pouring herself a cup of tea. Neston looked through the window with curiosity. The fairy smiled and gestured Neston to enter the house.

"Hello, I am Neston", said Neston as he entered the kitchen. "I am going to capture the witch Caligula, with the help of Brave Hunter." He made a gesture with his fists. The fairy looked at him with admiration.

"I am very glad that you are going to catch the witch and free our fairies."

As she said this, three fairy children entered the kitchen.

"Mummy, who is this?", asked the oldest fairy Brady, pointing at Neston. They stared wide-eyed at Neston because they had never seen a human child before. They flew circles around him and looked him up and down.

"He is so big", said one of them.

"He doesn't have any wings", said another.

"How is he going to fly?", asked the three fairy children simultaneously. Mother fairy stood up from her chair and took Neston by the hand.

"Children, this is Neston and he is going to catch Caligula the witch together with Brave Hunter." The fairy children looked at Neston with huge eyes and sighed:

"Oh, is that true?" All three were speechless.

"You are very brave!", finally Brady exclaimed. They all knew that this was a very dangerous thing to do. They then began to bombard him with all kinds of questions.

"Where do you come from? How old are you? Have you fought many witches?"

By now, Neston felt very important and told colourful stories about how brave he was. Meanwhile, mother fairy took the biscuits out of the oven and gave them to the children. While they nibbled on the biscuits and sipped lemonade, Brad, the middle fairy child, asked:

"Would you like to play 'touch and drop' with us?"

"That sounds great fun", Neston chuckled, "but I don't know how to play it."

"Oh, it is very easy. One person is appointed

to chase us and try tapping one of us. If you are tapped, you have to drop to the ground. The person who stays in the air the longest has won."

Neston jumped up excited:
"I would love to play it but I don't have any wings, I can't fly!"
"But with my magic flying stick you can", whispered the youngest fairy Bonnie. "When we are little and our wings are not big enough to fly, we get a magic flying stick. It takes you into the air when you hold the stick in both hands above your head. I don't need my stick anymore because I can fly without it now."

Bonnie flew to her room and a moment later she came back with a red stick that had a golden knot on both sides.
"We'd better step outside to practice", suggested Brady. "We have more space there." They all went outside and explained to Neston how to use the stick.

Bravely Neston started to practise. He held the stick tight and then flew in the air. But instead of flying he made all kinds of strange circles and turns.
"Help, help", he shouted. "I get air sick, I want to get back on the ground!" The three fairy children laughed their hats off.

"Ha, ha! Is this the brave boy who is going to catch the witch? Ha, ha, ha, he can't even fly!", laughed Brady. Bonnie, the youngest, felt sorry for Neston.

"You have to hold on to both ends of the stick and pull it towards you. That way you automatically land on the ground", she yelled at Neston. It worked, Neston landed beautifully in the field.

"Phew, that was quite a ride!", he mumbled as he held the stick tighter. "But I think I know how it works now." And poof, he was gone again. This time more successfully. After a while he got the hang of it and flew through the air as if he had done it all his life.

While Neston played with the fairies, Brave Hunter had been taken to the castle of the king and queen of Jingleland. The fairy king and queen welcomed him in the Chamber of Knights. The thrones, on which they sat, were made of diamonds and pearls that filled the room with a magic blue light. A fresh scent of pine and lavender was in the air. Both the king and queen wore the most beautiful gowns that Brave Hunter had ever seen. The queen had a silver crown on her angel hair.

"Welcome to Jingleland Brave Hunter!" The king flew towards him waving the sceptre in the air.

"We are very grateful that you want to help us catch Caligula the witch", the fairy queen said waving her colourful fan.

"It is so horrible that all our fairies are put in jars. My dearest lady-in-waiting, Lotte, is also now in a jar and that makes me very sad." With a small handkerchief she blinked away a little tear.

"There, there", said the king. "Brave Hunter is going to help us. Soon your favourite lady-in-waiting will be back in the castle." The king then pointed with his sceptre to one of his servants:

"Please, bring our guest food and drink. Take a chair, Brave Hunter and I will tell you all we know about Caligula the witch."

While Brave Hunter nibbled on the food, the king told him about the witch Caligula.

"Every year the mighty witches from across the mountains, organize a witch ball, where everybody can show off their most powerful and special tricks", the king began.

"Last year they chose our woods for this meeting; a place only about ten stones' throw away from our fairy village. Suddenly our peace and quiet was shattered. Witches flew low over our village on their brooms, screaming and yelling. They tried to steal our laundry from the washing lines. Biscuits and cakes that were cooling off in the air disappeared. At night we could see large campfires, where from smoke, disgusting smells and sounds were emerging. I scnt one of my bravest fairies to the meeting to find out what the witches were up to. They saw that the witches were conducting some sort of ritual, where everybody was making their own potion. That's where that horrible smell came from. After everybody had tasted the potion, they started to dance like madwomen around the campfire; they kept on singing the same song over and over again:

'*We are old and ugly and our hair is curled,
but with a mug of fairy juice
we will feel on top of the world.*'

Slowly it became clear to our spy why they had chosen to be so close to our village this year. The old witches felt their strength was weakening and so were looking for a substance to make them young and alive again. They wanted to make a potion, using us fairies, which would make them young again.

The witch Caligula, a mighty and strong witch, was appointed to prepare this potion for the next witch ball where all the witches could drink it. All year long she has been collecting fairies and as you know she puts them in jars. The rest of the day she busies herself collecting herbs. I have sent out our bravest fairies to conquer the witch. But none of our fairies has ever returned. They too are all put in jars. In a few days it will be time for the next witch ball for the witches from all over the mountain. I am at my wits' end Brave Hunter, because on that day the fairies who have been captured in jars, will disappear in the cauldron." The king blinked a tear away.

"That is why you are our last hope. Brave Hunter, please help us to catch that horrible witch and be rid of her for ever."

Brave Hunter sighed deeply. What a sad story. Of course he had to help capture the horrible witch Caligula and free all the fairies from the jars. Tonight he would investigate and find out for himself what was going on. But one thing had to be done first.

"Majesty?", Brave Hunter said, "may I ask you to send one of your fairies to the Village of Oak-trunk? To tell Neston's parents that he is travelling with me. Otherwise they will be worried sick!"

"Of course, we'll send our royal fairy courier immediately."

IN THE WITCH'S HOUSE

"But Brave Hunter, I am really not scared at all of the mean ugly witch! Please, can I come along with you tonight?" Neston looked at Brave Hunter with wide eyes. They were sitting on the royal veranda that bordered the royal garden.

After Neston had played with the fairy children, he had flown to the palace with his new flying stick. The fairy servants had shown him to his own room in the palace. It all looked so lovely. The bed was made of seaweed and soft white sand. From his room he had a view over the royal garden and the veranda on which he was now sitting with Brave Hunter.

First Neston showed off his flying stick and told Brave Hunter about the new friends he had made. Brave Hunter laughed hard about Neston's flying skills. Then Brave Hunter told the story about the mean witch Caligula and said that he was going to investigate tonight. Neston was desperate to join him.

"No Neston, it is much too dangerous. Before you know it, you will be in a glass jar too! I will be setting off alone to hatch a plan to capture this witch Caligula and her fellow witches."

Brave Hunter got up to get his rucksack and then hit the road.

The moon was high in the sky and gave enough light for Brave Hunter to follow the path to the witch's cottage. The moon was shining on the diamond roofs of the fairy houses and put a lovely glow over the fairy village. In the distance he heard crickets chirping.

"It all looks so beautiful and peaceful, what a pity that the witches have chosen this spot for their witch ball", Brave Hunter thought to himself. He inhaled the sultry night air that filled his lungs. The scent of lavender and pine mingled in his nostrils. Brave Hunter looked up and saw a clear sky full of stars.

"I wonder if my uncle and aunt in Corsica can also see the clear starry sky?", Brave Hunter mused. "I have to catch those mean witches as soon as possible so I can go on to Corsica."

The king had given him a case with the same magic powder that Alice had in her case.

"When you get close to the witch's house, put some of this powder on your cheeks so you grow back to your own height", the king had said. "But I want to remind you that you must put some of the powder in your hair before returning to Jingleland!"

Brave Hunter took the case from his ruck-sack and put some of the magic powder on both cheeks. Immediately he felt himself growing as he walked purposefully along the path that led to the witch's house.

The branches of the trees were a little spooky in the moonlight. They seemed like arms wanting to grab you. Now and then you could hear the call of an owl or a bat flying closely beside your head. But apart from that it was deadly quiet in the forest. The path was becoming narrower and narrower. The sounds of the animals disappeared. Brave Hunter smelt a strange smell. He put his nose to the wind and sniffed the air.

"Hmm, what a stench", he mumbled to him-self. "It smells like rotten eggs and cow dung. I'm sure it is Caligula, busy boiling some kind of potion." Brave Hunter decided to follow the smell and indeed, not much later he saw, through the bushes, the witch bending over a large cauldron, fumes evaporating into the night.

Brave Hunter hid himself well behind the bushes, so that Caligula couldn't see him, and spied on her. Suddenly the witch stuck her crooked nose in the air.

"I smell human meat", she said to her black cat. "But that cannot be possible, no humans are ever seen here in Jingleland!" She looked around with her sharp black eyes. Brave Hunter rolled himself up like a little ball, to make himself as small as possible, and held his breath. Almost immediately, the witch looked his way but then she shook her head.

"No it can't be a human, I must be imagining it." She started diligently stirring the potion and murmured all kinds of spells.

Brave Hunter was sitting silently behind the bushes.

"Phew! That was close. The witch almost saw me. And who knows what she'd have done to me. While she is here in the wood I'll go to her cottage to have a look there", Brave Hunter thought.

The cottage was hidden behind all kinds of branches and bushes. The tiles were hanging off the roof and the windows were full of cobwebs and flies. Brave Hunter pushed down the door handle; it squeaked a bit. For a second he looked back. Had Caligula heard him? Fortunately, everything remained quiet. The door squeaked even more as Brave Hunter stepped inside. It was an enormous mess in the house. On the left of the room was a large stove with lots of pots and pans on it. On the large round table, which was in the middle of the room, were baskets containing bunches of herbs and mushrooms. A dusty book also lay on the table. Near the window, there hung a cage with a crow in it. On the other side of the room was a bookshelf full of jars and in those jars were the fairies.

The fairies in the jars were looking at Brave Hunter longingly. One of them asked curiously:

"Who are you? A friend of the witch Caligula?"

"No, I am definitely not that", said Brave Hunter as he shook his head.

"I am a friend of your king and queen. They are very sad that you have been taken prison by the witch. They have asked me to free you and capture the witch."

The fairies began to talk excitedly; would they finally be freed? One of the fairies gestured the other fairies to be silent.

"The witch studies that book on the table for hours - maybe it explains how to catch a witch", said the fairy, pointing at the book.

Brave Hunter walked to the table and sat down on one of the wobbly chairs and took the book in his hands. The cover read:

*"The Great Magic Book of
the Mighty Witches from over the Mountains"*

"Hmm, this could be interesting indeed", Brave Hunter mumbled. He leafed through the book that contained large letters and many pictures. The book was full of spells and recipes for herbal-drinks. There was also a spell to turn someone into a toad: You had to stamp three times on the ground, while saying:

"Sweaty feet and heavy load
from here on in, become a toad"

Brave Hunter scratched his head.
"I should remember this spell, it might come in handy." Brave Hunter studied the spells for an hour before one of the fairies called:
"I hear the witch coming back!" And yes, in the distance could be heard the squeaky voice of the witch, who hummed a song about old witches gaining youth.

Brave Hunter looked around him in fright. He had completely forgotten the time and hadn't thought about the fact that he was sitting in the house of Caligula the witch. He had been so caught up with reading the book.
"Where is the best place to hide?" The fairies thought quickly. Suddenly someone yelled:
"In the coal-shed, she never goes there."
"Yes, yes in the coal-shed", the fairies yelled in unison.
"There, next to the bookshelf is a door that

leads to the coal-shed", said the fairy, who had heard the witch first.

Brave Hunter just closed the door of the coal-shed as the door handle of the cottage turned and the witch entered.

"Hmm, again I smell a human", she said sniffing the air. She looked around her with her sharp eyes and asked rudely:

"Have you seen a human, little caged birds?" The fairies claimed ignorance.

"A human, what is that?", asked one of the fairies.

"We did see a bird flying in, maybe that's what you smell?", suggested another fairy. In no time all fairies were talking over each other to distract the witch's attention. But the witch was tired from collecting herbs all day and was snappy.

"Shut up soup vegetables! I am going to bed because I am tired!" The witch disappeared up the stairs to bed.

The fairies sighed with relief. Brave Hunter had heard everything from the coal-shed. He waited until the witch was sound asleep then, when he heard her snoring he sneaked outside.

THE WITCH CHILD NORMA

The next morning the sun was shining through the grubby windows of the witch's cottage.

"Wow, it is going to be a beautiful day, but goodness me, I still have a lot to do." Caligula stretched.

"Just a couple of days to go before the witch ball starts and I don't have enough fairies", Caligula brooded.

"More witches than usual have signed up for the ball. Everybody wants to try the potion to regain youth. Hmm, how am I going to solve this problem? I can't say that I only have enough potion for half of the witches. I am sure the other witches will get very angry with me and do something terrible to me. How can I get more fairies?"

Caligula got out of bed, walked towards the kitchen sink and grabbed the water jug. She threw some water on her face.

"Brr, beautifully cold", she crowed as she shook her head, water drops flying everywhere. With a rusty old comb she combed her long jet-black hair. She then got a black velvet dress from the wardrobe and slipped it on. It was a beautiful ball dress, which used to belong to her sister Desirée.

Desirée lived in the valley of the squirrels and rabbits. The valley bordered gnome land and laid about a day's walk form Caligula's cottage though only twenty minutes by broom. If you saw Desirée, it would be hard to imagine that she and Caligula were sisters.

They both had jet-black hair, a long face with dark brown eyes and long dark eyelashes. But if Desirée smiled, you could see beautiful shiny white teeth, while Caligula had only a couple of black stumps. Desirée's eyes were clear and open, while Caligula always screwed her eyes up as if hatching some plan. Desirée's hair was always neatly combed, while Caligula's hair was all over the place. Desirée always wore the latest fashion of Milanhex, while Caligula usually wore Desirée's hand me down clothes.

Their characters were as different as their appearance. Caligula was a mean witch who used her magic gift for her own gain. Desirée, on the other hand, was a good witch who used her powers to help others.

"Hmm, that sister of mine, why does she have to be a good witch? If she wasn't, she could have helped me catch the fairies", growled Caligula.

"Hmm, wait a minute, maybe her daughter Norma could help? She is such a sweet little thing, nobody would suspect that she was working for me." Caligula rubbed her hands and took the crystal ball from the dusty shelf. She held her hands above the ball and said:

"Norma there, Norma steady,
my crystal ball is waiting ready"

A little girl appeared in the ball. She looked very much like her mother; jet-black hair and big wide eyes, only not brown but blue. She inherited those from her father, the Mighty Sorcerer. Norma had never met her father; he left before she was born. Her mother told her that he was a very wise man, always willing to lend a hand. Norma had a medallion of his, which she never took off. She believed that the medallion would protect her against danger.

"Are you calling me, aunty?", asked Norma cheerfully.

"Yes Norma, quickly come over here on your broom, I have a nice task for you", growled Caligula back.

"I am coming right away aunty", answered Norma.

Caligula had just finished her breakfast when she saw Norma hanging in the air on her broom.

"Hello aunty!", said Norma cheerfully as she

waved from the air. She circled above the house then landed in front of the old veranda. Caligula walked outside to greet her niece.

"What do you think of my air broom? It flies much faster than the antique one you use." Norma showed her aunt the broom.

"Look it has a special hair structure which ensures that the wind stays under it, so you can go extra fast!" Caligula shook her head and ground her teeth:

"I'll stick to my old fashioned broom." Norma smiled at her aunt and said cheerfully:

"By the way, mum sends her regards." Caligula nodded and growled:

"Yes, yes, what nonsense is she wasting her time with? Saving rainforests? A seals' sanctuary perhaps? A shelter for baby bears? Your dumb mother could use her gift much better then wasting it on these kinds of non-sense." Norma rested her broom against the veranda.

"At this moment she is helping the gnomes take care of the trees and bushes in human land."

"Yeah, yeah, no doubt", grumbled Caligula as she stumbled into her cottage.

Norma shook her head and followed her aunt. Norma always found it very exciting to visit Aunt Caligula. She lived in such a strange house with all kinds of pots and pans and there was so much to look at. And of course 'The Big Magic book', that was always in the middle of the table. A very different magic book from the magic books she knew from home! In those books were just spells about how to help animals, gnomes and fairies. Aunt Caligula's magic book was full of very different spells! In just a moment she would snoop around in the dusty magic book. Not that she wanted to do mean things. But it was great fun to be able to change your herb teacher into a frog, chuckled Norma as she walked into the house.

Norma looked around with surprise. She saw all kinds of jars on the shelf containing small creatures. She walked to the shelf and picked up a jar.

"Put that jar down immediately", shrieked her aunt as she put the kettle on the fire.

"You might break the jar!" Quickly, Norma put the jar back on the shelf

"But aunty, it is only a little fairy, you can't put them in jars!" Then Norma saw how many fairies there were in the jars. Most were sitting on the ground. Some were hanging against the glass side; or lying down to sleep.

"Aunty, why do you keep fairies in jars?", asked Norma again. Caligula knew that she couldn't say that she was using the fairies to make soup for the witch ball. Norma would have told her mother immediately. Her mother was much more powerful than Caligula, so she didn't want to make her angry. No, she had to make up something else, so she answered:

"Norma, those fairies have a contagious disease and to prevent it spreading, I am taking care of them here at home." Norma looked at her aunt with surprise.

"Yeah, yeah, it really is true", said Caligula quickly." It was so sad to see all those fairies sick that I decided to take them home with me so I could take care of them. Look this one is losing all its hair." Caligula pointed to a fairy, as she blinked away a tear.

"Oh, don't you feel sorry for them?" Then suddenly cheerfully:

"Come on, we are going to give the fairies my delicious honey to eat."

Caligula walked to the cupboard and took out a large pot of honey. Then she took the kettle off the fire and made a delicious smelling drink with all kinds of herbs. She took a special fairy dinner service out of the cupboard, with small cups and saucers, little plates, forks, spoons and knives. Together, aunt and niece made breakfast for the fairies.

"Has aunty changed that much?", pondered Norma. It is a real pity that all those sweet fairies are sick.

When all the fairies had had their breakfast,

Norma and Aunt Caligula sat at the table. They both had a cup of the steaming drink that Caligula had made for the fairies. Norma gulped the delicious liquid and asked:

"Aunty, why did I have to come so quickly and what kind of task do you have for me? Making breakfast for the fairies?" Caligula shook her head.

"No Norma, I wish that was it. In order to avoid contaminating more fairies with this horrible disease, all the fairies in Jingleland must be sprayed with the potion I have made. But as you know, I don't have time to do it myself. In a couple of days there will be the annual witch ball and even today the first witches are going to arrive. That is why I would like you to sprinkle the fairies with this potion. And as soon as possible, before more fairies get contagious."

Caligula walked over to a cabinet and took out a sprinkler.

"You have to take this with you and spray twice on each wing. Don't tell them that I have sent you, because I don't want them to know that I have turned into a good witch. And you mustn't say that I am your aunt or let anybody know that you know me. Is this clear?" Caligula gave Norma a piercing look.

"You'd better walk to the village, that way they won't notice you. Follow the path here on the left and you'll come to Jingleland. You will recognise it immediately from the horrible......oh, I mean the lovely smell of lavender and pine. And of course you have to make yourself little before you go into the village." Norma nodded, she realised that the lives of the fairies were depending on it. It would be such a pity if more fairies ended up in jars. The fairies in the jars were becoming restless and suddenly all the fairies started screaming:

"No, don't do it, no don't do it!" Quickly Caligula pushed Norma outside.

"You see, the illness causes them to have strange fits. Go quickly spraying all the fairies in Jingleland so they won't get those fits. Make yourself small before going in!"

Caligula shut the door behind her and Norma went on her way with the spray.

"Bad, bad, fairies", grumbled Caligula, walking towards the table.

"You think that you are smart trying to warn my niece. Ha, that stupid goose is now going to bring me all the fairies. You see, if she sprays my potion on the fairies' wings, they will all fly straight to my home. Ha, so I can put them in jars as well. All of Jingleland will end up in jars and I will have enough potion for all the witches at the annual witch ball. Ha, ha, ha, what a stupid goose Norma is and what a wonderful mean witch I am! Ha, ha, ha!"

ALICE AND NESTON MEET NORMA

"Wake up sleepy head!" Alice pulled on Neston's arm. "Time to get dressed, the sun has been up for ages!" Alice flapped her wings. Neston rubbed his eyes and said sleepily:

"What time is it then?" Alice fluttered above his face and answered impatiently:

"It is already six o'clock, I have been up for an hour and you are still in bed. Come on, out of it!" She grabbed the blankets in her hands and flew up with them.

"Oh, six o'clock, that is way too early", mumbled Neston. He turned over. Six o' clock is no time to get up. He fell straight back to sleep and dreamt about his flying skills.

All of Jingleland had come to watch how well he could fly. Never before had they seen anyone fly so well and with so much grace, style and courage. He somersaulted three times in the air when it started to rain.

"There you are, now you are awake." Alice had squeezed out a dish cloth above his face. Neston jerked up at once.

"Why did you wake me up when I was dreaming so happily about flying and adventure", he muttered.

"Because I have a plan and I want to go on

an investigation with you." Neston was now wide awake.

"Yes, let's go to the witch's house." Neston jumped out of bed. In seconds he was washed and dressed.

"Come on, let's go straight to Caligula's house." Neston pulled at Alice's dress.

"No silly", called Alice. "You can't just go there like that. You will end up in a jar."

"Well, I won't fit in it!" Neston pulled a brave face.

"She'll just change you into a toad! Do you want to go through life croaking and jumping?"

"Come on, let's have breakfast first and then I will tell you all about my plan." Alice flew through the colourful shell door while Neston was following her on foot.

During breakfast Neston told his story of Brady, Brad and Bonnie and the flying stick.

"So can you now fly, like me?", asked Alice as she bit into some delicious fairy bread.

"Yes, and that might come in handy when we are going to catch the mean witch", said Neston bravely, stirring his tea.

"What kind of plan do you have to catch the witch Caligula, Alice?"

"Now", Alice said sternly, "I didn't say that I want to catch the witch. I just said that we should go on an investigation. You see it will be some days before the witch ball."

Alice breathed deeply. "But I believe that today the first witches will arrive. My idea is to mislead the witches, so no one will arrive at the witch ball."

"What a great idea", yelled Neston enthusiastically. "And how do you intend to mislead them?" Neston looked at Alice inquisitively. Well, that Alice didn't know either, so she shrugged her shoulders.

"Let's explore the vicinity of the witch's house, I am sure we will get an idea."

Together they went outside as the sun had already started to rise steadily. It promised to be a radiant day. At the fairy bakery they bought some bread for the journey then walked towards the path that led to the witch's house. They had to go over a hill before reaching the start of the path. It was still early and Neston and Alice were all alone.

"What a wonderful smell", said Neston.

"Yes, do you remember, it is that special scent that makes all living creatures happy." Alice jumped in the air. Neston gestured with his head.

"I feel like jumping into that brook over there. Will you come with me Alice?"

The brook lay down the road, surrounded by trees and little beaches with a few little waterfalls. It looked very tempting.

"But we don't have time for that, silly. We have to explore the surroundings." Alice's wings were trembling impatiently.

"Oh, a little bit of cooling off can't do any harm." As he said this, Neston walked down to the brook, took off his clothes and jumped into the cool crystal water. Alice shook her head and followed Neston.

Suddenly Neston disappeared underwater and after a while Alice began to worry.

"Neston, come up, you are scaring me!" She scanned the water to see if she could see his head.

"Here..................I am!" Neston was hanging onto a branch of a tree that was standing in the brook. Alice flew towards him.

"Don't ever do that again, do you hear! I thought something terrible had happened."

"Don't you worry, I can take care of myself, I am Neston after all!" Neston chuckled, letting the branch go and splashing into the water.

While Neston swam to the side and got dressed, Alice sat on the beach. She took a little twig and rubbed the soft sand away. Harder sand appeared and she started to draw a map. When Neston sat down with her, she said, pointing with the stick at the map:

"Look, here is the witch's cottage. A little further away is the circle where she has her magic cauldron." Alice clacked her tongue whilst drawing. "And this is the path that leads to the house and the circle." Neston looked at the drawing.

"Hmm", he said, "the circle where the witches will gather is quite far from the witch's house." Neston picked up some little stones and started throwing them in the water. He skimmed the flat ones over the water so they bounced a couple of times, before dropping to the bottom.

"What are you doing Neston?", asked Alice irritated, "we have to hurry up to explore the area."

"Yes", answered Neston, picking up another stone to skim. "But when I throw stones in the water, I always get good ideas and................ I believe that I am getting a good idea!"

The stone dropped to the bottom and at the same moment they heard someone sing. The sound was coming from the witch's woods and was getting closer.

"Who is coming from the witch's woods?", asked Alice in surprise. Neston shrugged his shoulders.

"It doesn't sound like a wicked witch and it also doesn't sound like a fairy." Quietly they crawled up to the path and hid behind a big tree. In the distance they saw Norma arrive.

"I don't know her", whispered Alice, "I have

never seen her before. She looks a little bit like a witch with that jet-black hair. But her face is much friendlier than Caligula's." Neston nodded in agreement.

"But if it is a witch then it is a very pretty witch", he whispered softly. Alice looked at Neston who was staring at Norma open mouthed. Then she pulled at his sleeve.

"Come on, let's follow her and see what she is up to."

Cautiously Neston and Alice followed Norma. Unaware of this, Norma was walking with her spray towards the village. Norma looked around. She was now in the green valley that just had been crossed by Neston and Alice.

"It is so beautiful here", she thought, as a lamb walked up to her. She tickled it under the chin. More lambs, sheep and goats came up to her. One by one she stroked them all and spoke to them kindly.

"I wish I could be here with you all day but...............unfortunately I don't have time, because I have to save the fairies." Norma sighed and followed the path to the village.

From a distance Alice and Neston heard what Norma had said to the animals. Alice couldn't believe her ears.

"Did you hear that Neston?", she asked in amazement. "She was saying she has to save the fairies. I don't understand that at all. How is she going to do that?" Neston shrugged his shoulders and quickly walked on because Norma was taking huge steps towards Jingleland.

Norma had never been to Jingleland, although she had heard many stories about it. Her mother came to help the fairies when they were sick. When Norma was big, she would do the same and help all the animals, fairies and dwarfs. Norma walked into the village. In the distance she saw the first fairy walking. It was Dora, the wife of the potter. Her husband made all kinds of pots for flowers, grain, and sugar etcetera. He has just made a beautiful vase and Dora was looking for some beautiful flowers to put in it. She took her basket to go flower picking in the hills.

"Good morning, have a good day", said Norma to Dora.
"Good morning child, are you lost? Can I give you directions?", asked Dora smiling.
"No Madam, I have come to help you fairies." As she said this, Norma sprayed her potion on Dora's wings. Immediately the potion started to work and Dora was taken into the air and flew into the woods. Norma walked on and saw the grocery store. When she opened the door the little bells above the door tinkled. The grocer

and his wife were behind the counter. In front of the counter a couple of fairies were talking excitedly about the arrival of Brave Hunter. It went quiet as Norma came through the door.

"Good morning, how are you?", called Norma cheerfully. The fairies nodded good morning back. Then one of the fairies asked:

"Aren't you Desirée's daughter? You look just like her." Norma nodded enthusiastically.

"Yes, she told me about this lovely village, that is why I am pleased to help you." While she said this she sprayed the wings of the fairies.

"Oh, oh what's happening to me?", called the fairy. She then flew through the door in the direction of the woods, together with all the fairies in the store.

"How strange that they all fly outside", pondered Norma as she walked out of the store. Neston and Alice had also seen everybody fly out of the store in the direction of the woods.

"She can look sweet and cute", growled Alice. "But I know that she is helping Caligula get more fairies into jars." Neston nodded.

"Yes, they are all flying to the witch's cottage. Something must be in the sprinkler, so they are somehow bewitched. We have to warn Brave Hunter!"

A PLAN HAS TO BE HATCHED

"All fairies were healthy when I left." Brave Hunter paced up and down the Chamber of Knights where the king and queen were.

"As far as I'm concerned they were well taken care of." The queen sighed with relief.

"I am glad to hear that, I worry day and night about our fairies."

"Do you have any idea how you plan to stop the witch?", the king asked. Brave Hunter stepped to the window and looked outside.

"She has a magic book, you know. I have been going through the book for a long time, to see if I can find something to beat the witch with." The king now also got up and asked with interest:

"What a good idea and..............have you found anything to beat the witch with?" Brave Hunter turned around and slapped his hands together.

"Now", he finally said, "it is full of magic spells. Only the problem is that most spells need a magic stick or herbs and potion. And......that we don't have. The question is of course if those spells, where you don't need a stick or potion, will work." The king looked at Brave Hunter questioningly. Brave Hunter pressed his lips together and continued:

"If they are not spoken by a witch." The king looked at Brave Hunter and asked cautiously:

"Which spells do you know where you don't need a magic stick or potion?" Brave Hunter raised his eyebrows.

"Yes", continued the king, "because then you can try out a spell on me to see if the spell really works." The queen jumped up from her throne in fright.

"No please, you are not allowed to do that, who would rule the country?" The queen looked anxiously at her husband.

Janus, the king's aide, shook his head sadly. Since the last witch ball it had never been the same in the palace. The palace used to be a cheerful and happy place but had now for more than a year been under deep sadness. First there was the fear by the fairies about the low flying witches and their bizarre noises. The fairies were relieved, when the witch ball was finished, and all the witches went back home.

But the peace and quiet didn't last, because soon fairies started to disappear. The king had called on a whole team of agents and spies to find the missing fairies. Eventually, a spy found out that, the witch Caligula had put all the fairies in jars. And all those jars were standing in the witch's cottage on a shelf. When the king heard this he immediately sent out an army of fairy soldiers to free the fairies. Nobody came back from this expedition. A number of expeditions followed but still no one came back. The king was at his wits' end. His golden hair became greyer and greyer and lines appeared around his mouth from worrying.

Often at night the king paced up and down with a worried frown on his face. On one of those nights he had said:

"Janus, the worst thing is that I don't know what the witch wants to do with our fairies. That insecurity makes me feel very scared and helpless."

Then Janus had made a decision. He would find out what the mean ugly witch was up to with the fairies. The fairies always heard strange noises coming from the woods around the time of full moon. So Janus had waited till it was full moon and then he had crept up to the witch's cottage. And there, in an open place in the forest, he had seen the witch dancing around a circle of jars containing fairies. And she accompanied it with the most awful song:

> " *Fairies big and fairies small,*
> *You soon won't be here at all.*
> *Youth and beauty will be mine,*
> *in my heart for all of time.* "

"Ha, ha, haaaaaa!" An awful witch-laughter had followed. Janus saw how sad the fairies in the jars looked, and it broke his fairy heart.

Then the witch got herself into the circle and murmured all kinds of spells. She sat with crossed legs on the ground. Her head and arms turned to the sky, while she had her eyes closed. It seemed as if she was in some sort of trance. Eventually she opened up her eyes and put her arms in her lap while she looked at the fairies one by one.

"Bad, bad, fairies, you won't be sitting in the jars for much longer." She made a cooing sound and continued in a loud voice.

"No, during next week's witch ball we are going to make soup out of you." Again, that horrible laughter. It had given Janus goose bumps.

After that, he had carefully flown out of the forest, back to Jingleland. He had been very relieved when he was safe and well behind the gates of the palace.

"Phew, that was very exciting indeed." Then he had reported to the king, who had been a little angry at first

"Janus, you could have been in a jar right now!" The king shook his head and continued pondering.

"It is very clear now that we need help fast,

otherwise we will never see our fairies again. But nobody should know this horrible news, Janus, otherwise we will worry more fairies. I will get my daughter, Alice, to seek help."

Then the king went to his bedroom. And yesterday Alice had come back with Brave Hunter, who now wanted to try a spell on the king. Can you imagine, the king as a toad, frog or bat? No, that must not happen.

"Forgive me, your royal highness", said Janus with a trembling voice. "I would like to be your guinea pig." Brave Hunter, the king and queen all looked at the servant. Then Brave Hunter shook his head and said:
"I can't do that. I might be able to change you into a toad, but I don't have a clue how to change you back into a fairy." Janus's face was serious and he took a step forwards.
"If it will disarm the witch I will do it with pleasure." Janus looked at the king and queen.
"Really, I don't mind, the fairies have got to be freed and the witch caught!"

The king looked at his queen who nodded and said firmly:
"We have to start somewhere to capture this horrible witch and if this spell would really work........"
"Yes", Janus replied. "Please, let us try it."

The king sighed and nodded:

"Ok, let's give it a shot. We don't have any other choice at this moment. Anyway we can always ask Desirée to turn you back into a fairy."

Brave Hunter stood right in front of the servant and looked him deep in the eyes, stamped his feet three times and said:

"Sweaty feet and heavy load
from here on in, become a toad"

Janus looked at his hands and feet, but he was still a fairy. Brave Hunter tried it again and stamped three times.

"Sweaty feet and heavy load
from here on in, become a toad"

Still Janus didn't turn into a toad. Brave Hunter sighed and looked at the king and queen.

"I am afraid that you have to be a witch for the spell to work." The king nodded sadly.

"Well, we'll have to come up with another plan."

At that moment the door opened and Neston and Alice entered the room of the knights.

"Oh, Brave Hunter", called Neston, running towards his friend. "Someone is spraying the wings of the fairies. And all those fairies are fly-ing towards Caligula's forest." Alice continued with excitement:

"Yes, Dora, the grocer and his wife and many more are disappearing into the woods. The girl that sprays them claims that she is saving them. But we think that she is helping Caligula the witch to catch more fairies." Neston nodded fiercely.

"Yes and if we don't do something fast, soon all the Jingleland fairies will be in jars."

Brave Hunter sat on the couch.

"A girl that sprays-.........", he sighed. "Does the witch have a daughter?", he asked the king, who shook his head.

"But who is this girl then?", he pondered.

"What does this girl look like, Alice?", the queen asked.

"She has jet-black hair and looks kind of friendly. The unusual thing is that she has blue eyes." The queen looked straight through Alice.

"Blue eyes huh?", she mumbled thoughtfully.

"Blue eyes?", she repeated. Then she jum-ped up and called out in excitement:

"I think I know who she is. She must be Desirée's daughter and therefore Caligula's niece! You see, her father is the Mighty Sorcerer of the High Mountain. And he is known for his shiny blue eyes."

"But dear", said the king in amazement, "Desirée is a good witch, she would never have a daughter do something mean."

Now the king looked at Brave Hunter.

"Desirée is Caligula's sister. But Desirée is a good witch. She comes here to help us when we have sick fairies. She has a daughter, Norma, and when Norma is older she will help her mother take care of the sick. Because Caligula is her sister, we didn't dare to ask Desirée for help to disarm her sister. But that she would send her own daughter to help Caligula catch the fairies, I would have never guessed! I still cannot believe it", sighed the king eventually.

At that moment they heard a murmur in the inner court of the palace. A group of fairies had gathered in front of the gate.

"King, king, come outside. King, king, come outside!", they called out.

"They have found out that fairies are disappearing", said Neston. He walked towards the window to look outside. The whole square was full of fairies. They were all shouting over each other:

"King, king, come outside!"

The king got his cloak and sceptre and walked to the balcony door. Brave Hunter opened the door and raised his hands in the air as he stepped onto the balcony.

"My wife hasn't returned from picking flowers", someone called out.

"And my children have disappeared", yelled another voice.

"My husband hasn't come home from shopping. The grocery store has been abandoned." From every corner these things were called out.

Brave Hunter brought his hands to his mouth and yelled:

"Silence please, silence please, your king wants to speak to you."

"Shh!", the crowd called.

"Shh! The king wants to say something. Silence please." The fairies quietened down.

The king stepped forward and cleared his throat.

"Dear fairies, the queen and I are deeply shocked and concerned about what is happening to our country. We know that at the moment many fairies are disappearing, but we have just found out why. I have asked Brave Hunter to help us catch the witch. He really wants to help us but he needs everybody's help. Do not panic, stay calm!

I request that everybody goes home and

closes the doors and windows. When we need your help we will let you know with the fairy flute. But most importantly, everybody must stay at home and not go outside until it is safe!"

There was some shuffling.
"We will do that king, long live the king!", someone in the crowd called. And then all the fairies shouted together:
"Long live the king!"

The king and Brave Hunter stepped back into the Knight's room.
"I am glad that you are here to help us, Brave Hunter", said the king relieved. Brave Hunter nodded encouragingly but wondered what was to happen next.

CALIGULA PREPARES FOR THE PARTY.

"Dandelion, white dead nettle, horse chestnuts, parsley and clover." Caligula read from her grocery list. Well grocery list.........she had to search for these things herself in the woods. Fortunately her best witch friends were coming this afternoon to help her with the preparation.

She had known Babs, Trix and Dien even before they could fly on a broom. Caligula chuckled.

"Oh, how wonderful I am! It is marvellous that Norma is catching more fairies so we will have enough for everybody." Suddenly Caligula realised that she needed more jars to put the fairies in. She walked to the cellar door. When she opened the door a stale smell rose. Caligula inhaled deeply.

"Hmm, my favourite smell!"

The little staircase went straight down. The cellar was very large, dark and moist and full of cobwebs. A couple of bats had been woken from their sleep and narrowly missed smacking into Caligula, as they grumpily flew outside. A family of rats fled into their holes. The cellar was packed with all kinds of things that Caligula had collected: An old spinning wheel with the wool still on the reel, a stone salamander, Caligula's first trick, her old broom in the corner and her witch cradle on the side. A little further in lay her school magic books and old school reports.

Caligula looked around her.
"Where did she leave those jars? O yes, behind the boxes containing old clothes." She stepped over the mess and waved her arms.

"Jars here jars there,
go to the kitchen up the stair."

One by one the jars floated out of the cellar up to the kitchen, where they neatly stood in a row on the sink.

Caligula was just walking up the stairs when she heard her crystal ball calling her.
"Caligula, are you there?" Caligula ran up the stairs to the corner of the room where here crystal ball stood on a black tablecloth.
It was Trien's voice. Trien was the most feared witch of all. Together with her three sisters Truus, Toos and Trees they formed an invincible team. They were meaner than mean. Even Caligula was scared of the foursome, but most of all, of Trien.

Quickly she walked to the crystal ball.
"Yes Trien, here I am. What can I do for

you?”

"Well Caligula, you should not have kept me waiting this long, do you hear me?” Trien put a crooked finger in the air, and continued:

"You do have everything under control there, don't you Caligula? We want our youth back and to become even more beautiful than we already are, of course.” Caligula nodded quickly:

"Yes, yes, Trien, I have everything in the house, don't you worry.” Trien said fiercely:

"As you know, my three sisters and I do not want to wait when we arrive. So the moment we arrive we want to have the best spot and have the potion immediately.” Trien growled and said resolutely:

"Caligula......... I am counting on everything going smoothly.” And off she went.

Caligula shivered.

"Those horrible sisters are mean and nasty witches. No, Caligula didn't like them at all. They always thought they were better than everyone else. And if something did not suit them, they bewitched anybody who was in their way, into a frog or whatever. Grr!” Caligula shook her head back and forward and at that moment the door swung open and Dora flew in.

"Oh, well done Norma, you understood very well!” Caligula quickly took a jar and put Dora in it.

"Ha, ha! You are the first fairy. I am sure more will follow. Oh, what a clever idea to send Norma. I should have thought about that before." Dora raised her fist to the witch.

"You are not getting away with this, you ugly old witch." Caligula held the jar close to her face.

"Ugly now perhaps, but not for long with your help, ha ha ha!" She slammed the jar, with Dora in, onto the shelf with the other fairies. Straight after that the door opened again and more fairies kept flying in.

Caligula put each one in a jar. When the last fairy had flown in and been put in a jar, Caligula said to herself: "Well done Norma, very well done, you will soon see for yourself how many fairies you have brought me." Suddenly Caligula realised that this was not a good idea at all.

"Oh no, because if she sees the fairies that she has sprinkled, then she will know that the fairies are not really sick at all. She will be very angry and call her mother straight away on her mobile crystal ball. Oh no, that shouldn't happen!"

Caligula groped in Norma's rucksack and took out the mobile crystal ball and hid it under a loose floorboard in the room.

"It is about time that my niece becomes a real witch and I, Caligula, will teach her what that means. Ha, all that nonsense about helping animals, gnomes and fairies. No, Norma has to learn to skim low over the ground with her broom at night and scare all the animals. Brew herbs that will turn living things to stone. Fill the night air with delicious fumes that scare all living creatures. Enjoy the terrified cries in the night when she flies up against the full moon on a broom. Turn herself into a mouse or elephant. Yes, it is about time that I teach her all this. At first she will struggle against it, but eventually she will see that it is for her own good. After all, she is a witch."

Caligula also decided to hide Norma's broom, so she couldn't fly away. She walked outside to get the broom from the veranda when she heard voices above her head.

"Cooey Caligula, cooey Caligula."

They were her three friends: Babs, Trix and Dien, flying high on their brooms above the cottage. They looked very colourful with their tall hats and long dresses. The dresses were made of different pieces of cloth in a variety of shapes in one colour. Babs was in all blue; her hat was dark blue with an even bluer little ball. Her dress, which covered the whole broom, was made of different pieces of cloth in various blue shapes. The edge of the collar of the dress was white. Trix's dress was exactly the same but in green and she had a dark green hat on. And Dien was all in purple.

They pushed the noses of their brooms down and landed in front of Caligula.

"Ah, mean witch of mine!" Babs gave Caligula a thump on her arm. Caligula thumped her back.

"Ha! Dirty slimy serpent!", Trix thumped Caligula."Horrible to see you again, stinking rat!"

"Green slimy lizard, the displeasure is all mine", squawked Caligula back.

"Double twisted rain worm!", Dien croaked.

"Revolting purple reptile", crowed Caligula. They were clearly thrilled to see each other.

They then went and stood in a circle and put their arms around each others shoulders, bent forward so their crooked hats were almost touching and slowly turned around, chanting squeakily:

"We are the witches from over the moun ains.
We make nasty potions and horrible spells.
Four friends forever, for bad and for worse.
Dare meet us and suffer a terrible curse."

A horrible laugh followed the song. When

they had finished laughing, Dien looked at the broom that Caligula was holding.

"Whose broom is that Cal?", she asked. Her friends had always called her Cal ever since witch kindergarten.

"It is Norma's", said Caligula, walking to the veranda. "I was just hiding it when you girls arrived."

"Norma?", asked Babs surprised. "Isn't she the daughter of that sweet sister of yours?"

"Yes that is right", chuckled Caligula. "She is helping me to catch the fairies. Only she doesn't know that she is catching them. You see I have given her a sprayer containing magic potion. She sprays this bewitching potion on the fairies' wings. That mix will see to it that all the fairies fly to my home. Only, Norma thinks that, the fairies need to be sprayed to prevent them from getting sick. She has no idea that the spray makes the fairies fly to my home. So if she comes back soon, she will see all the fairies in jars, and will want to fly home and tell her mother. But she mustn't, do you see? That's why I wanted to hide her broom."

The witches screamed out in admiration.

"What a brilliant idea, Caligula", hissed Dien. "It is about time that that goody two shoes niece of yours becomes a genuine witch", snapped Babs. The witches were now all standing on the veranda.

"I also think it is about time to make her into a real witch. And girls, I am going to need all the help I can get." Caligula turned around and walked to the door.

"We'd be pleased to help you Cal", answered Dien, as the witches followed Caligula.

At that moment Norma was just on her way back to the witch's cottage. The potion in the spray had all gone. She had sprayed so many fairies. Every fairy she encountered got some spray on its wings. Norma did find it a little bizarre that every time she sprayed a fairy, it suddenly flew away. She thought that perhaps they were a little shy. She turned herself back into her usual size and with huge steps she continued along the path.

Norma found Jingleland more beautiful than her mother had said. And all the fairies were so nice; always friendly, greeting you good morning and asking how you are. Well, except that they flew away as soon as she had sprinkled them. Norma was glad that she was able to help the fairies this way. When she got back to the cottage she would call her mother to tell her what she had done.

Norma approached Caligula's house and saw a couple of brooms in front of the veranda. They must belong to her friends; Babs, Trix and Dien, thought Norma. Norma knew that the four of them had a sort of a club in which they planned all kinds of things. She heard Babs's voice in the distance.

"So, Trien expected that on her arrival she should get her potion immediately? How dare she?" Babs stamped her feet with anger.

"Yes, and she wants to have the best seats." Caligula put her crooked finger in the air impersonating Trien.

"I resent those four witches so much", sighed Trix. "It is only because she is so powerful that we have invited her."

"Don't worry", said Dien, walking through the room. "They will arrive late anyway, so we won't have to put up with their company for too long."

"When are you expecting the first witches, Cal?" Dien was sitting on the kitchen table. Caligula took a wooden spoon and dipped it in the large kettle on the fire.

"Tomorrow afternoon", she said, filling the four stone mugs with the liquid.

"I have most of the ingredients at home, such as fungus, mushrooms, frog spawn, salamander legs and black charcoal." She put the four mugs on the kitchen table.

"But as you know, I need a couple of fresh ingredients."

"That is why we came early, to help you out,

Cal." Trix pulled up a kitchen chair.

"Which ingredient do you need?", she asked as she sat down. Caligula started to count on her fingers:

"Dandelion, white dead nettle, horse chestnuts, parsley and clover. I need masses because so many witches are coming this year."

"And this is your freshest ingredient." Babs pointed with her witchy head to the jars where the fairies were. The witches made a cooing sound.

Caligula walked over to the shelf and lifted one.

"These, my mean fellow witches, go in at the last minute. It has to be crunchy to be most effective." Babs sat down on the kitchen table and said:

"Are you sure it works, do we regain our youth and beauty?" With large steps Caligula walked over to the table and slammed her fist down.

"I, Caligula, have worked very hard. Day and night I have been busy with potions and spells. I have studied every magic book in the world. Collecting the right fungus and mushrooms; studying and analysing herbs; during full moon I have placed fairies in a circle and mumbled spells to give them even more power. How dare you doubt it?"

Furiously Caligula looked at Babs.

"Take it easy, I was just wondering if you had ever tried it out." Caligula looked shocked at Babs and then pulled herself up to the table. She put her elbow on the table and put her head in her hands. No, she had never tried it out. She assumed that it would work. But what if it didn't? Caligula shook her head as if to get rid of a negative thought.

"No", she said determinedly. "It just works!" And with that, the discussion was over.

NORMA BECOMES A REAL WITCH
OR DOES SHE.............?

"Good afternoon everybody!" Norma walked into the witch's cottage. She walked over to the table and shook the witches' hands.

"How do you do?", she asked politely. Norma knew her aunt's friends well. They were a funny bunch together. They came up with all sorts of plans, which nearly all failed. Norma's mum said that they failed because the witches were such airheads.

"Come and join us Norma." Caligula gave Norma a cup of herbal tea.

"Well aunty, I have sprayed many fairies today." Norma took a sip of her herbal tea.

"I hope that no more fairies will get sick." The four witches snorted with laughter. Trix put her finger in the air and proclaimed.

"Well done child, I am sure they won't get sick anymore, ha, ha, ha!" And again they all snorted with laughter. Norma didn't understand at all.

Caligula started setting the table for lunch. When they had all filled their bellies she said:

"If you girls", and she nodded to Babs, Trix and Dien, "go and look for the herbs that I need, then Norma and I will feed the fairies."

"Good idea", said Dien as she got up from the table.

"Do you have a couple of baskets for us to put the herbs in?", asked Trix.

"Oh, don't bother, I will use my magic", said Babs walking to the door. In a second, three baskets were standing by the door. The three friends took a basket each and stepped outside.

"What nice friends you have, aunty" said Norma as she got the fairy plates.

"I am sure a lot has to be gathered for the witch ball? Are there many witches coming?" Caligula nodded and walked to the oven where she took out a large loaf. She cut the loaf into small pieces.

"There are many more witches coming this year." Norma put the pieces of bread on the small plates. Then they filled the fairy cups with delicious soup and a fairy bowl with custard.

"You take good care of the fairies, aunty", said Norma, as she walked to the fairies with a tray full of cups and plates. Then suddenly she saw Dora who looked at her shaking her head.

"You came to help us hey? Well some sort of help this is!" Norma put the tray down and walked over to Dora in surprise.

"Did you become sick, even though I sprayed you?", she said with amazement.

"Sick, sick, sick, you mean bewitched!" Dora shook her fist.

"You can look innocent and sweet and put on a nice little voice, but you are just as bad as your aunt over there." Dora pointed at Caligula with her little finger. Norma stared speechlessly at the jars. Now she also saw the fairies, who were at the grocery store and the children who played in the square. And there was the fairy, who was fishing; he still had his little rod. That is why they all suddenly flew away. By spraying the fairies she had sent them to her aunt!

Norma turned around and said with latent fury:

"Aunty, what does this all mean? All the fairies I have sprinkled are now here in jars, even though the idea was to save them." Norma's eyes were shining full of anger. Caligula walked towards Norma and put her forefinger in the air.

"Listen Norma, it is about time that you became a real witch. Yes, the fairies who, were sprinkled were enchanted by it. Tomorrow is the great witch ball and you are a witch. So you should be happy that you could do something so important for the witches."

Norm was looking at Caligula incredulously.

"And what is going to happen to the fairies?",

she asked fearfully.

"Don't look so sad Norma!" Caligula turned around and took a jar from the shelf.

"Tomorrow at full moon, the fairies will be used for my special witchpotion and you have the honour to be there." Caligula waved her arms as she put the jar back. Norma shook her head and responded:

"I will call my mother immediately. She will put an end to this." She walked over to her rucksack to get her mobile crystal ball.

"I have taken that out", sneered Caligula. "I knew that you would call your mother!"

"Then I will go home right away to warn her." Norma took large steps towards the door.

"And I have hidden your broom", yelled Caligula at her.

She walked over to Norma and shook her gently back and forward.

"Come on little witch of mine, be a big witch. Your mother has turned you into a softy. But you are, and always will be, a witch. That is why I will show and teach you how to be a witch."

Norma thought feverishly. She couldn't warn anybody and she couldn't go anywhere. If she bolted now then her aunt would surely lock her up in that spooky cellar of hers until the witch ball was over. She heard her mother's voice in her head: Norma, when there is trouble and doom stay calm. The shortest way is not always the best way.

"Oh", thought Norma to herself.

"What should I do? What should I do?" She looked at the jars on the shelf and saw the fairies staring sadly into the distance. If she didn't do anything, the fairies would be used tomorrow as soup vegetables. And if she made trouble, she would be locked up. How could she stop the witches before the fairies were thrown into a cauldron? Think Norma, think!" And then, as if by magic, she had a brain-wave.

"Aunty, you are totally right. It is about time I became a real witch and that is why I thought it would be a nice idea if I made the starter. To show all the witches how skilled we are in making potions. The main course by the almighty witch Caligula and the starter by her niece Norma." Caligula took Norma's hand and danced around.

"Yippee, I knew you were going to see that this is much better." Caligula then stopped dancing and asked:

"What do you want to make, Norma?" Norma shook her head and shrugged her shoulders a little.

"Oh nothing special, a potion that will give each witch a divine voice. They will be able to sing like hummingbirds." Norma looked at

Caligula with a huge smile.

"Hmm, good idea", nodded Caligula. "First, a starter for a golden voice and then the potion for eternal beauty and youth." She jumped into the air and crowed:

"Norma, they will never forget us! We are a great pair; my friends will be so surprised. Oh, I am going to tell them straight away!"

Caligula walked over to the shelf where her crystal ball was, she put the ball on the table and held her hands above it.

"Trix there, Trix steady,
my crystal ball is for you ready!"

"Yes!", the voice of Trix sounded through the room.

"Here I am Cal, we have found lots of herbs and chestnuts. Our baskets are almost full." Trix held the full basket in front of her crystal ball.

"Only we have one small problem, we can't find dandelion anywhere. Babs is gathering parsley, Dien horse-chestnuts and clover and I am searching for white dead-nettle. Have you fattened up the other ingredient?" Trix made a cooing sound. Caligula chuckled:

"Trix, I have wonderful news. Norma is making the starter for the witch ball!" Trix looked surprised.

"A starter, what kind of a starter?" Caligula nodded enthusiastically and said hastily:

"She is making a potion that will make our voices sound like bells. Isn't that wonderful! Trix grinned and her ugly witch-teeth stuck out as she said:

"Finally that niece of yours has seen sense. It is about time that she used her gift for more useful things!"

Then she turned her head away from the crystal ball and shouted:

"Babs, Dien, come on over, I have good news. Norma is making the starter for the witch ball; a potion that will give us golden voices."
Now Dien's head appeared in the crystal ball.

"A golden voice, Cal? Can she brew that?" Caligula chuckled:

"You bet! She has lessons everyday. And don't forget she has her father's genes. He's the Mighty Sorcerer."

"Who knows, she might turn us into toads?" It was Babs who pushed Dien away from the crystal ball. With two staring eyes she looked into the crystal ball.

"Cal, how can we believe that she can make a potion that gives us a divine voice? Maybe she'll turn us into some kind of creepy beast." Caligula shook her head.

"She can't do that Babs, she doesn't have

that kind of power. As you well know, all witches have a natural defence system against the evil tricks of other witches. Only my sister and Trien have the power to break that protection. By the way, I am convinced that Norma is on our side."

She smiled at Norma bearing her ugly witch teeth. Norma nodded back sweetly.

"Of course aunty I want to become a real witch." Caligula nodded.

"Do you hear that Babs, Trix, Dien she wants to become a real witch!"

"I think it is great Norma, welcome to our club", said Trix cooing.

"Yes we will accept you in our witch club", crowed Dien. Caligula nodded in agreement.

"You see girls, I knew that Norma would see the light. I will come over to show you where the dandelions grow.

While Caligula was talking to her friends, Norma supplied the fairies with food and drinks. They all looked at her angrily. Norma pretended that she hadn't noticed and continued handing out soup and custard.

"So Aunty Caligula, I have served all the fairies with food", said Norma as she walked to the kitchen table. Her aunt put the crystal ball on the shelf.

"Well done child." Caligula walked over to

her broom.

"I have to pop out to show my friends where the dandelions grow." Norma nodded.

"Yes, I had already heard that. I also have to go searching for the herbs I need. Can't I get my broom back?" Caligula shook her head and put her long forefinger in the air.

"We will help you look for the herbs later, so you won't need your broom at all!" Norma put her head on one side and said sweetly:

"But aunty, you are so busy and I don't need that many herbs, just very special ones." Caligula hesitated but then threw her head back and said resolutely:

"We will go to look for the herbs together and that is the end of it."

Caligula had hardly left before the fairies became restless.

"What are you up to, helping the witch?", asked Dora.

"Help us!", called a couple of fairies in panic. "Soon we will be thrown in a boiling potion!" Norma nodded.

"Yes of course, I will help you, I am very sorry that I have brought some of you here. Believe me that was never my intention."

"Why don't you use Caligula's crystal ball to call your mother?", said a soft voice. The question was from Lotte, the queen's lady in waiting. You could see that she was a very important fairy, because she carried a beautiful cloth on which crowns were embroidered. Norma looked in Lotte's direction.

"It is Caligula's ball and only responds to her. That doesn't work."

Norma threw back her long black hair and was about to say something when a low voice came from one of the jars.

"Free us immediately from these jars!" It was Duncan, a colonel of the king's army. His army had been sent by the king to free the fairies. But the witch wasn't easy to catch. Caligula had smelt their arrival. And when his men were close to the cottage, she had thrown a fishing net over them. They had put up a fight with their swords, but that hadn't helped much. They were all put in jars. But now the chance had come for which Duncan had been waiting.

He pushed himself up and stood up straight in the jar, put his hands on his hips, pushed his shoulders back and his chest forward. He frowned a little then looked forcefully at Norma.

"Norma, I order that you free us all from these horrible jars. I will immediately send my men to get your mother." Norma walked over to Duncan and looked at him with curiosity.

"And uh......who are you?"

"Duncan, colonel of the secret royal brigade

and I order you to free us!"

"And what do you think the witch will do when she comes back and sees all the empty jars?", asked Norma.

"Our country is protected against spells and evil", roared Duncan.

"Maybe, but Caligula did succeed in catching you fairies here in the jars. Tomorrow afternoon hundreds of witches will arrive. And when the witches find out that their favourite drink can't be made...... believe me, you don't want to get caught up with so many angry witches. By the way, the potion that I sprayed on some of you, worked fabulously! No, we have to handle this differently."

Norma walked to the kitchen table and took a seat.

"And I have a plan", she said as she put the chair in front of the jars. The fairies stretched forward, they were all very curious as to what the plan might be. Norma sat on the chair, folded her hands in her lap and asked:

"What kind of potion do you think I will make?" But before any fairy could answer she said:

"I brew a potion that bewitches them into a weeping willow. Isn't that smart? Before you are all thrown into the cauldron, all the witches will be weeping willows, so they will never finish the main course." Norma put her hand

on her thighs and bent forward a little. She looked at the fairies in anticipation; for a moment it was silent, then they all started to chatter.

"Good idea, then we are rid of those creepy witches for ever", one of the soldier fairies called out.

"Yes, and we can build a lake on the cooking place", said the fairy with the fishing rod.

"And it will be safe to go into the woods again to look for berries", said another fairy.

"But you don't possess that power at all!" It was Duncan who roared out above everybody.

Suddenly all the fairies were deadly quiet. That was true. They themselves had overheard that only Desirée and Trien had that kind of power. Sadly, they sat in their jars. Norma waved her hands and shook her head.

"I am not the average witch, you know, but half witch and half sorcerer. So my powers are much stronger than the average witch. When I am big I will be much stronger then any other witch."

"We don't care about the future!", yelled Duncan. "It is about now!" As he said this he put a finger in the air. Norma looked at Duncan and nodded.

"Yes, you are completely right there Duncan." Norma drummed her hands on her thighs.

"But actually, I know how you can beat the natural defence system of the witches." The fairies were standing up in their jars again and looked at Norma with big eyes.

"You see, if I have the nails and hair of Trien and use them as an ingredient...." Norma jumped from her chair and did a little dance.

"Then my potion would be powerful enough to change all the witches in weeping willows." Duncan ran his fingers through his hair.

"Hmm, and I'm sure that Trien will just hand over her nails and hair so you can change her into a weeping willow?", Duncan pouted sulkily:

"So that isn't a good idea either!"

Norma looked at Duncan and after a while said:

"Yes I believe that you are right, I have been much too optimistic." She sank back in the chair and put her head in her hands. Then in a soft voice Lotte said:

"We could ask our fairy king for help, couldn't we?" Norma looked up in a daze.

"Ask the king for help?", she said softly more to herself than to the fairies. Slowly Norma got up.

"He will never help me after I have lured so many fairies to this place. And even if he would help me, how do we get the nails and hair of

Trien?" Norma looked at the jars. Next it was Dora who let herself been heard.

"If we don't do anything, then we will definitely disappear into the soup!" More fairies start yelling.

"Yes, get help from our king!" Norma nodded.

"And what do you THINK THAT HE WILL DO WHEN I KNOCK ON THE GATE? '*HELLO, I AM NORMA AND THIS MORNING I SPRAYED MASSES OF FAIRIES, WHO ARE NOW ALL NEATLY IN JARS AT CALIGULA'S PLACE. ISN'T THAT FUN? AND HEY,...............BY THE WAY, CAN YOU HELP ME LOOK FOR HERBS? YOU SEE I AM MAKING THE STARTER FOR THE WITCH BALL. AND FINALLY, COULD YOU GET ME SOME HAIR AND NAILS FROM TRIEN?*' No doubt the king will throw me straight into the cellar." Lotte shook her head.

"I will go with you and explain everything to the king. I am convinced that he will help you."

Now all fairies started to shout in unison.

"To the king, to the king, to the king!" Norma held the palm of her hand in the air as a stop sign.

"Ok, I'll go with Lotte. And ask the king to help look for herbs and to come up with a plan to get the Trien's nails and hair." Duncan jumped in his jar.

"If you let me out as well then I can go and warn your mother." Norma nodded.

"That is a good idea, Caligula won't miss two jars. And maybe you will reach my mother in time. How long do you think it will take you to fly there?"

Duncan thought hard and then said:

"If things go as planned I should be there by tomorrow afternoon." Norma nodded:

"That will be too late, by then most witches will be here. My mother is not able to fight such a huge number of witches. Pity we can't reach her now." Norma sighed, but then said resolutely:

"That is why it is of the utmost importance that we make this potion."

She took Duncan and Lotte out of the jars and put the empty jars in the cellar. She prepared a rucksack with food for Duncan.

"This is for the journey." Duncan hung the rucksack on his shoulder. Norma looked worried.

"Be careful Duncan, make sure that no witches see you." Duncan put his fingertips against his forehead and saluted.

"I, Duncan, colonel of Jingleland, will see to it that Desirée is warned." Then he walked out the door.

Norma left Caligula a message that she was looking for herbs and would be back for dinner. Then she went on her way with Lotte.

IN THE KING'S PALACE

Brave Hunter, the king, queen, Alice and Neston were sitting at the large table in the Chamber of Knights. The afternoon sun shone through the window and the whole chamber was bathed in light. The pearls along the sides of the ceiling radiated a blue glow over the table.

They had just finished eating. The cook had prepared a delicious lunch. Warm soft fairy buns filled with egg, tomato and cucumber, two jugs of fresh orange juice and milk. A plate filled with apples, pears and peaches. A little plate each of vanilla custard. They didn't have any appetite. Everyone was lost in their own thoughts. It was deadly quiet in the Chamber of Knights. The servants took away the untouched buns and custard.

The fairy king sighed deeply and took off his crown. Brave Hunter took a sip of milk.

"King", he started to speak, brushing away a moustache of milk with the back of his hand:

"I assume you have a fairy army." The king nodded and pulled a sad face.

"Yes I do, but most of the soldiers are in jars with the witch Caligula." Brave Hunter put his glass down and continued:

"Could you call on the general of the army?" The king looked at Brave Hunter curiously.

"Dear man, what's left of the army is no match for the witch. What do you want them to do?" Brave Hunter continued:

"I think it is wise if we track down and catch Caligula's niece, before more fairies disappear. I would have a fairy courier get her mother. If she is indeed as nice as you all say she is, then she would never agree with what her daughter is doing."

The king snapped his fingers and shouted:

"Servant, get the general and one of our fastest fairy couriers." The servant clicked his heals together and said:

"Of course your majesty." And then disappeared through the door.

While Brave Hunter was talking to the king, Neston kept thinking about the map of the witch's cottage. Should he tell the others his idea? Maybe they would laugh at him? After all it is a crazy plan. But better than no plan at all. Neston gathered all his courage, cleared his throat and then said:

"I have an idea to trick the witches." At once the whole table was silent. All were staring with large eyes at Neston and were full of anticipation about what he was going to say. Neston swallowed and took a sip of water.

Brave Hunter nodded encouragingly at him; the king and queen also gave him a little nod. It seemed that even Janus, the king's aide, was nodding at him. Neston put his glass down and started stammering:

"Uh.......it is maybe......a kind of crazy idea but.........uh.........I thought." Then he stopped and shook his head, "no, it is too silly to tell." Alice, who was sitting next to him, pulled on his arm.

"This morning you were being so mysterious while I drew the map."

"A map of what Alice?", asked the queen who was sitting right opposite Alice.

"A map of the area surrounding's of the witch's cottage and the witch circle." Alice looked at Neston again.

"Come on now, tell me what you are thinking. I am very intrigued by your little scheme! I promise I won't make fun of you."

Neston threw an incredulous look at Alice, but then started to tell:

"Indeed, Alice drew a map of the surroundings. It showed that the witches circle and the witch's cottage, aren't all that close." The king shrugged his shoulders and said:

"So what?" Brave Hunter also looked at Neston with curiosity.

"Now", Neston continued, "if we get the witches who are coming, to go to another place?" For a moment it was silent, then a smile appeared on Brave Hunter's lips as he nodded comprehendingly.

"I know what you want to do." Now Neston sat on the edge of his chair.

"You see, the witches are coming tomorrow during the day to Caligula's house." Everyone on the table nodded his head.

"They don't know exactly where the witch circle is. So they will fly to Caligula's house first." The king grumbled:

"Yes, that is obvious enough." Undisturbed Neston continued his story.

"If we see to it that the witches don't fly to Caligula's house, but straight to the circle of witches? We put directions by means of arrows made from pebbles with the writing 'WITCH CIRCLE', and we send them far away from Jingleland. We put a large cauldron on that place so that the witches think that they are at the right witch circle."

Neston looked triumphantly round the table. Alice clapped her hands with joy; the king made an approving sound and even the queen looked impressed. Only Brave Hunter looked worried.

"One thing bothers me", he said at last. "At some point they will find out that Caligula hasn't shown up with her potion. I fear..........."

Before he could finish his sentence the door opened. The servant, who had gone to get the general and the courier, stood in the doorway.

"The general is here for you, your majesty", he said politely taking a bow. The colonel was beginning to go bald.On the sides of his head was some brown hair, which was cut very short. What he was lacking on his head he had let grow under his nose. A large brown moustache decorated the colonel's face. The copper buttons on his blue uniform shone in the sunlight. He clicked the heels of his black polished shoes against each other and stood in position in front of the king.

"You have called me your majesty", a voice roared.The king put his crown back on his head and walked to the throne. As he lowered himself onto the cushions he said:

"At ease general."

The general relaxed and walked to the throne.

"General", began the king, "as you know at this moment many fairies are disappearing. It looks as if Norma, Desirée's daughter, sprayed some potion on the wings of our fairies. I would like you to find Norma and bring her to me." The general nodded.

"Will be done your majesty, I will start searching for Norma immediately." He clicked his heels again and left the chamber.

NORMA ASKS THE KING FOR HELP

"I hope they will find her", said the queen. She got up from the table and walked to her throne. Her throne was next to the king's. The king's throne was on a platform. The queen looked at the king with a worried look on her face as she said.

"We have to get to Desirée as quickly as possible." The king nodded.

"The courier will be here any moment." He had hardly finished his words when a servant opened the door and announced the courier.

"Your royal highness, Courier Fast-as-Lightning is in the corridor." The king raised his sceptre.

"Let the good man enter."

A lively fairy flew into the room. He circled the room and then landed in front of the king and queen's throne.

"Fast-as-Lightning at your service!", he said bowing. He held his red and yellow striped hat in his hands. The king nodded his head and said:

"Fast-as-Lightning, go as quickly as you can to Desirée, the good witch; and bring her here immediately. Tell her that her daughter is putting a spell on our fairies." Fast-as-Lightning nodded.

"I will leave straight away your majesty and get Desirée here as fast as possible." The king raised his eyebrows.

"No minute should be wasted!" Fast-as-Lightning nodded even harder.

"I understand king, there is a lot of pressure." The king was about to wave his sceptre to signal Fast-as-Lightning to go, when a lot of noise was heard from the corridor. Everyone in the Chamber of Knights was silent as they looked at the door. The noise was getting closer until the door flew open and the general stood in the doorway. The servant at the door was waving his hands nervously and stuttered with a scarlet face:

"I, I wwwwanted ttto stop hhhhim kiing but he ddddidn't want tttto lisssten."

The general pushed the servant aside and took big strides into the Chamber of Knights. Only then the king saw that the general had two fairies with him. He looked again and screwed his eyes up. It seemed as if one fairy didn't have any wings. Then he saw the queen suddenly jump off her throne and run towards the fairies.

"Lotte", she called. "Lotte, is that really you?" Lotte nodded and her eyes filled with tears.

"I have missed you so much majesty", she said with a croaky voice. The queen took her hands and with tears in her eyes, she

whispered:

"Good to see you again Lotte, I have been worried sick about you." She squeezed Lotte's hands. Lotte blinked a tear away.

"It has been so horrible with that witch, but fortunately Norma has freed me." Only then the queen noticed Norma standing there and stuck out her hand to her.

"Welcome to Jingleland, Norma." Norma was just about to take the queen's hand when Alice ran up in front.

"Welcome, welcome, NOT welcome at all", she roared giving Norma an angry glance. "She was the one we saw this morning spraying the fairies." She pointed with her forefinger at Norma.

"That is the reason so many fairies have disappeared! And now they are all in jars at the witch's house."

The general now took big steps towards the throne, as he dragged Norma with him.

"Majesty, this is Norma, I caught her sneaking into the palace." Norma pulled herself loose from the general and said with controlled anger:

"I wasn't sneaking at all!" She turned around to the king, bowed and said:

"Majesty, I came to ask you for help."

"Help?", everyone called out simultaneously. Norma continued:

"I didn't know that I was bewitching the fairies. You see my aunt had said that the fairies in the jars were sick. She asked me to sprinkle the fairies in the village so they wouldn't become sick as well."

Neston raised his eyebrows and shoulders and nodded at Alice with an approving glance. Alice pouted and didn't seem convinced.

"But", continued Norma, "when I came back to my aunt's cottage", she shuffled her right foot on the floor, "I saw the fairies I had sprayed in jars on the shelf." She looked with begging eyes around the Chamber of Knights.

"I really didn't know I was bewitching them when I sprayed them." She put her hands on her hips and said in a high voice: "Really, you have to believe me."

Everyone in the Chamber of Knights was dead silent and they all stared at Norma. And then, to give her words more power, she said:

"I wanted to warn my mother with the mobile crystal ball. But aunty hid it along with my broom." Norma shivered. "She wanted me to become a real witch!" The king smiled at her and said:

"We also wanted to warn your mother. I summoned courier Fast-as-Lightning to get her as quickly as possible." Norma shook her head.

"That isn't necessary your majesty. The

colonel from your army is already fetching my mother."

"Duncan, my colonel?", bellowed the general. Norma nodded:

"Yes I have freed him and Lotte from the jars." The queen looked inquisitively at Norma.

"Why didn't you free everybody from the jars?" Norma shook her head.

"That was far too dangerous. I would have jeopardized the safety of the whole of Jingleland."

The king waved his sceptre at the servant.

"Fetch a jug of lemonade and some biscuits, our guests are bound to be thirsty." Then he got up from his throne. "Come, let's sit at the table of knights and find out how we can help Norma." Everybody sat around the table. The servant came in with lemonade and biscuits.

When everyone had been served with drinks and biscuits, Brave Hunter asked:

"Norma, what do you need our help for?" Norma brushed a couple of crumbs from her mouth.

"You see it is like this", she said taking a sip of lemonade.

"My aunt thinks that I'm going to make a potion for the witch ball. A potion that will give all the witches beautiful voices." Neston banged his glass on the table and asked:

"But why?" Norma licked her lips and continued:

"You see, aunty thinks that I have become a mean witch............"

And then Norma told in great detail, her story and her plans to catch the witches. They all listened intently. You could have heard a pin drop in the Chamber of Knights. "And that is why I came here to ask your help", she said finally.

Brave Hunter picked up his pipe.

"Good plan", he said, lighting his pipe. "Smart idea, then all the witches will be eliminated and we won't have to worry about any revenge. Collecting the herbs won't be a problem. We can set everybody in Jingleland to work."

"But then all the fairies would have to go outside and that would be far too dangerous", remarked Neston.

The others nodded.The queen shivered:

"Yes and then all the witches would come on their brooms, oh, I can't bear the thought of losing more fairies." The others looked anxious. Brave Hunter shook his head.

"We won't have to be afraid of the witches", he explained. "If I have understood Norma correctly, they are too busy collecting herbs."

Norma nodded in agreement.

"Indeed, that is why my aunt asked me to spray the fairies. She didn't have time herself." She put her glass down and sighed.

"By the way, she wants to help me look for the herbs." Alice said gently:

"You sent them to the other side of the woods to search?" Neston grinned and looked around the table.

"Yes and we'll search on this side!" Everyone nodded in agreement.

Brave Hunter started speaking.

"Searching for the herbs won't be a problem. But getting hold of Trien's nails and hair is another story." Norma pulled a solemn face.

"Yes and Trien and her sisters always arrive last.Trien doesn't like to wait and always wants to be served immediately." Brave Hunter made an approving sound:

"Hmmm." He looked at Neston and gave him a big wink. "I believe that Neston has given us an idea." All eyes were focused on Neston, who began to blush. He looked confused.

"I have an idea about how to acquire Trien's nails and hair", Brave Hunter announced to his audience. Everybody's attention was now focused on Brave Hunter.

It was late afternoon before he had finished explaining and finally the king said:

"So, is it clear to everyone what he or she must do?" The atmosphere was cheerful and a buzz sounded through the Chamber of Knights. The low afternoon sun shone in Norma's eyes. She looked outside.

"Oh it is way too late", she said in a panic. "I really have to go back now before my aunt gets suspicious." She pushed her chair back and got up. Then she took the medallion from her neck and walked over to Neston.

"Here Neston, wear this medallion. It belonged to my father and will protect you against evil forces." She hung the medallion around Neston's neck.

"But make sure that the witches don't see it- put it under your shirt." Neston nodded and put the medallion under his shirt and whispered shyly:

"Thank you Norma." Norma turned to the group.

"So, tomorrow afternoon you will put the herbs on the Sunny path?" The king nodded.

"Everything will be alright Norma, we will put the fairies to work." Norma looked at Brave Hunter and Neston.

"Do not underestimate Trien." She bit on her bottom lip. "She is a very powerful witch."

"We will be on our guard", said Brave Hunter calmly.

A NEW DAY DAWNS

It was still very early in the morning when Caligula went into the kitchen. She was so nervous she hadn't slept a wink all night. Today all the witches were to arrive for the annual witch ball.

"Oh, I hope that everything will go smoothly", she mumbled, taking the kettle from the fire. It was still dark outside and her three friends and niece were still fast asleep. She heard Trix snoring from the attic. It was as if someone was sawing wood, so much noise it made. Between Trix's snores, you could hear Dien making smacking noises. Caligula poured herself a cup of tea and shuffled to the table. She flopped onto the wooden chair and stirred her tea deep in thought.

"How many witches will arrive today?", she wondered. "Fortunately we've been able to collect plenty of herbs. I think it should be sufficient for the potion." She looked up at the shelf in front of her, where the jars of fairies were. Most of them were still sound asleep. Caligula's movements had woken a few fairies.

"Your last day, soup vegetables of mine", she hissed through her teeth. She looked at the sad faces of the fairies. For a moment she felt a pang of guilt. Actually she had grown quite fond of the little creatures. After all she had taken care of them for a long time and soon that would all be over.

"I must not be so sentimental", she mumbled to herself. Caligula shook her head and took a sip of tea. She looked around and grinned.

"I will serve you a delicious breakfast." She got up from the table and started cooking for the fairies.

Norma lay wide awake in her bed. She couldn't sleep with all that snoring above in the attic.

"What a noise those witches make when they sleep", she mumbled to herself under the blanket. "Almost as much as when they are awake." When Norma had come home yesterday afternoon, her aunt hadn't asked where she had been. They were so busy preparing for the witch ball. And by the time they had dinner, the witches were so engrossed with all their gossip that they had forgotten about Norma.

"I should try to sleep for one more hour", Norma sighed, "it is going to be a long exciting day." She turned over and pulled the blanket round her.

On the other side of the woods someone else was also lying awake. Not because there was too much noise in the palace. No, it was dead quiet but Neston lay wide-awake staring at the ceiling. The moon shone its beams through the windows casting shadows on the walls and ceiling – they seemed to be moving. Neston had run through Brave Hunter's plan hundreds of times in his head. What if things went wrong? Luckily he had Norma's medallion, he thought to himself. It felt heavy; just like his eyes. In no time Neston had fallen into a deep sleep.

When Neston opened his eyes, the sun was shining on his bedspread. He rubbed his eyes and jumped out of bed. The palace was full of noise. When Neston had washed and dressed, he walked to the dining room. It was a hive of activity; all the tables were occupied. On one table there was a heated discussion taking place. Neston saw Alice fly from one table to another. She handed out pamphlets and talked excitedly to all the fairies.

"Hey, Neston!", called Brady. Neston waved back and walked over to the table.

"Brady, good to see you", said Neston as he shook Brady's hand. Brady pulled a chair from under the table and said:

"Sit down human child and have breakfast with us." Neston lowered himself into the chair.

"Last night Alice summoned us to be here today", proceeded Brady. "My brother Brad is here as well", Brady pointed to a table a little further up.

"I guess you have to go looking for herbs", said Neston grabbing a bun out of the basket.

Brady nodded.

"Exactly, we will be divided up for each hill." He chuckled a little and made a face.

"I don't quite understand it but it seems to be very important." Neston took a bite out of his bun and mumbled:

"Hmm, hmm, indeed Brady, it is very important."

Just at that moment Alice flew to their table.

"What is important Neston?", she asked. Neston swallowed his bun and said clearly:

"Collecting the herbs, Alice." He then got a glass of milk and drained it in one glug. He rubbed away his milk moustache with the back of his hand and said

"I understand that you already have done a lot of work." Meanwhile Alice handed out pamphlets and said with a sigh:

"Indeed I have been busy. Last night I told all the fairies to be here this morning; then I made pamphlets about the herbs we need and brought everything to the printer." Everyone at the table now had a pamphlet. She looked at Neston and said: "I trust we will find all the herbs in time." Neston nodded.

"Good work Alice, I am sure you will succeed." Alice smiled at Neston and flew to the next table to hand out pamphlets there. Neston finished his breakfast and said:

"Good luck today Brady." He got up. "And

give your brother my kindest regards." Neston nodded at the furthest table. Brady grinned:

"I will pass the message on." And then a little more seriously. "And you too Neston, and good luck with whatever you have to do. I don't know exactly what, but the rumour is that it is quite dangerous." Neston nodded:

"Thank you Brady, I will take good care of myself. See you tonight!" He stuck his hand up and left the dining room. There was a lot of activity in the palace; plenty of coming and going in the hallway. Neston walked through the hallway towards the Chamber of Knights because he thought he would find Brave Hunter there.

Indeed Brave Hunter was in the Chamber of Knights, in consultation with the king and his general. They were bending over a map.

"Look here is the gorge where they have to cross over." The general pointed to a brown spot on the map. They can't fly across it because it is too high." The general rubbed his chin.

"My idea is to wait here for them." He marked the brown spot with a cross. "And here, right in front of the gorge are some caves where you can hide." He drew a circle on the map. "You can hide here until Trien arrives." The king handed some binoculars to Brave Hunter and said solemnly:

"You can see them coming from a long way

away with these." Brave Hunter took the binoculars and hung them around his neck.

"No doubt Trien won't be the only one to fly through the gorge", Brave Hunter ground his teeth: "but there is only one with a red broom!" He nodded at the king and said:

"Thank you your majesty. I'm sure they'll come in handy." The king gave an approving nod.

"It is all right, my man." The general rolled up the map and handed it to Brave Hunter, who put it in his rucksack.

"Is the cloth that I asked for ready?" The king nodded.

"Yes it was brought by the printer this morning." He clapped his hands and called:

"Servant, bring the cloth in." A servant came in with a case and handed it to the king, who took off the lid and pulled the cloth out of the case. It was a grey blue cloth, the colour of rocks and stones. A white circle was drawn on the cloth with a big cross in the middle. On the side was a large arrow pointing to the left. Brave Hunter nodded approvingly.

"Fine, exactly as I intended." He rolled the cloth up and put it back in the case, which he hung on the rucksack. The king stood up while Brave Hunter put the rucksack on his shoulder.

"Be careful", called both the general and the king as Brave Hunter walked out of the door.

THE DEAD VALLEY

Brave Hunter walked through the hallway towards the royal sunroom.

"Hey Neston", he said cheerfully when he saw Neston approaching.

"Good morning Brave Hunter, I was on my way to see you", smiled Neston. "I figured that I would find you in the Chamber of Knights."

"Yes", nodded Brave Hunter. "I've just come from the king and general." He knocked on his rucksack, "the cloth and map are in here." Neston saw the binoculars swinging around Brave Hunter's neck.

"Present from the king?", he asked pointing to the binoculars. Brave Hunter held the binoculars in his hands.

"Yes, we will need these very much. After all, only Trien and her sisters are allowed to see you." He took Neston by the shoulders.

"Come on buddy, let's go!"

The nails and hair of Trien had to be trimmed with special golden scissors. This was the only way to preserve their magic power. Norma would have hidden Caligula's golden scissors near the sheepfold. Neston stood on his toes.

"The little scissors should be here", he said while his hands searched the ridge.

"Got it!" Neston held a red box. Carefully he opened the lid and on the red silken tissue lay a pair of golden scissors shining in the sun. Brave Hunter opened up his rucksack.

"We'd better put them away in here", he said as he took the box.

"If we keep on walking, we should be at the gorge before twelve o' clock." Neston jumped a little in the air.

"Yes, Norma figured that the first witches would arrive from around twelve o'clock."

Brave Hunter took a little case out of his rucksack. Neston recognised the case immediately.

"Ha, we are going to get our old height back." Brave Hunter rubbed some of the magic powder on his and Neston's cheeks. Within an flash they had their old height back. Brave Hunter lifted the rucksack, which had grown with them and started walking along the path. Neston scurried behind him.

The trail they were following lead to the east. To begin with the woods were on the left of the trail and a meadow lay on the right. But soon the landscape started to look wilder. The trees made way for large stones and boulders. The meadow quickly disappeared. Brave Hunter and Neston had to climb and clamber over the stones and boulders.

"Phew!, It's getting so hot", Neston wiped his hand over his forehead. Brave Hunter looked up.

"Yes the sun is already high in the sky." He put his rucksack down and opened the drinking bottle that was attached to the side of the pack. "Here, take this!" He handed Neston the bottle.

Neston took a gulp of the wonderful cool water.

"Hmm, that is nice", said Neston and he rubbed his mouth dry with the back of his hand. Meanwhile Brave Hunter had taken a map out of his rucksack. While he was studying it he mumbled,

"Hmm, the gorge is on the other side of this mountain." He pulled a face at Neston. "Just a little bit further Neston and we can rest in the cave. We are doing well." Neston grimaced and gave the bottle back to Brave Hunter. Brave Hunter took it, had a sip and then said:

"Yes, we are in the valley of death." He smacked his lips: "An impenetrable wilderness where no one will set foot." Neston screwed up his eyes against the sun and said grinning:

"Except two idiots like us." Brave Hunter took his rucksack and nodded.

"Indeed Neston, move on forward."

After fifteen minutes they were on top of the

mountain ridge. Down below them lay a barren plain. The wind was very powerful here and blew with great force through the gorge. Whoo, whoo, it sounded as if a large herd of horses were thundering past, so much noise it made. Pieces of bushes and other debris were dancing in the wind.

Neston and Brave Hunter descended the mountain. When they reached the base, they saw the entrance to the cave.

"In here Neston", gestured Brave Hunter. The cave lay directly opposite the gorge. The entrance of the cave was partly closed by a rock. Brave Hunter and Neston walked along the stone and stood in a large dark space.

"Finally some peace and quiet", sighed Neston. "That wind makes an enormous amount of noise."

Brave Hunter put his rucksack against the stone and took the binoculars in his hand. With his belly he leaned against the rock and brought the binoculars to his eyes. His head was sticking out just enough to be able to look outside.

"Hmm, I do have a good view of the gorge from here." A small sunbeam wriggled between the stone and the cave wall.

Neston took a blanket out of his rucksack

and put it on the ground in the sunlight. He placed a thermos of soup and a bag of buns on the rug and then sat with his back against the wall, letting the sun shine in his face.

"Hmm, everything is peaceful and quiet in here", he thought. Then he pulled a serious face and said:

"I suppose that the first witches will arrive at any moment." Brave Hunter turned around and sat himself next to Neston on the blanket.

"Hmm, it sure is nice here in the sunshine", he said with a sigh.

"We are safe here aren't we, Brave Hunter?", asked Neston suddenly frightened. Brave Hunter nodded reassuringly.

"Don't worry about that. No witch is going to find you here." Neston took the bag of buns and held it in front of Brave Hunter.

"A bun, Brave Hunter?"

"Well, I sure have an appetite after all that scrambling."

He took a delicious bun out of the bag and sank his teeth into it. Neston took the thermos jug.

"Will you see when Trien arrives Brave Hunter?", he asked pouring soup into the bowls. Brave Hunter took the steaming soup and said calmly:

"With my binoculars I can see for miles. Don't you worry about that." Neston gulped his warm soup.

"No doubt we will have to wait a couple more hours as Trien will arrive at the last moment." Brave Hunter gave Neston a big wink.

"We will have to stay down here for a while!" Neston smiled and then said more seriously:

"Trien and her sisters will arrive last, so that will be at the end of the afternoon."

Brave Hunter was just about to take his pipe when they heard a piercing row in the distance.

"The first witches are arriving", said Neston startled. He jumped up and leaned against the rock. In the distance he saw something move through the gorge. Brave Hunter stood behind him, staring through the binoculars.

"It is a large group of witches", he said softly to Neston.

"Here, have a look", he handed Neston the binoculars.

With trembling hands he took them. Yes he could see them clearly now. There must be at least twenty witches with tall pointed black hats. Their long black dresses hung over the brooms and their sharp shoes pointed up. They were getting closer. He could even hear them chattering.

"You said that very well", crowed a witch.

"Yes", replied another witch, "and when I am fed up with all the quacking I just turn him into a mouse." All the witches laughed.

"And if I can't stand the squeaking, I'll bewitch him into a plant!", squawked another witch. Even louder they laughed and then they flew across the cave towards the woods.

"Pooh, what a bunch of cackling old chickens they are!", mumbled Neston and he gave the binoculars back to Brave Hunter.

THE WITCHES ARRIVE

Norma was sitting with Babs on the veranda. She rocked back and forth in her rocking chair. Caligula was with Dien in the kitchen clearing up from lunch. Trix stood in front of the house staring into thin air.

"I'm sure we will hear them arrive", called Babs.

"You don't know that, you don't know that", hissed Trix. Babs shrugged her shoulders.

"It is up to you." She screwed her eyes up and said to Norma:

"You were an early bird this morning." Norma turned to face the witch and nodded slowly.

"Yes", she said stretching. "I had a lot to do." Babs looked up at Norma and asked:

"And do you have everything you need for your soup?" Norma sighed:

"Yes, everything is under control."

Norma closed her eyes and thought back to the morning. She had risen early even before the other witches. Caligula had been busy running around feeding the fairies. When her aunt was bending over the cauldron, she had quickly snuck into the cupboard where the little box with the golden scissors was kept. Just before Caligula had turned around she slid the

box into the pocket of her dress. She had grabbed a chunk of bread from the table and sneaked outside.

She had then walked straight to the sheepfold to hide the box. She had sneaked into the palace just as Alice came in with a pile of pamphlets.

"Ha Norma", Alice had said cheerfully. "You are also up early this morning." Alice had explained that she had gathered all the fairies to look for herbs. In the pamphlets were the names of all the herbs. She would hand them out at breakfast.

"You don't have to worry Norma", Alice had said. "All the herbs will have been collected at the beginning of the afternoon." They had agreed that Alice would put the full basket at the entrance of the Sun path.

Norma sighed and rocked a little harder in the rocking chair. Brave Hunter and Neston had better get hold of the hair and nails of Trien.

"There they are, there they are", Trix jumped a little in the air. Norma then also heard the cooing and chattering in the distance. Caligula and Dien ran outside.

"You hoo, you hoo", waved Caligula. The other witches began to wave and yell.

Norma remained quiet in her rocking chair and surveyed the scene. A large group of witches landed in front of the house.

"Hello Caligula, Trix, Dien and Babs", yelled a couple of the witches as they rested their brooms against the veranda. Caligula jumped up.

"Ha girls", she cooed and, along with Dien and Babs, ran towards them.

"Are we the first?", asked a witch with a dark blue hat. Caligula nodded:

"Yes, I expect everyone to arrive within the next four hours."

"Oh, oh, yes, how cosy", yelled a couple of witches dancing around.

"Here comes another group", crowed Trix pointing in front of her. She had hardly finished talking when Dien yelled that there were more witches coming the other way.

Soon it seemed that from all corners witches were flying to Caligula's cottage. In no time, the area in front of Caligula's house was full of witches. Some witches sat on the floor; others leant against their brooms. It was a sea of brightly coloured dresses and tall hats. The noise was deafening; each witch yelling louder than the next. With great excitement, stories were exchanged about new potions and spells. The latest witch fashions were also a topic of conversation.

Caligula walked around, with red blushed cheeks providing everybody with drinks. She busily waved her arms and everywhere tables appeared with jugs of bat-tea. Dien trailed behind her and magicked up cobweb cookies on the tables.

Norma got up from her rocking chair as Caligula walked up to the veranda.

"Aunty?", she said, "I want to start preparing my soup. Is my cauldron in the witch circle?" Caligula nodded nervously picking at her dress.

"Yes I put it there early this morning. The large pot is mine, but you can use the small one." Norma pursed her lips and nodded.

"Ok, I will go and get everything ready. I will see you over there!"

Norma walked to the Sun path; the place where Alice would put the baskets of herbs. From a distance she could see the baskets ready for her.

"Ha Norma", said Alice who flew towards her.

"Well well, aren't you mighty big today!", she laughed flying around Norma.

"I am not going into Jingleland, I didn't make myself smaller", said Norma, taking large steps towards the baskets.

"This way I am much quicker", she winked at

Alice. Alice clacked her tongue.

"At about twelve o'clock I have sent all the fairies home. Because you told me, that the first witches would arrive around midday. Everybody has been working really hard to collect as many herbs as possible."

They reached the filled baskets. Alice jumped on a basket and looked around grinning.

"This should be enough to turn all the witches into weeping willows." Norma looked approvingly at the well filled baskets. She picked one up and recited a spell. The basket rose up and disappeared into the woods. Alice looked with astonishment at the rising basket and whistled.

"Yeah, it really is great when you can do magic. Will the basket fly to the witch circle?" Norma nodded and glanced at Alice.

"I assume that you heard the witches arrive?", she asked. Alice smiled.

"How could anyone not hear that noise?" Norma grinned while she sent another basket to the witch circle.

"Indeed, they make a hell of a noise. And those clothes........" She chuckled: "I have never ever seen such a multi-coloured collection in my whole life."

Once again she took up a basket, which flew

into the woods.

"I would like to have the soup ready before the witches arrive at the witch circle." She sighed and glanced at Alice.

"They must not see which herbs go into the cauldron." Alice grabbed the herbs and threw them back into the basket. And more to herself than to Norma she mumbled.

"I just hope that Neston and Brave Hunter are back in time with Trien's nails and hair."

TRIEN AND HER SISTERS ENCOUNTER NESTON

Brave Hunter leant against the stone and peered through the binoculars. Neston was sitting on the rug with his back against the wall. For the last few hours they had kept changing place. One group of witches after another flew through the gorge, towards Caligula's house. However for the past half hour not one witch had flown over.

Brave Hunter looked at Neston.

"I think that Trien will arrive at any moment." Neston grabbed his rucksack and said.

"I will get out the cloth." Brave Hunter nodded.

"Good idea, I will also make you smaller." Brave Hunter took the case from around his neck. He lifted the lid and put a bit of powder in his palm and blew it in Neston's hair. In no time Neston was as small as a fairy.

"My flying stick", said Neston pointing to his rucksack. Brave Hunter took the flying stick from the rucksack and gave it to Neston along with the little red box containing the scissors. Then he picked up the cloth and went outside. Neston flew behind him.

Brave Hunter spread the cloth out by the gorge.

"Trien should been able to see this from high up." Then he looked sharply at Neston and said seriously:

"Be careful and don't rush into anything." Neston swallowed and nodded.

"Are you wearing your medallion?" Neston took the medallion from under his shirt.

"Fine", smiled Brave Hunter. "Keep it hidden under there." Neston's lips trembled as he said:

"You will be in the cave, won't you?" Brave Hunter looked with concern at Neston.

"If you find it too frightening you really shouldn't do it." Neston shook his head.

"No, the fairies need to be saved." And then he said, a little more bravely.

"I am not scared!" Brave Hunter gave him a pat on the shoulder.

"Well said, I know you can do it. I will go back to the cave now and signal to you when I see Trien and her sisters arrive."

Brave Hunter took up his place behind the stone and looked through the binoculars to see if Trien was arriving. He would rather have stood on the cloth himself but Trien would never have believed that he was a servant of Caligula's. Neston was still a child and almost as small as a fairy. Small enough for the flying stick and young enough to be Caligula's servant. Brave Hunter sighed deeply:

"Where are they?" Fifteen minutes later, Brave Hunter spotted a red broom in the distance. He half closed his eyes and counted four brooms.

"That must be Trien with her sisters Truus, Toos and Trees", he mumbled to himself. He whistled to Neston a signal that Trien was arriving.

A little further up in the sky Trien hung on her broom. Her hair fluttered in front of her piercing eyes. She had a crooked nose with a big, fat wart on it. Her eyes lay deep in their sockets. Her cheeks were hollow and full of warts and bumps. When she opened her mouth you could see a row of brown stumps. And her lips were cracked and dry. If there had been a contest for the ugliest witch, Trien would win it easily.

Trien sighed. She knew she was uglier than ugly. That is why she had pinned all her hopes on Caligula's potion. Just a little more time and she would be beautiful and young.

"Grr, I just hope, for Caligula's sake, the stuff works", she hissed through her teeth. She looked back at her sisters and yelled:

"Girls we are almost there!" The sisters roared with laughter. Then suddenly Truus said:

"Trien, look over there in the distance on the ground." Trien looked where Truus was pointing and saw a big cross on the ground. She pointed the nose of the broom down and screamed.

"We are going to land here girls!" When they got closer to the cross they saw that it was a cloth with a big cross and an arrow on it. Trees suddenly yelled:

"Hey, there's a fairy on it!" The witches landed right next to the cloth. Neston, who was standing on the cloth, swallowed:

"They seem so big, when I am so small", he thought. The witches stood in a circle around him.

"Who are you?", crowed Truus. Neston gasped for breath.

"I am Caligula's servant", he said softly.

"And why has Caligula put you here?", hissed Trees. Neston breathed in deeply and said:

"To point you in the right direction."

Trien rubbed her pointy chin.

"Hmm, you are not a fairy because you don't have any wings", she said fiercely to Neston. Neston nodded:

"Oh yes I am a fairy but without wings." He continued with more strength in his voice.

"The fairies have abandoned me because I don't have any wings, but Caligula has taken me in. Look I can still fly, without wings."

Neston held his flying stick in front of him and circled in the air and landed on the cloth. Toos threw a sidelong glance at Trien.

"If he is a servant of Caligula, no doubt she will have put a safety layer over him for protection." Trien nodded:

"Let's test it!" She put her hands up and murmured:

> *"Frog egg and wortle tree,*
> *fly around like a honeybee"*

Then she put her hands down and an electric wave ran towards Neston. Even before the spell had reached Neston, it turned around and hit back at the witches.

"Kabam!", it sounded through the gorge. The hit knocked the witches backwards. Trien lay on the ground with her legs in the air.

"Caligula, has certainly protected you well. I didn't know that she had such power", she mumbled. Dazed, Trien got up. She wiped the dust from her dress and walked back to Neston who was standing shaking on the cloth.

The power with which the witches were thrown back, had also surprised him.

"The medallion must have enormous strength", he thought to himself. Trien stood in front of him with her eyes screwed up and looked straight at him.

"Caligula has protected you very well." She pointed at Neston with her crooked finger.

"If she has that much magic power, the beauty potion will surely work very well Trien", said Truus. The other witches nodded in agreement. But Trien shook her head and walked slowly around Neston, mumbling.

"Servant of Caligula. Hmm, servant huh?"

Neston started to feel hotter and hotter; it was clear that Trien didn't believe the story. Would she turn him into a frog or a rabbit? Nervously Neston rubbed his thumb over the medallion. Caligula was getting closer and closer. He smelt her stinking breath. Drops of sweat fell from his head and he thought:

"Oh, I wish the witches would turn to stone."

And then something strange happened: at that very moment the witches were turned to stone. Truus stood with her mouth half open and her hands in the air. She looked like a statue. Trien stood with her neck sticking out looking at Neston while her crooked finger in the air. It seems as if Toos was scratching her head and pointing at Trees.

Bewildered Neston looked at the witches and carefully stepped from the cloth.

"How is this possible?", he murmured full of surprise. He looked down at his thumb that was still on the medallion. Then he heard behind him.

"Amazing!" It was Brave Hunter who had come out of the cave. "Amazing", Brave Hunter repeated. "They look like statues." He knocked his knuckles on the stony back of Truus and it made a hollow sound. He looked at Neston and asked:

"What happened Neston, how was this possible?" Neston shrugged his shoulders and said quietly:

"I don't understand it myself. I was so scared. Trien didn't believe that I was the servant of Caligula. I don't know if you saw it, but she kept walking around me. She came closer and closer. Her horrible prying eyes really scared the hell out of me, Brave Hunter. And then I wished that the witches would change in stone."

Neston swallowed and pointed at the medallion under his T-shirt.

"I believe that this medallion has a lot of magic power." Brave Hunt nodded slowly.

"Yes, your wish has been granted." Neston had a good look at the stony witches.

"I need the nails and hair of Trien, but I don't think stone nails will work." He sighed deeply and looked at Brave Hunter, who bit his bottom lip and asked:

"Why don't you wish that the witches

weren't stone anymore, but turn them into dolls?" Neston nodded:

"That is a good idea." He closed his eyes tight, rubbed his thumb over the medallion and said out loud:

"I wish that the stony witches would turn into dolls."

Slowly Neston opened his right eye. "And did it work?", he asked. Brave Hunter was standing near Trees and knocked on her arm.

"No", he shook his head, "she is still as hard as stone." Neston shrugged his shoulders:

"How strange." He looked down at the medallion disappointedly.

"So it doesn't grant all wishes." Then Brave Hunter looked startled at Trees's shoes.

"Neston, Trees's shoes are no longer stone. And those aren't either", he called, pointing at Truus's socks. "Quick Neston get on the cloth. I think the magic spell is over and the witches will turn back into their old selves." Brave Hunter and Neston didn't lose a second. Quickly Neston jumped on the cloth and Brave Hunter ran to the cave.

Brave Hunter had just left when Trien started to blink. She shook her head a little and looked at her crooked finger hanging in the air. Behind him Neston heard Truus say:

"Come on Trien, don't go on about

servants....." Trien shook her dirty hair.

"Hmm, ignorant goose", she growled.

"What if he hasn't been sent by Caligula?" Truus looked at Trien and shrugged her shoulders. She asked Neston:

"So we have to go that way?" She pointed to the mountains. Neston looked around and said solemnly:

"Yes, Caligula has made a special place for you. You see, she thinks that important witches like you, shouldn't drink out of the same pot as all the other witches."

He looked intensely at the witches' faces. Would they believe him or not? But Toos, Trees and Truus looked approvingly at each other.

"Caligula values us well", crowed Toos cheerfully.

"Indeed we don't want to mingle with the common witches", chuckled Trees. Trien crunched her teeth and pointed at Neston.

"And you, little fairy, will come with us!" She had a mean look on her face and hissed:

"You'll fit on my broom!", a horrible laughter followed.

The other witches nodded and yelled:

"Yes, we'll take you with us, we'll take you with us!" The four of them made a circle around Neston and danced as they sang.

"We are the witches four,
we'll make you beg, 'no more'.
With us you will fly today,
to the magic pot, yippee yay!"

Terrified, Neston looked at the witches who were jumping around him with eyes shining. What would they do to him when they found out that there wasn't a cauldron at all in the valley? Neston got hotter and hotter; his knees were shaking and his hands were trembling. Softly he rubbed the medallion and wished:

"I would like the witches to change into dolls." And yes, just like before the witches stood deadly quiet. Only this time they had not turned into stone but into dolls.

Neston looked at the witches and got out of the circle. He pinched Trien's cheek and said amused:

"So little witchy, there isn't much you can do now." Then he heard Brave Hunter's voice:

"Neston, Neston, quick, cut Trien's nails and hair." With large steps he came up to Neston.

"We don't have much time because the enchantment won't last long." Neston nodded and quickly took the red box out of his pocket. He took out the golden scissors and cut Trien's nails and hair. Carefully he put them into the red box and handed it to Brave Hunter.

"Brave Hunter, here you go, that should be all the ingredients we need for the potion." Brave Hunter put the case in his pocket. He looked at Neston seriously:

"Soon the spell will be broken." Neston nodded intensely.

"I am so afraid Brave Hunter, they want to take me to the magic pot." Neston swallowed and continued, "and there isn't a magic pot, they will surely turn me into a frog or something like that."

Brave Hunter took Neston by the shoulder and said calmly.

"Listen, I think that the medallion works when you are in real danger. When you stand on the cloth again you will have to wish with all your might that the witches won't want to take you with them. And..... don't forget that just a while ago they tried to change you into a honeybee but they failed!" Brave Hunter gave Neston an encouraging wink and disappeared into the cave.

Neston stood on the cloth again and rubbed the medallion with all his might and murmured.

"The witches will go to the valley without me, the witches will go to the valley without me." He looked at the witches one by one. They were still standing there like dolls. He sighed deeply and said loudly.

"Witches you will go to the valley without me!" Neston had to chuckle. "Would they have heard him?" Diligently he kept rubbing the medallion. Slowly the first signs of life appeared.

Truus clapped her hands and shouted.

"Come on girls let's go to the potion. We don't need this scrawny little fairy!" The other witches yelled:

"Yes, yes let's go to the potion and we'll go just the four of us!" Toos jumped in the air.

"We don't want prying eyes, Caligula's servant can stay here!"

Neston held his breath, the medallion seemed to have worked well. He looked at Trien who looked back at him. She shook her head and snapped.

"And where do we have to go?" Neston breathed deeply and continued:

"Between the mountains is an open meadow. There stands a copper pot filled with potion, which will give you beauty and eternal youth." He looked around the circle and saw the witches nod hopefully.

"The potion is made from the finest ingredients." Trien raised her eyebrows and glanced sideways at her sisters. They were in an elated mood crowing about how special and wonderful they were. Then she turned to Neston and looked penetratingly at him.

"And how long does it take?" Neston swallowed. He had not prepared himself for this question. What could he say? It must not be too close or they would find out immediately that they had been tricked. And too far would make it suspicious.

Feverishly Neston thought. Then suddenly a smile appeared around his mouth and he said calmly:

"Now, that depends."

"Why?", Trien shrieked.

"Well", said Neston, "are you going to fly or walk?" Trien raised her eyebrows.

"Walking, walking? We are going to fly of course!", she roared at Neston. Neston shrugged his shoulders.

"It is up to you of course, but if you reach the copper pot walking then the potion has the utmost power. Then you will become the most beautiful witches in the whole world."

Trien stared at Neston. Neston clacked his tongue and continued:

"Yes, that is the other reason why Caligula put the cauldron in a special place for you, so the other witches don't know that you have to walk to it. Otherwise, everybody would be the most beautiful and we don't want that! Do we?"

Neston held his breath and looked at the witches with tension.

"Of course I will walk", cooed Toos. "I want to become the most beautiful." Truus hit the ground with her broom.

"I too will walk because I want to be the most beautiful."

"I will walk with you", squeaked Trees above all the quacking of Truus and Toos. Trien hissed through her teeth at Neston:

"And how far is it on foot?" Neston scratched his head and pretended to be thinking.

"I estimate five hours." Trien's eyes became as wide as saucers.

"Five hours", she roared, "what is this, a game for idiots?" Neston bit his bottom lip:

"Then I would fly, if I were you, you will be there then in an hour." Toos pulled a face:

"You can fly Trien, we will walk." Trees nodded.

"Yes because we want to become the most beautiful."

All three took their brooms and started walking towards the mountains. Trien growled:

"I will walk with you girls." She got her broom and stumbled behind her sisters muttering:

"Five hours, five hours, then it will be midnight!"

When the witches were out of sight, Brave Hunter appeared.

"Well done Neston!", he gave Neston a pat on the shoulder. Neston looked at him beaming.

"At least we will now have enough time Brave Hunter." Brave Hunter nodded approvingly.

"Really clever of you, that story about walking and all to become more beautiful."

Neston nodded and held the medallion in his hands, rubbed his thumb over it and murmured:

"I wish that we were in Jingleland." But nothing happened. Brave Hunter grimaced:

"No Neston it isn't a wishing medallion, as I said before. I think it only works when you are really in danger." He took the case from his neck and said smiling:

"I am afraid that you have to go back to Jingleland under your own power."

He put the special powder on Neston. Neston, who immediately grew back to his own size, said ponderingly:

"Five hours should be sufficient time to have all the witches drink from Norma's potion." He glanced at Brave Hunter.

"Trien and her sisters will be furious if they find out that there isn't a copper pot." Brave Hunter put on his rucksack and started walking.

"Yes, they won't be too happy about it, but", and he gave Neston a big wink, "by then we will be ready to give Norma's potion."

Neston kicked away a stone and said chuckling:

"They'll become the most beautiful weeping willows in the whole world!" Brave Hunter's laughter roared through the valley.

THE MAGIC CAULDRONS MUST
BE FILLED

Norma was busy with the kettle. The fire underneath was burning well and the brew was simmering nicely. All the herbs that the fairies had collected were in the pot. The sun had already disappeared behind the horizon and slowly it was becoming darker.

"Where are Brave Hunter and Neston with the hair and nails?", she muttered. They have to be here, before all the witches arrive at the witch circle!" From a distance she heard the witches yell and scream.

"They're having a lot of fun", thought Norma. Then she heard a branch cracking. She looked at the bushes where the noise was coming from and asked softly:

"Brave Hunter, Neston are you there?" The shadow in the bushes stepped forward and to Norma's surprise she saw Caligula approaching with large steps.

Norma stood as stiff as a board and looked at her aunt.

"Has Aunt Caligula heard me?", she wondered. "I'd better act dumb", thought Norma. She inhaled deeply and said with a strong voice:

"Ha aunty, have you come to make your

brew?" Caligula stood near Norma's cauldron.

"Hmm that smells good Norma", and she sniffed above the pot.

"What do you have in it?" Norma sighed with relief. Luckily her aunt hadn't heard her. She shook her head and said with a secretive smile.

"No aunty, I won't tell you!" Caligula sighed:

"Wizards secrets hey?" Norma grinned waving her wooden spoon in the air.

"Indeed aunty, wizards secrets." Caligula smiled.

"Well done, you are turning into a real witch. Because the golden rule is?" Caligula looked questioningly at Norma and both said in unison:

"A witch never gives away her secrets!"

Caligula cooed out of joy. Wonderful how she has got her niece back on track. Humming, she hopped to her own cauldron.

"What a batwing day today was", Caligula thought. There had never been so many witches at the witch ball. All the witches were extremely excited and looking expectantly at the potion. They had all come for her, Caligula and her special brew! Caligula sighed with satisfaction. And to anyone who was listening, she told of her niece's special brew.

"Your voices will sound like bells", she announced. And the admiration on some of the witches faces made her glow inside. Indeed a batwing day today!

Caligula waved her arms in the air and mumbled a spell. One basket after another came flying through the air. They piled on top of each other near the cauldron. Norma looked in the air and pointed at the flying baskets.

"The herbs and mushrooms for the potion?" Caligula, who was still waving her arms, crowed back:

"Yes, everything goes in the pot straight away except for **one** ingredient." Caligula shrieked and then exclaimed: "The fairies will be put in the cauldron after all the witches have had your drink." Norma nodded and called to her aunt.

"When will the witches come to the witch circle?"Caligula dropped her arms and answered:

"As soon as the moon is high in the sky." She bent down, looked at the wood under the cauldron and murmured a spell. The wood immediately caught fire. When the water in the pot started to boil, she emptied one basket after another above the pot. The brew started to bubble beautifully. Impatiently Caligula stirred the pot, while she mumbled one spell after another.

Norma was watching her aunt from the side.

"Could Brave Hunter and Neston be here already?" As long as her aunt was there, they

wouldn't dare come forward of course. Norma frowned and stirred the pot deep in thought.

"And if they are there, do they have the nails and hair of Trien? Or has Trien caught them? Fortunately Neston had her father's medallion which will certainly protect him." Suddenly Caligula stopped stirring. She put her crooked witch nose in the air and sniffed:

"Sniff, sniff I smell human meat." She turned her face and sniffed at all sides. "Where is it coming from?", she hissed.

Norma looked startled at her aunt, who of course could smell Brave Hunter and Neston. Quickly she murmured a spell to change the direction of the wind. A trick she had learned from her wizard teacher. She shook her head and said fiercely.

"No aunt, you are mistaken, people do not come here! You are smelling my brew, it is starting to work." Norma waved her arms. "The herbs are mixing now and that is where that strange smell is coming from." Caligula sniffed again and pouted:

"Hmm indeed, I think I have been mistaken, I don't smell anything anymore." Then she continued:

"Is your potion ready?" Norma nodded intensely.

"Yes,.......it is...uhhh-..........ready."

Caligula walked over to Norma and looked at her.

"Nervous Norma?" She patted Norma on the shoulders.

"Don't you worry, everything will be all right. I will go and get the witches and you'll see that it will be a success!" Then she disappeared into the bushes.

Norma sighed with relief and whispered:

"Brave Hunter, Neston, are you there? Come on out, the coast is clear." There was some rustling and cracking but then Brave Hunter and Neston stepped into the open field. Norma ran towards them.

"Oh, I am so relieved to see you", she shouted. "I was so scared that Trien had caught you." And then she asked in one breath, while jumping up and down:

"Do you have the nails and hair of Trien?" Neston pointed at the medallion that hung around his neck.

"Without this I would not have been here", he said with a smile. And then a little more seriously: "what an enormous magic power this medallion has!"

"That's right", agreed Brave Hunter, as he opened his rucksack.

"They wanted to turn me into a honeybee." Neston waved his hands. "But the spell glanced off the medallion and threw all the witches to the ground." As he said this, Neston dropped to the ground with both legs in the air. Norma chuckled:

"That must have been a pretty sight." Neston nodded as he got up.

"Yes and what happened then, was even more curious." Norma looked at Neston not understanding. But meanwhile Brave Hunter had taken the red box out of the rucksack.

"Here Norma, Trien's hair and nails", he said solemnly handing over the box.

"You've done it", she said softly, taking the box. "Wonderful", she whispered. But then she looked at Brave Hunter and Neston with worry. "I would love to hear your stories later but now you have to leave straight away." Norma looked timidly around her. "Caligula is getting all the witches and they'll be here any moment." Brave Hunter nodded:

"Yes we will leave for Jingleland right now." He looked seriously at Norma: "Be careful and good luck!" Neston, who was still wearing the medallion, also wished Norma luck. And before Norma had reached her cauldron, they had disappeared.

When Norma threw Trien's hair and nails into the cauldron, a huge flame leapt out.

"What a power!", shouted Norma in admiration, as she stirred the pot with all her might.

THE WITCH BALL BEGINS

"Where are Trien, Trees, Truus and Toos?",
shouted Caligula desperately, gazing into the
sky.

"Well, can we start without them?",
suggested Babs, also staring into the sky.
Caligula shrugged her shoulders.

"Hmm and then later I'd have to deal with a
furious Trien?"

"Well, you could start with Norma's drink",
suggested Trix.

"Indeed Cal, they don't even know about the
drink and all the witches are getting
impatient." Babs pointed at a large group of
witches who were sitting in front of the
cauldron. All the witches had their own wooden
bowls in their laps. Potions work best from
your own magic bowl. That's the reason
witches always take their own wooden bowls
with them.

"How do you intend to stop an angry crowd
of witches Cal, if their wooden bowls stay
empty?"

Caligula looked around the large group of
witches in front of her. Indeed the witches were
getting impatient. There was some calling that
they wanted to start. If they could start with
Norma's potion it would quieten them down.

Caligula scratched her head. And that would give Trien a little more time to come, she thought. She nodded approvingly at Babs and Trix.

"Let's do that", and she walked over to Norma.

Norma was fiercely stirring the cauldron when Caligula came over to her.

"Norma, it seems that Trien and her sisters are running late", said Caligula with a sigh. Norma shrugged her shoulders.

"So", continued Caligula, "we will start serving your drink." Norma clacked her tongue.

"That is fine but......." she glanced sideways at Caligula.

"What but", snapped Caligula. Norma breathed deeply and said:

"One has to wait for my sign before drinking." She turned around to explain: "You see I have to say a spell, just before one drinks the potion." Norma coughed softly and continued: "If that is not done properly, it will all go wrong." Caligula shrugged her shoulders indifferently.

"That is not a problem I will take care of that." She stepped away from the cauldron and went and stood in front of the group of witches. She put her hands in the air as a sign of silence.

"Silence, silence", shouted Babs, Trix and

Dien in unison.

It worked; slowly the hustle and bustle softened.

"My dear fellow witches", began Caligula. "As some of you all ready know, my niece Norma has made a drink for a starter." Sounds of acknowledgment came from the group.

"Yes, yes, our voices will sound like bells", crowed a witch. Caligula nodded:

"Indeed the potion will give you all golden voices." Then she put her finger in the air. "But you only can drink from the potion after Norma has said her spell. If you don't do obey, things might go seriously wrong." The witches nodded their heads understanding. They knew that you have to follow the magic rituals exactly. Caligula waved her arms and crowed:

"Now you can stand in line to fill up your bowls."

Before she had finished the sentence the first witches were at Norma's cauldron. Norma filled one cup after another with her potion. After a time, all of the witches had filled their bowls and were sitting on the ground again. Nobody had tasted the stuff, because nobody wanted it to go wrong. Norma stepped in front of the group and put her arms in the air saying dramatically:

"Witches, I feel very honoured that I can offer

you this drink. After you have tasted it, you will never be the same again." Norma waved her arms wildly and mumbled something in the air. Then she said with a loud voice:

"You can empty your bowl!" She had hardly finished speaking when she heard a loud crash. It was Caligula who had tripped over a pile of wood and lay flat on the ground. Her wooden bowl was rolling along the ground. Norma ran to her aunt.

"Have you hurt yourself?", she asked worriedly, helping her aunt get up. Caligula scrambled up and rubbed the sand from her skirt:

"Those damn logs", she crowed grimacing. "Where is my bowl?", she asked, looking around.

"Here is your bowl aunty", Norma bent down and picked the bowl up from the ground. She handed the bowl to her aunt who said angrily:

"This fall will haunt me for the rest of my life. What a flop!"

She turned around towards the group of witches feeling very ashamed. Suddenly her mouth dropped in surprise.

"Norma, Norma", she stuttered, "what have you done?" Caligula blinked. Instead of a group of witches, she was facing a field of weeping willows.

While Norma was helping Caligula get up, all

the witches had gulped the drink at once. Everyone was so excited that only Norma had heard Caligula's fall.

"Norma, Norma", hissed Caligula, "what on earth have you done?" Norma backed away a little and said:

"Uh aunt I believe, uh that it has gone uh, a little bit wrong." Caligula half closed her eyes and hissed:

"A little bit wrong, a little bit wrong? You call this a little bit wrong?", raged Caligula pointing to the weeping willows. "This is the disaster of the century!" Caligula waved her arms around in despair.

"You have put me to shame! Babs did so warn me about it."

Caligula was out of her mind and ran up and down. Then she shouted at Norma:

"Undo the spell immediately!" Norma was trembling with fear. She had never seen her aunt this angry.

"Don't you hear me Norma", yelled her aunt now

"Undo the spell or, or...."

"Or what Caligula?", a voice came from above. Caligula and Norma looked up and saw Trien, Toos, Trees and Truus hanging on their brooms in the air.

They landed in front of Caligula and Norma.

"Finally you are here", crowed Caligula. Trien got off her broom and stamped on the ground.

"Finally? That servant of yours sent us to the other end of the world!" Caligula looked confused.

"Servant? I don't have a servant." Trien screwed up her eyes and glared at Caligula.

"I had already figured out that you couldn't be behind it. Your servant was too well protected against our magic spells."

Then she turned to Norma.

"But look, who we have here?" Trien pointed at Norma.

"What a surprise", she lisped, "the daughter of the Mighty Sorcerer of the High Mountain and my archenemy!" Her staring eyes transfixed Norma's. Norma saw the anger in Trien's eyes and took a step back.

"Sisters, finally we can get revenge on that self-willed and horrible wizard, who is always in our way!", yelled Trien.

The sisters, who had been following everything from a distance, were getting closer.

"Ha, so you are his daughter, wretched thing", snapped Toos. The witches were now standing all around Norma. We will turn you into a stinking rat, and cut off your tail and send it to your father." The witches screamed with pleasure. Norma reached for her medallion but realized with horror that Neston still had it. The four witches held each other's hands and formed a close circle around Norma. Caligula, however, pulled Norma away.

"You are not going to touch my niece! Nobody is going to be turned into a rat." Caligula's voice was trembling with anger. Caligula stood in front of Norma, to protect her from the four mean witches.

The four sisters look aggrieved at Caligula.

"How dare you to come between us?", Trien shrieked. "Don't have the silly idea that you can stop us on your own!", Trien looked around triumphantly. "We will change your niece into a rat and you into an owl." Trees chuckled:

"Good idea, then she can eat her own niece!"

Suddenly a voice came from above:

"I see that I have arrived just in time." Above the witches head, a broom was circling. It was Desirée. She landed between Caligula and the other witches.

"Mama!", screamed Norma.

"Norma", gestured Desirée, "hide yourself in the bushes." Norma hesitated, but her mother's glance told her not to waste a second.

Desirée looked at Trien and said resolutely.

"I request that you to leave the district immediately."

Trien glared at Desirée and hissed:

"We'll stand wherever we want to." Desirée shook her head.

"I repeat, leave the district." Trien crunched her teeth:

"And you, we will turn you into a spider." At the exact moment she said this, she put her hands up and a fireball raced towards Desirée. Desirée deflected the ball without any problem. Then Trien shouted at her sisters:

"Come on girls, let's finish them!" Fireballs poured down on Desirée and Caligula, but the two witches deflected them all.

Desirée glanced at her sister:

"Caligula we will go into battle together but keep in mind what you are fighting for." Caligula nodded. Again a torrent of fireballs hurtled towards both sisters, but this time they didn't only deflect all the balls but hurled their own in return.

Back and forward the fireballs went. The field and dark sky were lit by red and yellow balls. It seemed like a firework display was in progress. Norma, who had hidden herself in the bushes, could only see fire, smoke and balls. Her mother and aunt were hard to distinguish from the other witches. The battle seemed to go on for an eternity. Then suddenly she heard her mother speak out above the noise.

"Four witches evil that I see,
Slimy frogs you all will be!"

She had hardly finished the words when the banging and fireballs stopped. When the smoke cleared, she saw her mother and aunt standing in front of four frogs with witch hats on. Caligula clapped her hands and called:

"Giddy up, giddy up! Into the woods." The frogs croaked and jumped out of the field.

"They won't bother us anymore", chuckled Caligula. Desirée patted her sister on the shoulder.

"Well done sissy, I am glad that you haven't forgotten the wise lessons of our father!" Caligula crowed back:

"How can I forget that, he drummed it into us everyday." She put her crooked finger in the air and then both sisters said in unison:

"Hate and envy is not the key,
pure hearts conquer as it should be."

Meanwhile Norma came running out of the bushes and jumped on her mother.

"Fortunately you came just in time."

WHAT HAPPENS TO THE WITCHES

Desirée looked frowning at Caligula.

"What a horrible plan you had! You should be deeply ashamed! Throwing fairies in cauldrons for a potion!" Desirée shook her head. She grabbed Caligula by her elbow and pushed her towards the witch's house.

"First we are going to free the fairies that you have locked up." Norma skipped after her mother and aunt.

"Oh, her mother did look angry, she had never seen her mother this angry!", thought Norma.

"And then you will apologize to the fairy king and queen", she heard her mother say to Aunt Caligula. When they got closer to the cottage they heard a peal of laughter. They could see through the trees, fairies flying towards the fairy village. When they reached the little house they saw Brave Hunter and Neston in the doorway. Caligula sniffed the air and crowed:

"So I did smell humans after all!" She waved her fist at Brave Hunter and screamed:

"What are you doing in my house?" Brave Hunter grinned and said:

"We are freeing the fairies of course, what else?" When the three women reached the cottage, Brave Hunter held his hand out to Desirée.

"It is an honour to meet you, Norma's mother." Desirée laughed:

"And you must be Brave Hunter. The one who has been snooping in my sister's magic books." Caligula's mouth dropped open.

"What?", she screamed stamping her feet.

"You have been in my house, I will turn you into a lizard!" She put her hands in the air but Desirée brought her hands down and said fiercely.

"Nobody is going to be turned into a lizard." Then Neston introduced himself and said proudly.

"We have freed all the fairies." Desirée nodded with approval.

"Good; Neston and Norma, do you want to fetch the fairy king and queen? They can decide on the punishment for Caligula and her friends the weeping willows."

After about three quarters of an hour Neston and Norma were back with the fairy king and the general. The queen stayed in the palace to receive the returning fairies.

"Desirée, how nice to see you again", the king said. Desirée was clearly glad too to see the king.

"Majesty I am so pleased to meet you again. It is a pity that the circumstances are so unpleasant." She nodded in Caligula's direction.

"My sister here has a lot to answer for." The king coughed softly

"Yes, we didn't have the nerve to tell you about it, since she is your sister." Desirée nodded understandingly and pushed Caligula forward.

"I believe that this witch has something to say." Caligula pulled on her shoulder.

"Do I really have to do this?", she hissed at Desirée, who nodded assertively.

"Yes, there is no escaping it." Caligula stood in front of the fairy king and with bent head, whispered.

"I really regret very much what I have done to you and the fairies." The king said calmly:

"What you have done is unforgivable. Fortunately all the fairies are unharmed and you have been taking good care of them during their captivity." For a moment there was silence, then Desirée said.

"I want to punish her and the other witches for what they have done. Is there anything that they can do for Jingleland?" The king raised his eyebrows.

"Hmm........." Then the general stepped in front and asked:

"May I be so free majesty as to make a suggestion?" The king nodded.

"But of course, my man!" The general licked his lips and said solemnly:

"Build a lake to swim and fish in." He

glanced at Caligula. "Right where this house is." Before Caligula could respond Desirée replied:

"It will be done." Caligula looked furiously at Desirée but Desirée ignored her:

"From this day forth Jingleland will be out of bounds to my sister and all the other witches." She bowed to the king and said:

"I will see to it that this is done." Before he left, the fairy king asked Desirée:

"Would you like to stay with us for a while as our honoured guest?" She nodded and said with a smile:

"That would be my pleasure. I will come to see you as soon as I have finished everything here."

When the king and general had left, Desirée looked around the circle and said calmly:

"I think that you should go back to Jingleland now, so that I can finish my business here with Caligula and the other witches."

"Do I have to go as well?", asked Norma softly. Desirée nodded:

"Yes, you go too." Brave Hunter agreed:

"Fine, we don't want to be in your way." He tapped Neston on the shoulder and took Norma by the hand. "Come on, we must leave these two sisters alone for a while."

THE GOODBYE

There was a lot of activity in the inner court of the palace. Fairies fluttered back and forward with plates and cups. A large buffet was set up on the left side of the square. The tables were laid with large blue crystal plates, filled with all kinds of goodies. Fresh strawberries with cream, cream puffs, chocolate puddings, cookies, cake and other delicious things, there was too many to mention. In the middle of the decorated table was a fountain, spraying lemonade into the air. In the middle of the court was a stage, where a group of fairy musicians were playing, filling the courtyard with lovely songs.

Everywhere you looked there was singing, dancing and smiling fairies. Brave Hunter stood alone in the Chamber of Knights and looked out of the window over the inner court. He saw the fairy musicians playing, as if their lives depended on it. The fairy with the trumpet had red cheeks from all the puffing. The fairy playing the drums was shaking his head so hard that his long nose almost hit the drums. The fairy singer was running back and forth on the stage, as if she was running the marathon.

Brave Hunter chuckled; it was indeed a

funny sight. Near the buffet he saw Neston, Alice and Norma with Brady, Brad and Bonnie. Neston was gesturing excitedly.

"No doubt he was telling the story of the witch battle", smiled Brave Hunter. His thoughts went back to the previous day. When they had parted from Norma, he and Neston had not gone back to Jingleland, but they had, after they had made themselves little, hidden in the bushes. It had indeed been very exciting when all the witches had gathered in front of the cauldron. Fortunately nobody had smelled them and they had been able to observe everything.

Norma's potion had worked fantastically. As soon as Norma had given the signal that the witches could drink the potion, every single witch put her lips to the cup. What a miracle that all the witches had been turned in weeping willows simultaneously. The firefight between the witches had been very intense and exciting. And he had sighed with relief when those creepy witches had become frogs.

After that he and Neston had gone to Caligula's house to free the fairies. The joy of the little creatures had been enormous. Some fairies had been in captivity for almost a year. They couldn't wait to fly back to Jingleland and see their friends and families again. Brave

Hunter sighed:

"I am so glad that everything has turned out well. The witches have gone and the fairies now have a beautiful lake in which to fish and swim. And now I must go straight to Corsica to help Uncle Antonio." He saw the king, queen and Desirée sitting on a stage. The queen looked up and saw him standing there and waved at him. Brave Hunter signalled that he was coming.

"So, you want to leave immediately?", asked the king. Brave Hunter nodded:

"Yes, your majesty, I have already lost a lot of time and my uncle and aunt need my help urgently."

"It is a pity that you have to go so soon, but I understand that you can't stay any longer", said the king. At that moment Desirée took a golden plaque from her sleeve.

"Here, this will give you access to wizards' county. You will cut out a whole stretch of road and it will save you a good deal of time." She paused but then continued:

"I will send the Mighty Sorcerer of the High Mountain a message that you are on your way. You'll be able to stay with him." She handed him the golden plaque.

"Thank you", said Brave Hunter taking it.

Meanwhile the king received a case from a

servant. "And this, my dear man", he said pointing at the case, "is a map of the area so you won't lose your way." The queen stood up and handed him a parcel.

"This parcel is for your aunt in Corsica, it will relieve her rheumatism and", the queen gestured with her arms at the servant, "we will fill your horses carry bags and your rucksacks with all kinds of goodies." Brave Hunter looked a little embarrassed and whispered:

"Thank you, your majesty."

Meanwhile Neston, Alice and Norma had reached the stage.

"Are we leaving immediately Brave Hunter?" Neston hopped from one leg to the other. Brave Hunter nodded:

"We have no time to lose. Fortunately we have a pass from Desirée to travel through Wizard County."

"Through my father's county?", asked Norma. Brave Hunter looked at her inquisitively, but Desirée answered:

"Yes Norma, through your father's county."

"Oh mum, can I go with them to see my father? I really would like to meet him." Norma looked at her mother with big begging eyes.

"I promise that I will do my best in the witch school." Desirée looked at Brave Hunter and asked:

"Would you mind if she travels with you?"

Brave Hunter shook his head.

"No, not at all, as a matter of fact we welcome the company, eh, Neston." He winked at Neston. Neston smiled at Norma and said clearly:

"Bet you!" Norma made a little jump in the air and took Neston's hands and started to dance.

When they had finished dancing Alice flew to the queen and whispered something in her ear. She looked puzzled and bent to her husband. After a few minutes of whispering the king sat up straight, cleared his throat and said solemnly:

"Brave Hunter, if it is all right with you, could my daughter come along too?"

"Your daughter?", he asked questioningly.

"Yes", answered the king and pointed at Alice. Brave Hunter, Neston and Norma looked confused.

"So you are a princess?", Neston said finally. Alice nodded, her face glowing as she pointed at the king and queen.

"Yes, they are my mother and father." She put on a more serious face and looked at Brave Hunter with big brown eyes.

"I would like to travel with you." She swallowed and continued:

"Please, Brave Hunter?" Brave Hunter looked at Alice and said cheerfully:

"We think it would be great if you travelled with us."

Alice flew to her friends and started to dance again. Then Brave Hunter muttered:
"I don't want to spoil your dance but we really have to go now!"

The group of travellers stood on the edge of the woods. The whole of Jingleland had come to wave them off.
"You will come back won't you Neston?", it was Brady.
What do you think?", chuckled Neston.
"I am going to practice with my flying stick and then I'll get revenge." Brave Hunter's horses had been brought in from the meadow and were now fully packed with provisions. After a final goodbye they all headed off. "Be careful!", they heard the queen call out.

As soon as Jingleland was out of sight, Brave Hunter took out the little case and put some powder on Neston, the horses and himself. Norma used her magic power and they all returned to their real size. Alice was sitting on the horse's neck and they all went forth to their next adventure.

DO YOU WANT TO KNOW
HOW THE STORY CONTINUES?
THEN READ:

'Brave Hunter
and the Giants'

www.Brave-Hunter.co.uk
www.Brave-Hunter.com

Brave Hunter
and the Giants

José Hofstede

illustrations by Ton Derks

Brave Hunter
and the Dragons

José Hofstede

illustrations by Ton Derks

Brave Hunter
and the Sea Snakes

José Hofstede

illustrations by Ton Derks

Brave Hunter
and the Pirates

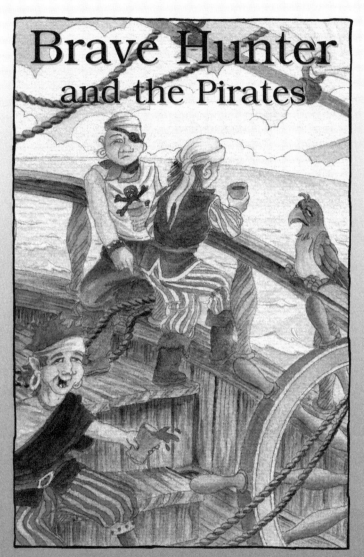

José Hofstede

illustrations by Ton Derks

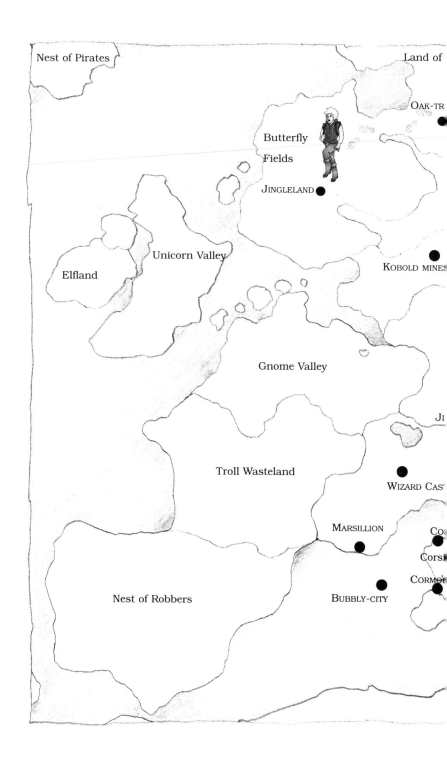

Nest of Pirates

Land of

OAK-TR

Butterfly
Fields

JINGLELAND ●

Unicorn Valley

Elfland

KOBOLD MINES

Gnome Valley

J

Troll Wasteland

WIZARD CAS

MARSILLION ●

CO
●
Corsi

CORMO
BUBBLY-CITY ●

Nest of Robbers

THE HIGH PLAINS KILLINGS

Chato, a notorious comanchero chief, brutally slaughtered some sodbusters on the wagon-train that Luke Culpepper, an ex-US marshal, was guiding across the Pecos in New Mexico. Now Luke was determined to bring Chato and his villainous gang to justice, but he had only the assistance of Baldy Springer, his mule with a nose for Indians and a washed-out Pinkerton agent. Soon Luke's life would be hanging by a thread and justice no more than a hope.

GH00750927

ELLIOT CONWAY

THE
HIGH PLAINS
KILLINGS

Complete and Unabridged

LINFORD
Leicester

First published in Great Britain in 2002 by
Robert Hale Limited
London

First Linford Edition
published 2003
by arrangement with
Robert Hale Limited
London

The moral right of the author has been asserted

British Library CIP Data

Conway, Elliot
    The high plains killings.—Large print ed.—
Linford western library
    1. Western stories
    2. Large type books
    I. Title
    823.9′14 [F]

ISBN 1–8439–5026–X

Published by
F. A. Thorpe (Publishing)
Anstey, Leicestershire

Set by Words & Graphics Ltd.
Anstey, Leicestershire
Printed and bound in Great Britain by
T. J. International Ltd., Padstow, Cornwall

This book is printed on acid-free paper

For Dawn, Paul, Beth, David
and the critter, Rosie

1

Luke Culpepper settled back in his saddle opining it was time he got the wagon-train rolling again. He had taken on the job as wagon boss for the twelve German families who had been left stranded at Fort Riley, Kansas after their original wagon boss had got himself shot dead in a saloon, for accusing one of the men he was playing poker with of being a four-flushing cheat.

The Germans, all farmers, were on their way to their new holdings at Carlsburg, on the west bank of the Pecos, New Mexico, and being that he was heading for Texas, it would be a chance to earn some extra cash — which wouldn't come amiss, as he was figuring to start a new life. Luke smiled to himself. As well as being well paid, the Germans had seen him well fed.

1

And it was certainly a heap safer and easier on the nerves than his four-year stint as a US marshal.

He had worked out of Fort Smith, Arkansas, serving papers on bad-asses defying the law in the Nations, for 'Hanging' Judge Isaac Parker. He had bullet and knife scars, and lumps of lead still in his body, showing how dangerous a calling it was. Eventually, Luke decided he'd had a bellyful of cold camps and cold beans for sustenance, and the stomach-tightening strain of having to be always on the alert in case some wanted man bushwhacked him; he handed in his badge.

He decided to go back to his home state, Texas, where he hoped he could get a job as a marshal's deputy in some dead-dog town well away from any cattle trail so he wouldn't be up most of the night cold-cocking rowdy drunk trail-hands and hauling them off to the jailhouse, or throwing down on a man who fancied himself as an up and coming pistolero. If that didn't pan out, he would work the strip of land left to him by his late pa.

Luke rode slowly along the wagons, checking the families in each Conestoga. He didn't want to leave any sodbuster lying drunk on the floor of some saloon here in Monahan, their last halt for supplies in Texas. He had guided his charges this far without any setbacks or trouble and he wanted to keep it that way.

By following the well-used Chisholm cattle-trail south, Luke had brought the wagons safely across the wild, lawless territory of the Nations. Then, by travelling west across Texas, along the route of the Butterfield stage line, running between a line of army posts, the train had made it to Monahan without having had to fire a shot to defend itself. Now he had to lead the wagons north, along the Pecos. Then it could mean earning his due. As a Texan, he was well acquainted with the West Texas saying of there being no law

3

west of the Brazos and no God west of the Pecos.

Luke rode back to the head of the train at a steady trot, calling out as he passed each wagon, 'We're movin' out in five minutes.' He drew up his mount to wait until the families had finished strapping on all their cooking pots and pans on the sides of their wagons. When he was satisfied everyone was ready, he raised his hat above his head and yelled, 'Let 'em roll!'

He heard the sharp cracks of whips and guttural German shouts and, with the rattle of pots and pans and creaking wheels the wagon train rocked into movement. Luke waited until all the wagons had rolled past him, nodding back at the smiling, hand-waving children alongside the wagons before riding out ahead of the train, clear of the dust clouds it raised in its passage. He rode straight-backed, eyes alert, Winchester laid across his saddle horn, ready for quick use.

2

Luke reckoned he had done a good job of nurse-maiding the Germans, calculating that another half-day's trailing and the sodbusters should be bouncing over the soil they had trekked all the way West to plough. Noting no signs of any large bodies of riders, shod or unshod, he relaxed his guard slightly and began to contemplate his plans for the future.

Suddenly his mount gave a coughing snort and stopped dead in its tracks. Luke's brain had only time to register the sight of two arrows sticking out of its neck, when he gasped out in pain himself, as an arrow plunged deep into the fleshy part of his right shoulder causing him to lose his grip on the reins. Then with blood gushing out of its mouth, the horse collapsed beneath him, throwing him side-ways out of his saddle.

Luke hit the dirt hard and painfully and was powerless to stop himself rolling down the bank. Every spin of his body drove the snapped short arrow deeper into his body and he plunged into the Pecos barely conscious. The ice-cold waters cleared his pain-fogged brain enough for him to hold his head above the swirling water as he was carried, cork-screwing in the eddies, downriver.

Gasping for breath, numbed by the cold, almost ready to give up the agonizing struggle of staying afloat, the current swept him on to a small, sandy, weed-covered spit of land close to the left bank. Exhausted with pain and loss of blood, he could do no more than struggle a few feet on to the island and, with the river tugging at his legs, passed out.

Two ranch hands looking for strays saw him lying there. By using their ropes as life-lines they waded into the chest-high water and hauled him to safety. Strapping him on to one of their horses, they high-tailed it back to the ranch, keen-eyeing all around them for signs of the men who had arrow-shot the stranger.

3

Luke came to lying on a cot in what he took to be a ranch bunkhouse, with bandages strapped tight across his shoulder. It felt as though a branding-iron had seared its mark in his flesh and a dull pain throbbed incessantly in his right leg. The rest of his body ached as though he had been kicked hard several times. He groaned as he tried to lever himself up in the cot and with a gaze blurred by tears of pain he saw an elderly ranch hand wearing a cook's well-stained apron, stoking up the pot-bellied stove in the centre of the room with logs of wood.

On hearing Luke groan, the cook glanced across at him then poured out a cup of coffee from a smoke-blackened pot.

'I reckon you could do with a drop of this,' the old man said, as he came up to the cot. He grinned at Luke. 'I've put in a slug of the hard stuff I keep in the cookhouse just to ease my achin' joints. You're bound to be more than a mite sore; I had to dig deep to get that arrow head outa your arm. And you've got a lump tore out of your right leg by another feathered stick. But you ain't runnin' no fever so it looks as though your wounds ain't about to go bad on you.'

'How long have I been lyin' here, mister?' Luke asked worriedly. 'I was actin' as wagon master for some German sodbusters headin' for their new holdings just north of here when those goddamned Injuns jumped me. Are they OK?'

Luke saw his answer mirrored in the old cook's eyes before he spoke. And Luke wished he had drowned in the Pecos.

'Most of 'em are, Mr Culpepper,' replied the old man. He grinned at Luke's surprised expression. 'Those sodbusters told us who you were. You bein' hauled out of the Pecos, arrow shot and brought here warned the boss that killin' trouble was happenin' on Bar X land so he quickly rounded up the crew and headed upriver loaded for bear.' The cook's face hardened. 'We managed to drive off the comancheros before they massacred all the Germans; shot dead some of the murderin' sonsuvbitches as well. That was two days ago, Mr Culpepper.'

'Comancheros?' Luke said. 'I thought it must have been Injuns who bushwhacked me, seein' I got an arrow stuck in my hide.' He sank back on the cot, the whiskey-laced coffee forgotten, his mind a deep pit of black despair. His carelessness had got women and children killed.

'Naw, it was Chato's comancheros who jumped you, Mr Culpepper,' the cook replied. 'Though he is part Injun, as are most of the bloodthirsty scum who ride with him. You were meant to be killed silently so as not to warn the Germans they were headin' slap bang into an ambush. Chato likes all the edge before he makes his move. You ain't the first man by a long chalk Chato's sneaked up on unawares. He's one cunnin' sonuvabitch. Why, there's a whole company of horse soldiers tryin' to hunt him down. All they've done so far is ride round in circles lookin' up each other's asses.'

The old cook's words didn't comfort Luke any. He still believed he had let down the people who had hired him to lead them safely to their new homes. He and no one else was responsible for the deaths of those who lay in shallow graves on the banks of the Pecos.

'That m'be so, friend,' replied Luke. 'But it somehow don't ease my conscience any. I feel it's kinda beholden to me, like the Good Book states, to get blood for blood. I know it won't bring back those folk the comancheros butchered, but I'll sleep more restful if I can send some of those comancheros to Hell where they belong; Chato in particular.' He favoured the old cook with a wry grin. 'I reckon you must think I'm loco intendin' to go off on a wild-ass hunt, but right now I couldn't put my mind to do anything else.'

The old cook grunted non-committally. He wasn't about to waste his breath arguing with a crazy man who admitted the dangerous foolishness of his actions to try and ease an unsettled conscience. He opined that Chato would soon have another scalp hanging from his belt.

'It ain't my place to put a fella off what he reckons he oughta do,' he said. 'But what you're figurin' to do will have to wait until that shoulder of yours mends. The boss don't mind you stayin' on the spread until you're fit enough to travel. Now get that coffee down you and sleep some, that's the only medicine I can give you, bein' I can only doctor horses when I ain't cookin' for hungry, thankless cowhands. And I should be over in the cookhouse right now. If there ain't any grub on their plates the crew will blow my ears off.'

12

Luke drank the coffee, the whiskey it contained relaxing him enough to lie back and drop off into a light sleep enabling him to forget for a while about the fearful task he had set himself.

4

Baldy Springer heard his mount give a nervous snort. He spat a stream of brown juice between the pricked-up ears of the rangey-legged mule.

'You've got a smell of Injuns passin' this way as well, Jethro,' Baldy said, mockingly. 'You must be gettin' old. I picked up their sign as we were crossin' the trail leadin' into Emory Pass.'

Baldy cast an apprehensive glance over his shoulder at the saw-toothed peaks of the Black Ridge mountains filling the horizon behind him. He took off his hat and scratched at the puckered, fish-belly-coloured skin that covered his hairless head like a macabre skull cap.

'Though they ain't Injuns, Jethro,' he said. 'The tracks I seen were made by iron-shod horses, but too many of 'em to be a ranch-crew's trail.' Baldy's face screwed up in concentration. 'If they ain't Injuns' or cowhands' doin', Jethro,' he said softly, 'those tracks must have been laid down by a big bunch of comancheros headin' north to their hole-up on the Staked Plains. Though your nose ain't playin' you wrong, those sonsuvbitches are as close to Injuns in their murderous ways and habits as to be blood kin. And I don't mind confessin', I'm as skeered as you are knowin' we've just missed bumpin' into them head on.'

Jethro broke wind, loud and foul.

'You can keep your goddamned opinions to yourself, you, you, walkin' fleabag,' Baldy growled. 'You oughta be skeered; if the comanchros took you they'd eat you in a bad winter.'

Jethro snorted.

'I see 'em,' Baldy said. 'I m'be old but I ain't blind.'

The dust the pair of them had seen was heading in their direction, too big and slow-moving to have been raised by an Indian or comanchero war band. It

could only be some of Charlie Goodnight's cattle being driven to new grass
along the Pecos, Baldy thought. Though
he did wonder why they were being
driven so fast. If the hard men
Goodnight had on his payroll didn't
shoot him on sight for riding across
their boss's range uninvited, he maybe
could beg some coffee and beans from
their cook.

'We'll stay put here, Jethro,' he said.
'Smilin' real purty to let those trail
hands see that I ain't a look-out for
some gang of cattle-lifters.'

Ed Newton, riding point on the herd,
saw the lone horseman up on the ridge.
Suddenly it didn't seem like easy-raised
wherewithal for him and the boys,
sneaking off with a few score head of
long-horns from Charlie Goodnight's
vast herds spread all across southern
New Mexico, then driving them across
the line into West Texas where buyers
didn't ask for bills of sale.

If the man up ahead was one of
Goodnight's crew they would have to

leave the cattle and hightail it back to Texas before the watcher raised the alarm — or risk choking on the end of a rope slung across a branch of the hanging tree, or shot dead. Newton stopped his cursing and dirty-mouthing in mid-flow. The rider hadn't cut and run for it, and he couldn't see dust being raised by riders coming in fast to join him, so he figured the man must be a lone drifter. Whoever he was he would have to be got rid of, being as he could describe their likenesses to Goodnight and the old bastard's cattleman's law ran a wide loop, right across into Texas.

'Gino!' he yelled to the left swing rider. 'While I go ahead to have words with that fella, you circle around him, real easy like till you get close enough to cut him down.'

Baldy sat back in his saddle, face fixed in a jaw-aching, guile-less smile. Then his face tightened as he noticed the left-hand rider, a Mexican, was edging his mount round to come on to him from his rear. And seeing the bandolier of reloads slung over one of his shoulders also disturbed Baldy. No dollar-a-day trail hand could afford to buy as many shells, or be foolish enough to allow his hard-working cow pony to carry the extra weight. Alarm bells began to sound in Baldy's ears. If the Mexican wasn't a vaquero he could only be part of a border cattle lifting gang. That meant, he reasoned, there was more in the two riders' purpose than just coming across to pass the time of day with him. It would be hot lead not coffee and beans they would hand out.

Baldy had spent most of his life on the high plains of Montana and Wyoming stamping ground of the Sioux and the Crow, trapping for beaver and killing cattle predators for the ranchers. Territory where a man had to develop several senses he hadn't been born with, or lay claim to an early grave.

He had drifted south to New Mexico where there were ranches and town-ships, where an over-the-hill old man whose reactions were slowing down could sleep at night with both eyes shut. Or so he had thought.

A lone Apache buck, slipping off the agency and looking for a horse and guns so he could ride south into Mexico to join up with other broncos, jumped him while he was asleep, within a couple of rifle shots from Hondo. Baldy couldn't understand why the Apache hadn't killed him before scalping him, but the Indian's action had saved his life and got his attacker dead.

The fierce agony of the knife sawing away at the top of his head brought him fully awake, mad angry with fear and pain. He had grabbed for his own knife, stuck in the ground at his side, and slashed wildly behind him, disembowelling the Apache. Almost blinded by the blood and the flap of skin and hair hanging down in front of his eyes he left all his gear and scrambled on Jethro's back and made it to Hondo.

Baldy hadn't needed the doctor who treated his wound to tell him he was lucky to be alive. He also told him he could kiss goodbye to his hair ever growing back on his head. Losing his hair didn't upset Baldy any, if it had grown it would have turned white. His close, painful brush with the Grim Reaper had rewakened his instincts of self-preservation and once more he slept on his back with one eye open.

Baldy had both eyes wide open and all senses fully active and smelt trouble, killing trouble, riding in on him. Still smiling, he drew aside his coat and reached inside his shirt, gripping the butt of the Dragoon Colt and thumbed back the hammer to full cock.

Newton relaxed somewhat on seeing who it was sitting up on a raw-boned mule, an old saddle-tramp wearing a long, mangey buffalo-hide coat. Downing him should present no problem. He thin-smiled. The dirty old goat was long overdue for despatching.

The Mexican was the biggest danger, Baldy calculated. If he got behind him the sons-of-bitches had him boxed in.

He took a last confirming look at the two riders to make sure his instincts weren't playing him wrong and he wasn't about to gun down two hard-working trail hands.

Baldy's assaying didn't take long, he'd had killing looks cast his way more than once. He cursed. This was trouble he hadn't sought. If he did manage to shoot the Mexican and his *compadre*, he thought, how could he possibly hold off the four, five men with the cattle? He sure couldn't outrun them on Jethro. The old fleabag wouldn't race a gallop short of lighting a fire beneath his ass.

The Mexican was still more than a fair distance away for the certainty of a killing shot with a pistol but Baldy couldn't let his doubts delay his action any longer; at any moment the Mexican could pull out his rifle and blow him out of his saddle. In a single fluid movement he yanked out the Dragoon, laid the barrel across the crook of his left arm, then took a quick sighting on his target and squeezed off two shots.

In spite of his age and the speed of his action, Baldy had the grim satisfaction of knowing he had lost none of his skill as a marksman. The heavy calibre shells struck Gino full in the chest, tearing his heart apart before blowing fist-size bloody exit holes in his back. The smashing impact of the shells knocked him backwards out of the saddle and, with arms out-flung, he hit the dirt, already a dead man.

The deadly swiftness of the old man's pistol work threw Newton off balance for a few seconds; vital, lost forever seconds, allowing Baldy to twist in his saddle and throw down on him. The last thing Newton saw as he slumped across his horse's neck with a red-weeping hole in his forehead, was the gun flash of the shot that killed him.

Baldy didn't give the two bodies more than a cursory glance, whether they were dead or not didn't matter; they were no longer a threat to him. It was getting-to-hell-out-of-it time, and fast. He pulled Jethro's head round sharply, and dug his heels hard into the mule's ribs.

'Run, you son of Satan!' he yelled. 'Or you'll be gettin' a new owner! And he'll not be as kind-hearted towards you as me!'

Jethro drew back his top lip, baring yellow fangs of teeth in an angry, hurt snarl. He had never been kicked before, and sensing the fear of his owner was shocked into action. With a dirt-and-stones-raising, kicking-back-legs start, almost unseating Baldy, Jethro took off in a headlong gallop.

Although he was raising the dust, Baldy wasn't running scared; he opined he was carrying out what the army big brass would call a strategic withdrawal. He knew the *compadres* of the men he had shot would be out for his blood, seeking revenge, or more likely, he thought, to stop him from alerting the ranch hands at the nearest branding camp that some of their boss's cattle were being lifted.

Baldy had an eye for the terrain and how to use it to his advantage. The slight rise half a mile or so ahead would be where he would make his stand. With the big Sharps rifle that could bring a buffalo to its knees at 500 yards he could maybe make the sons-of-bitches keep their distance until nightfall. As an old trapper and trail breaker the darkness would be his ally. Only an Indian would be able to track him. Even the clumsy-footed Jethro could cover the ground silently in the dark, if pressed to do so.

The five rustlers with the herd had bunched up to watch Newton and Gino closing in on the rider. That the man would have to be killed didn't upset them any; taking precautions to protect their own lives came first.

The sudden killing of their *compadres* had them all rocking back in their saddles with disbelieving looks twisting their faces. Then they got over their shock and began cursing at the fast disappearing shooter. Winchesters were pulled out, heels dug savagely into horses' ribs and they raced after the man who could see them all hanged unless they gunned him down.

Baldy pulled hard on Jethro's reins as the mule breasted the rise, bringing him to a haunch-sliding halt. Before the dust of Jethro's sudden stop had settled, Baldy was out of the saddle, gripping the .50 calibre Sharps single-shot rifle. He slapped Jethro on the rump which sent the mule trotting a few yards down the slope so it was below the rim line, safe from any shots meant for him. Then he dropped flat to the ground behind the ridge.

Baldy laid a handful of shells alongside him and deftly thumbed a load into the Sharps. He took a quick look at his pursuers, coming at him in a loose half-circle, judging their distance, before bringing the Sharps up to the firing position. He raised the back sights and framed the nearest rider in them. He smiled grimly; the cattle-lifting bastards were about to hear the bells of Hell toll.

The deep boom of the buffalo gun and the blood-chilling whine of its shell's flight echoed across the plain. Baldy's target felt a moment or two of infinite pain as the heavy ball caved in his chest. The rustler, choking to death on his own blood, lost all grip on his horse and slid out of the saddle off his still fast-moving mount, hitting the ground in a bouncing roll.

Baldy quickly reloaded and picked out another rider and fired, but only winged his man. The winged rustler dropped across his horse's neck, howling with pain as he clutched his shattered left shoulder. His horse veered away to Baldy's left, still raising the dust. Baldy was satisfied with his score so far; he had cut the odds facing him down to three, and slowed down their style. The sons-of-bitches wouldn't be riding in on him in wild Texas fashion, reckoning on stomping him into the ground. Like him they were kissing dirt behind some mound. Though he was still between a rock and a hard place.

He had to hold them off with the Sharps for at least a couple of hours until it was dark enough for him to break off the action and sneak away unseen. He was banking on the rustlers quitting first, putting their own necks before seeking vengeance for him killing their *compadres*. They had a bunch of stolen cattle behind them to be driven across into Texas which they would lose if the shooting drew any of Goodnight's crew to the scene. Then, as well as losing the cattle they could also forfeit their lives.

Baldy lay, watching, listening and sweating.

5

It had been three days since Luke had
left the Bar X, his shoulder not yet fully
healed, but the urge to get on the trail
of Chato ate painfully at his stomach
like a cancerous growth. He had
thanked the ranch owner and the crew
for tending to his wounds and allowing
him to share their rations and had
ridden out to pick up the comancheros'
sign at the spot where they had attacked
the wagon train.

Feeling the way he did, gazing down
at the rough-made wooden crosses
— stuck in the mounds of freshly
turned dirt, he was glad the remaining
Germans had journeyed on to their
new holdings, escorted by a cavalry
detail. Expressionless-faced, mad or
not, his only task in this life was to kill
Chato and, if possible, as many of his
men as he could, even if it meant him

28

losing his own life doing it.

The clear trail of the comancheros petered out on the hard, sun-baked ground before he had crossed the border into New Mexico. Luke cursed Chato to hell and beyond. Then cursed himself for thinking it would be a walkover tracking down men who knew every trick there was in hiding their tracks. What he could see of the tracks they were heading north, so riding north seemed the right thing to do. Of course, Luke thought, the comancheros could have swung east, back into Texas, doing their killing there. Until he had clear signs they had cut away to the border, he would continue north. Otherwise he could be going round in circles like the horse soldiers.

The trail swung away from the Pecos and, on breasting a slight rise, Luke saw the longhorns roaming unattended on both sides of the trail, and the dark, crumpled bundles of two men. He opined the dead men were part of the crew with the herd. The rest of the men nursing the cows must be in hot pursuit of the bunch of rustlers who had gunned down the two men in their attempt to take the cattle. Luke jerked his left-hand rein to take a closer look at the bodies.

'You've read it wrong, Luke,' he told himself. The dead men were Mexicans and Luke hadn't seen men so armed up since the end of the war. He knew he was gazing down on a couple of *bandidos*, cattle-lifters. Then he heard the distant sounds of gunfire which could only mean the herd's crew had caught up with the gang of rustlers and were fighting it out.

It wasn't his fight, Luke thought. He would need all the luck in the world to track down and kill Chato; he didn't want to waste any of that fervently prayed-for luck taking part in a gunfight with a gang of border hard-cases. Luke made to cut away from the abandoned herd, then with a 'what-the-hell' smile, pulled his mount's head round in the direction of the small battle. He had handed in his tin star, but opined he still had peace-officer's blood running through his veins and poor, hard-working, underpaid ranch hands had enough grief to contend with trailing ornery cows all the way to the rail-head towns without having to fight off a gang of border cattle-lifters.

Baldy cursed as a Winchester shell kicked up a spurt of dust near him. The son-of-a-bitch Indianing up on his left, was getting too close for comfort, too close for him to raise his head to try and pinpoint exactly where he was before pulling off a shot without risking a slug in his head. And it wouldn't be dark enough to cut and run for it for another hour or so, that's if Jethro hadn't got tired of waiting for him and taken off on his own.

Then Baldy began to think like an Indian. A Sioux buck wouldn't lie scared waiting for his enemy to come in and kill him, he would take the fight to his foe. Reasoning that if it was his day for dying he would do it like a man, on his feet, not like a yellow cur dog, hard-faced, Baldy pulled out his Bowie and began crawling, low-assed, towards his 'enemy' on the flank. It would have to be a no-fuss killing, he thought. The other two rustlers seemed content to stay put, thinking they had him by the balls keeping him pinned down while their *compadre* sneaked in and finished him off with a well-placed shot. Before the bastards cottoned on to the fact that he had sprung their trap and their buddy was lying there with his throat slit he'd get out of this hairy situation fast, on his own legs if Jethro had quit on him.

Luke pulled out his rifle and dismounted. Keeping crouched down below the skyline, he walked up the ridge to drop on his belly and look over the lip. He was within 200 yards or so of the small battle being played out below him and could clearly see all the participants: saw the two riflemen firing on the old man, and picked out another man belly-crawling to outflank him.

The old man in his battered plains hat and long hide coat couldn't be a ranch hand, Luke opined. He favoured him being a ragged-assed drifter unlucky in his wanderings to meet up with a bunch of rustlers. Whoever he was, the old goat had made his mark on the gang, two dead men back at the herd and another body lying behind the riflemen. Right now, Luke thought, the old sharpshooter could do with some back-up. He brought his rifle up into his shoulder, drew a bead on his clearest target then squeezed off a shot.

It was a true killing shot. The rustler groaned loudly and dropped his rifle, stretching out his arms as though he had suddenly come over tired and wanted to catch up on his sleep. The other rifleman heard the crack of the shot and his *compadre*'s dying sigh as he was thumbing reloads into his Winchester. Shells fell from nerveless fingers as he realized that the shooter up on the ridge had all the edge. It was running-for-home time. Luke's second shot caught him in the back as he was getting up on to his knees to make a run for it. He gave a painful grunt and dropped down on to the dirt again, as dead as his *compadre*.

The rustler trying to close in on Baldy also didn't favour the odds he was now facing, and sprang to his feet to cut across to his horse, his wild-eyed gaze swinging between the rifleman on the ridge and the man he had been hoping to kill. Baldy got a clear sighting of him and raised himself up from the ground and threw the Bowie, grunting with the exertion. The panicking rustler glimpsed something glinting in the sunlight, speeding through the air towards him. Before his brain could register what it was and the danger to him, he felt a sickening pain in his neck and the warm stickiness of blood gushing down his throat. Suddenly he had no feeling at all, just a dim, distant sensation of his legs folding up beneath him and falling down into a never-ending dark pit.

Baldy, cautiously, got to his feet. Whoever the shooter was, he knew the killing business well. He tagged him as a regulator hired by Goodnight to put paid to the men who were helping themselves to his longhorns. And regulators, he knew, were men not particular of whom they shot down, being paid on a head count of the bodies they brought in slung across a horse's back, men past protesting to Mr Goodnight they were not cattle-lifters. An apprehensive Baldy raised his Sharps horizontally above his head, the plains' sign that his intentions were peaceful.

'I ain't with these fellas, mister,' he called out. 'The sonsuvbitches kinda sicced themselves on me!'

Luke came down from the ridge, mounted up, riding in close to the old man. He thin-smiled. 'You're sure garbed like some border hard-man,' he said. 'But no self-respecting cattle-lifter would be seen dead up on a slab-sided mule, so you can lower that cannon before you bust a gut.'

Baldy brought the Sharps down to waist height, quickly assessing his saviour, whose smile, though friendly, in no way lightened up the bony, drawn-skinned face. It was the face of a man, Baldy reckoned, with a lot of trouble chewing away at his innards.

'My name is Baldy Springer,' he said. He took off his hat. 'You can see how I came by my handle.' Luke flinched at the sight of the fearsome scar. 'But the Injun who gave me the haircut didn't live to boast to his red brethen at their lodge fires about it,' Baldy continued. 'But that ain't here or there; I oughta be thankin' you for pullin' me out of a tricky situation I just walked blindly into. I take it you been hired by Mr Goodnight to do some regulating for him.'

'No, I ain't a regulator, or a bounty hunter, Mr Springer,' replied Luke. 'Though I did wear a lawman's badge back there in the Nations. Just to be sociable, my name is Luke Culpepper.'

36

Then briefly he told Baldy of his mission, the vendetta against Chato and his comancheros. Luke favoured the old man with a ghost of a smile. 'I reckon you could say I'm still in the law-enforcin' trade, though now it's kinda more personal. I know it's a wild chance me findin' the sonuvabitch's hole-up when he ain't out burnin' and killin', but I've got to damn well try.'

Baldy grinned. 'Now that m'be wrong thinkin' on your part, Mr Culpepper. I caught sight of what me and Jethro, there, think were tracks made by a bunch of comancheros at a pass in the mountains. They were headin' north towards the Staked Plains, where, I opine, Chato has his hole-up. Of course, I could be wrong about the tracks, I wouldn't want to send you off on a wild goose chase, but I don't think so.'

'It's worth checkin' out, Mr Springer,' Luke said. 'It's the only lead I've had so far.' Then he began to wonder how a mule could read tracks, but wasn't nosy enough to ask the old man the secret of the mule's special talent.

'You'll m'be do that, Mr Culpepper,' Baldy said, casually, 'if you can convince those *hombres* ass-kickin' it in on us we ain't a coupla no-good cattle-lifters.'

Luke twisted round in his saddle and saw the dust pattern of several riders rein-lashing their mounts, approaching them. Luke's face lengthened with tension. He figured he was on Goodnight's land, and the biggest cattleman in the south-west employed ornerytempered men; men, who if they thought he and the old drifter were cattle-thieves they would only live as long as it took them to throw a rope over a branch of the nearest tree.

'Mr Springer,' he said, still eyeing the closing-in riders, 'try not to look so mean and lay down that buffalo gun. We're about to pass the time of day with a bunch of tetchy *hombres*.'

In a cloud of billowing, throatburning dust, the six riders drew up in a rough semi-circle in front of them. Gimlet-eyed, intimidating men, gringos and Mexicans.

'I take it you boys are some of Mr Goodnight's crew,' Luke said, watching the riders for the slightest signs of any hostile movement from them, such as hands pulling out pistols; Then his beholden trail would end right here along the Pecos in a blaze of gunfire for no goddamned reason at all.

Before he could say who he was and why he was here, the thickset man wearing a well-worn, blue, store suit, growled, 'We know who we are, mister. What I want to know is what you two *hombres* are doing on Mr Goodnight's land? Me and the boys have hightailed it from the west range on hearing the gunfire, passin' a bunch of the boss's longhorns and two dead men on the way. And I can see four more men, likewise dead, lyin' around. Now you two fellas just prove to me why I shouldn't have my boys string you up on yonder tree for bein' no-good cattle-lifters. And make it quick!'

To Luke's surprise it was Baldy who did the answering, backing up his words with the big Sharps. Somehow the old man had the rifle to his shoulder and was pointing it at the hardfaced spokesman.

'Pilgrim,' Baldy grated, 'if those boys of yours so much as fart, so help me I'll blow your spine clear across to that west range you spoke of.'

The ranch-hands caught short by the speed of Baldy's action sat tight in their saddles, as unmoving as though hewn from stone. Baldy gave a satisfied grunt.

'I came south,' continued Baldy, fish-eyeing the rider he guessed was Goodnight's straw boss, 'from the high plains territory of the Sioux and the Crow, seekin' a little peace and a restful night's sleep in my old age. And what happened, eh?' Baldy took off his hat. 'This goddamned happened!' he shrieked, angrily. 'Then those assholes lyin' there were intent on killin' me for stumblin' on them drivin' stolen beef.'

40

Baldy favoured the straw boss with a sneering look. 'When was the last time you saw a seventy-odd-year-old cattle-lifter ridin' a mule, a critter that would be hard pressed to make it to the Texas border in a week?' Baldy gave a shrill whistle and a dour-faced Jethro lumbered up from the dip as if to prove his owner's point. 'Why Mr Goodnight oughta give me and Mr Culpepper there a reward for gettin' rid of some rustlers for him and savin' a bunch of his cows.'

Normally, Macey, the straw boss, wasn't troubled with his nerves. He bossed over a wild outfit, men all shades of colour, but the sight of the loco old man's fearsome scar and what the lump of lead the Sharps threw would do to his innards this close up, had his stomach screwing up into a tight ball of intense pain. He could also judge if a man was a blowhard trying to bluff his way out of a tight corner. The old goat pointing the Sharps at him wasn't playing out a bad poker hand;

the son-of-a-bitch was holding all the aces, and the joker. Macy knew all mountain men were loco. He opined it was living up there in the high lonesome with the mountain bears and the bare-assed blood-thirsty red men. He was also a man who had survived an Indian haircut, which would make the old man madder than most of his breed. Macey didn't doubt he would kill him. Though trying not to show the mountain man hadn't thrown a scare in him, glaring, he growled, 'Lower your piece, you old rooster. I'm willin' to listen to your *amigo*'s reason for bein' close to a bunch of stolen cows belongin' to Mr Goodnight.' There was a loud creaking of saddle leather as men relaxed on their mounts as Baldy eased the hammer of the Sharps forward and lowered it to his waist.

'I'm Luke Culpepper,' Luke said. Then began by relating to the straw boss of his stint as a marshal for Judge Parker to allay the hardman's suspicions that somehow he was linked with the cattle-thieves. He had the satisfaction of seeing the straw-boss's face softening somewhat. Then stiffening again on hearing about the wagon-train massacre. 'I feel it was beholden on me,' Luke continued, 'to try and get close enough to Chato, at least, to be able to put a Winchester shell into his black, evil heart. Mr Springer has picked up some tracks north of here which could have been made by the comancheros. We were setting off to ride there when we saw your dust.'

Macey opined Mr Culpepper was every bit as loco as his crazy partner. He hadn't a cat in hell's chance of getting within cannon shot of the comanchero chief, and live. But he wouldn't be the first man whose so-called pride and honour had seen him dead. Though in spite of his gloomy forecast of the tall Texan's chances of succeeding in his mission, the loco *hombre* had the right to play out things the way he saw it.

'I wish you luck in your enterprise,

Mister Culpepper,' he said. 'You can get on the trail pronto; me and the boys will tidy up here. There could be Wanted flyers posted on the fellas you shot. If there's any reward money due you can call at the big house two miles west of here, if you swing back this way from the Staked Plains. You tell who comes to the door that Macey said you had to call.' Macey leant forward in his saddle. 'The same applies to you, Mr Springer, if you're still driftin' around these parts.'

Then Baldy surprised himself. Now he was getting old he had a hankering for company more conversational than Jethro. 'Well,' he said, 'bein' me and Jethro ain't doin' nothin' more than wander around in circles since comin' south, and I sure don't want another brush with a bunch of cattle-lifters, I reckon I'll tag along with Mr Culpepper.' Baldy gave Luke a gapped-toothed grin. 'That's if he don't mind an old mountain man as a trail-buddy and that ornery crow bait of mine don't object to travellin' around with a real horse.'

Luke thought that even if the old man had horns and sported a tail, a man who knew Indians would be a good tracker, and the dead rustlers proved he could handle himself in a tight spot. 'I'd welcome another gun, that's for sure, Mr Springer,' he grinned. 'And I reckon you're old enough to know what we could be ridin' into. Now, pard, I'd be obliged if you could get up on that fine piece of horse flesh of yours and show me those tracks you saw.'

Mentally, Macey shook his head, sadly, as the two newly made partners rode out. He had never seen men so cursed with a death wish before. And death would be their lot if the butcher they were hunting discovered they were on his trail. And it would be a slow, painful manner of dying.

6

'There they are, Mr Culpepper,' Baldy said. 'Tracks of at least thirty, thirty-five riders, just as I told you. And they ain't more than three days old, or the rain we had earlier on in the week would've washed them out. There's too many of them to have been made by a ranch crew. And they're headin' north as you can see, the way I figure Chato's goin'.'

Luke gazed long and hard at the stretch of loose earth churned up by the passage of many horses. If the tracks had been made by the comancheros, it meant, as Baldy had said, Chato was making for his hole-up somewhere on the Staked Plains. Though unless Baldy could read the sign right up to Chato's stronghold it wasn't much of a lead, he thought dourly. The Llano Estacado, giving the wild high country its Mexican name, was one big piece of territory to search. Though not as big as searching the whole of southern New Mexico, and west Texas where Chato did his raiding. It meant that Chato was up ahead of them, if Baldy was right.

'Could they have been made by an army patrol, Mr Springer?' he asked. 'Accordin' to the Bar X cook the cavalry are quarterin' the territory.'

Baldy shook his head. 'Naw, the soldier boys ride real neat and purty, in double file. These tracks were made by riders bunched up.' Then noticing his new partner's doubting looks, he said, 'If you're still unhappy about the way I've read the sign, Mr Culpepper, look at the way Jethro's ears are stickin' skywards. For all his darn cussedness this mule can smell Injuns ten miles away, even if their scent's a week old. I reckon Jethro smells the paint and stuff the red heathens daub on their faces when they're about to go on a killin' spree.' Baldy favoured Luke with a cocky smile. 'Now I figure it ain't too wild a thought to consider that Chato has Injuns, or part Injuns ridin' with him.'

Luke made up his mind. 'We'll head north then, Mr Springer,' he said. 'I've no reason to doubt your skill in readin' sign.' He smiled. 'Or that mule's sensitive nose.'

★   ★   ★

With the Black Ridge mountains hardly two hours' ride behind them, the two hunters came across the first sure, grim signs they were trailing Chato's comancheros. Splashing their way across a shallow creek, they had to skirt around a gunshot-dead cow lying with its hindquarters in the water. Riding up the slight slope from the creek, all-seeing eyed, rifles drawn, they saw the stone chimney standing like some gigantic grave marker in the middle of a heap of charred and smoke-blackened timber of what had recently been someone's home.

'You can relax, Mr Culpepper,' Baldy

said, laying his rifle across his saddle horn. 'There's no smoke or heat comin' from those ruins. They've taken all they wanted here, see?' Baldy pointed at the empty corral. 'They were after horses.'

Something caught Baldy's eyes in a patch of long grass and weeds to the left of the burnt-out house. Lifting up the Sharps again, he heeled Jethro into a walking pace across to have a closer look. Luke stayed where he was, rifle at the ready, as if in spite of his partner's assurance the comancheros could come fire-balling up from the creek hollering for their blood.

He jerked ass in his saddle on hearing Baldy's soft but carrying call of, 'They're here, Mr Culpepper.' Luke rammed the Winchester back into its boot and swung down from his horse and rein-led it across to where his partner was standing looking at the ground.

Hard-boned-faced, Luke gazed down at the two bodies lying in pitiful, twisted postures. The farmer had been scalped and his genitals slashed off. His wife, stripped naked, lay on her back, legs drawn up in her last living moments of agony. The terrible gash at her throat, showing dark against the paleness of her neck, told him of the fearful manner of her death after the comancheros had all used her. Mercifully, so he had been told, none of the German dead had been defiled. Any doubts he may have had about being beholden to see Chato dead, were gone. He would try his damnedest to strangle the murdering son-of-a-bitch with his bare hands if all other ways failed.

'Mr Springer,' he grated, 'you're the *hombre* ridin' point from now on in. Use all your trackin' skills; we're huntin' down a mad dog. Use that mule's ears if you have to, but get us close enough to Chato so I can put several Winchester shells in his dirty hide.'

'I don't need to get you in that close, Mr Culpepper,' Baldy said, as stern-faced as Luke. 'My Sharps can send

50

Chato to where he belongs from a mile away.'

They had seen the bodies decently buried and were riding north again, now and then picking up the trail of the comancheros. Luke knew the hard part would come soon. Chato, on nearing his hole-up, would hide his tracks and the old man would get the chance to prove his skill as a hunter. Luke's hopes were riding on the odd partnership of an old drifter and an ornery mule's sensitive nose. Luke thin-smiled. He might as well get down on his knees and pray for a miracle.

Jethro was the first of Luke's new partners to show him he wasn't riding with freeloaders. The trail had swung away from the creek and now on the right of them was a range of low, grassy-topped hills. Luke heard Baldy give a muttered curse, saw him jerk up straight in his saddle, and lift the big Sharps chest high.

'Trouble, pard?' he asked, looking in the same direction as Baldy, at the flat-topped ridges.

'Jethro reckons so, Mr Culpepper,' Baldy growled. Then Luke noticed the mule's ears standing rigid, heard the animal snort as if confirming its owner's statement.

Luke had never acted on a mule's instincts before but he could see that his partner had taken Jethro's warning seriously. He drew out his Winchester, albeit, a little self-consciously, and levered a shell into its chamber. Only then did he see what the mule had been catching a smell of a few minutes ago.

Set against the fiery ball of the sun, squint-eyed, he picked out the dark figures of a string of riders paralleling their trail along the high ground. He saw the Indians drop down from the ridge as if to cut across their path. Out of the blinding light of the sun, Luke could clearly see their feathered lances, and the long, eagle-feathered head-dress of the leading rider.

'Mr Springer,' he said. 'I owe you and that mule an apology. I thought you were ribbing me about his ears playin' him up when he gets the smell of an Injun.' He nodded towards the closing-in war band. 'Apache or Comanche?'

Baldy shrugged. 'I ain't familiar with the get up of the local Injuns, Mr Culpepper,' he replied. He grinned. 'And this bone-headed, walkin' flea bag don't know a Crow from a Comanche, the wild boys all smell alike to him. But I take all Injuns as natural-born white-eyes haters, which I reckon is only fair considerin' the way we whites have lied and cheated in all our dealin's with them. So I try and avoid meetin' up with them if I can.'

'Are they goin' to pay us a call, Mr Springer?' Luke asked. 'Nine to two are favourable odds for any bad-asses, red or white.'

'M'be a couple of the young bucks will come at us to kinda test our mettle and to prove to their chief they've got warriors' balls. That is, if we can't persuade them to seek their fun someplace else. Pull up, Mr Culpepper and we'll let them know just what they'll face if they intend liftin' your scalp.' Baldy favoured Luke with another gap-toothed grin. 'They sure can't lift my hair.'

Baldy brought the Sharps up to his shoulder and pulled off a load. The bang of the discharge and the banshee-like whine of the heavy slug in flight rang loudly along the ridges. Luke saw the wisp of dust the slug had kicked up the hillside well above the Indians, drifting on the light breeze.

'Could've took that chief's head clear off,' Baldy said. 'But it wouldn't be wise to rile them more than they are right now. Though it should make them have second thoughts about attacking us. I figure they thought they were still outa long-gun range.' Then reaching behind him he yanked out a sawn-off double-barrelled shotgun from his bedroll. He drew back the hammers and fired off both loads into the air. 'That should give them something to talk over,' Baldy said, as he thumbed two fresh loads into the shotgun breech and snapped shut the barrels. 'Now, Mr Culpepper,' he said, 'I'd be obliged if you could fire off a coupla shells from your Winchester. Then those boys across there will get the message that we ain't easy pickin's.'

Luke, determined to underline that message, fired off half a magazine load of shells in the general direction of the war band.

'Look!' Baldy cried. 'They've got the message, they're headin' back up on to the ridge!'

Luke breathed out a deep sigh of relief. He didn't hanker after a running fight with a bunch of broncos. His fight was with Chato and any luck he might have coming his way he wanted to save for the battle. Luke's hair at the back of his neck, like Jethro's ears, had stiffened up since sighting the Indians, and stayed bristled when he heard Baldy say, 'Of course, we could raise those red hellions again, Mr Culpepper. They're headin' north, the same direction as us.

Could be they're meetin' up with Chato on the Staked Plains to get themselves some guns and rotgut fire-water.'

Luke's face twisted in a grimace of a smile. 'What the hell's another nine killin' *hombres*, Mr Springer, when we're takin' on a whole durn gang of suchlike characters?'

'Ain't nothin' at all,' replied Baldy, po-faced. 'I figure Chato don't need any help to see us dead, if that's the way it's gonna be.'

This time Luke's smile had more warmth in it. 'I take it that means you ain't pullin' out of our partnership. I wouldn't hold it against you if you did. Though I sure would have a hard time makin' it to the Staked Plains on my own without Jethro's Injun-smellin' nose.'

'That you would, Mr Culpepper,' Baldy said. 'That you would.'

Jethro snorted and stamped his front feet.

'Now don't get all uppity,' Baldy

growled, good-naturedly, 'just because Mr Culpepper here spoke highly of you. You ain't got the savvy to know what you could be ridin' into. Like the wild boys we're huntin', those red devils across on those hills would eat you when the snows come.' He dug his heels into Jethro's ribs. 'OK, blowhard,' he barked, 'let's move out.'

A disappointed Chief Howling Wolf, keeping well off the skyline, watched the two white-eyes cut away from the high ground. He would have liked to have taken their horses and guns and the two boys in his band could have been blooded as warriors by taking the white-eyes' scalps. But he had seen the killing power of the long gun the older white-eye carried: the gun that fired in the morning and killed when the sun was past its height. He had seen the heavy slug it fired kill a running buffalo dead within its own length as far away as seven, eight arrow flights away.

Howling Wolf could not afford to lose any of his small band of warriors. He had dealings with the 'breed, Chato, in his stronghold in the high country north of here. And he wanted to ride into the 'breed's camp with some pride at the head of a war band, not just two of three warriors.

With the gold and silver ear-rings, bracelets and gold teeth, they had taken from the Mexicans they had killed south of the Rio Bravo, he would buy guns, horses and whiskey from Chato. Weapons and horses he would use to attract other broncos who would acknowledge him as their chief.

The chief's nostrils dilated at the thought of all the killing his enlarged war band would inflict on the hated Mexicans and the white-eyes. He drew his mount round and hurried it along to catch up with his warriors.

7

The trail twisted again, the hills dropping back far to their left. Crossing over a flat, unbroken range where an Indian, scalp-hunting, Luke thought, confidently, would be hard-pressed to jump them unawares. Luke rode along silently and, not wanting to take things on chance, wary-eyed. Although he didn't show it, sitting slumped back in his saddle, smoking a short-stemmed pipe, Baldy would be alert as he was in keeping a watch out for trail dust of any incoming riders.

Every now and again, Luke glanced, unconsciously at Jethro's now flattened-down ears. He grinned. That would set the drinkers rolling on the floor in any frontier bar if he told them he had only managed to hang on to his hair by watching a mule's twitching ears.

He was curious to know how his

partner came to lose his scalp, but reckoned it would be a touchy subject to raise, especially to an experienced hunter as Baldy. And again, in the short time he had known him, he had found out that the old hunter wasn't a gabby man, which suited him. He had a lot occuping his mind working out the tactics he would use when the day came when he found he was within striking range of Chato.

'It ain't any good frettin' about how you're gonna play things when you meet up with Chato, pard,' Baldy said. 'You'll find you'll do what is needed when that time comes as natural as this mule of mine breaks wind. Mark my sayso: you'll give yourself belly ulcers doin' otherwise.'

Luke gave Baldy a look of surprise. The old goat must have read his mind; had he Indian blood in him? 'I guess you're right, pardner,' he said. 'But I'm a worryin' man. Though I'll endeavour to hold back that trait until we're breathin' down Chato's dirty neck.' He smiled. 'That won't stop me from keepin' an eye on that mule of yours ears, Mr Springer.'

'You could do worse, Mr Culpepper,' replied Baldy. 'I figure Jethro's ears must have been jacked up real high the night that Injun jumped me. But, of course, it was dark and the old crow-bait hadn't the savvy to bellow out a warning.' Baldy suddenly raised an arm. 'There's smoke away to our left, see it?'

Luke swung round in his saddle, taking several minutes of keen-eyed gazing before he saw the thin column of smoke against the washed-out blue of the sky. He would have to stop thinking that his partner was over the hill; Baldy had eyes like an hawk. He straightened up in his saddle, giving himself a higher horizon. 'There's buildin's there, Mr Springer. Could be a ranch or a farm.'

'We oughta swing by there,' Baldy said. 'Warn them there's a bunch of broncos prowlin' around close by.'

Baldy grinned. 'M'be if they're kind-hearted plainsfolk we might be invited to sit at their table and share their vittles with them. I'd have to apologize for keepin' my hat on; I wouldn't like to scare any kids who might be there.'

'It's quite a spell since I partook of a meal I didn't rustle up myself, Mr Springer,' Luke said. 'Though we're more likely to get a load of buckshot whizzin' around our ears as a welcome. All the trailin' we've been doin' has us lookin' like a couple of West Texas stompin' men runnin' ahead of a hangin' posse.'

★　★　★

Sam Turner stopped his ploughing and unhooked the plough horse's reins from his shoulders as he saw the indistinct shapes of two riders in the heathaze heading towards him. He cursed profoundly but silently, not wanting his son, Earl, clearing stones out of the plough's path, to hear him dirty-mouthing. Another couple of hired guns, he thought angrily, riding in to beg, or threaten him for a free meal before heading north to Fort Sumner to kill for one of the factions in what the territory called the Lincoln County war.

Sam hawked and spat in the dust like a savage Indian. Wasn't there enough trouble for folk in this section of New Mexico — Chato and his bunch of killers, broncos on killing and burning raids and the hard, unyielding goddamned land without a war starting up?

Mr Antrim, a young pistolero, named on the Wanted flyers as Billy the Kid, who ran a gang of like-minded wild boys, kept the fire blowing hot. When things became too hectic for Billy and his gang up at Fort Sumner they came south, showing up on some small farm like his, banking on their notoriety as shootists to get their meals free.

Sam's face hardened in anger. The

incoming assholes would get the message that it would be better for their health if they kept on riding past the Turner place, or face the consequences.

'Earl!' he called. 'Go and get your rifle from the stump then come and stand by me. 'There's two riders comin' this way and they'll need persuading to keep on travelling.'

When the riders came close enough for Sam to see them more clearly, he thought they must be running short of pistoleros in West Texas. The old man in the long hide coat must have had help to get up on that mule. He hadn't the cut of a fast gun but looks, as he well knew, could be deceptive. Choirboy-faced Billy the Kid proved that.

The old man's partner, a tall lean man, was an *hombre* of a different stamp. He had the keen-eyed sweeping gaze of a man who knew when and where to jump if things got out of hand — and when to stay and make good use of that pistol he had sheathed on his right hip.

'It ain't quite the welcome mat they've laid out for us, pard,' Baldy said softly. 'The kid with the rifle looks more than a mite scared, could jerk off a load at us. And the big pistol his pa's got fisted will put a bigger hole in a man's hide than the Sharps. There'll be no chow for us on this fella's table.'

'It pays a man to take precautions to protect his property, Mr Springer. This place ain't all that far from the Texas Panhandle and men seekin' easy pickin's could regularly pass this way. And, as I said, we sure don't look like a coupla tree-stump, hot-gospel-preachin' men.'

'If they make a move for their guns, Earl,' Sam said, as the riders drew up beside the plough, 'send them on their way to Boot Hill.' Stepping closer to them he said, hard-voiced, 'The trail north to Fort Sumner is back a-way to your left.' He waved his pistol between Luke and Baldy, scowling-faced. 'This ain't an open house for no-good Texas drifters.'

Out of the corner of his eye, Luke glimpsed Baldy's right hand make a sudden sweeping movement and then he saw the long barrelled cavalry pistol in his partner's hand. The old man didn't favour a holstered pistol so Luke guessed he'd had the Colt stuffed down his shirt. He thought he still had a lot to learn about the staying-alive capabilities of Mr Springer.

'Now, pilgrim,' he heard Baldy say, in a passing-the-time-of-day voice, 'you've got two choices. Either you can take the wild chance that you'll shoot me dead before I blow that fine young boy of yours head off, or you can put that pistol back down your pants and tell your boy to lower his rifle while Mr Culpepper tells you why we're callin' on you.'

Sam did some more cursing. He had cursed more in the last few minutes than he had in a whole month. He had never seen a shirt-carried gun yanked out so fast before. The old goat was more nimble than he looked. The son-of-a-bitch had him well and truly over a barrel. It was crow-eating time unless he was willing to take a gamble on his boy's life. 'Lower your gun,' he told the white-faced Earl, and tucked his pistol into the waistband of his pants. 'We'll hear what Mr Culpepper has to say.'

'Put your gun away, Mr Springer,' Luke said. 'No man enjoys bein' talked to under threat.' He waited until Baldy had stuffed the Dragoon back in his shirt. 'We saw chimney smoke,' he began. 'And thought it was our Christian duty to go out of our way to warn the folks livin' there about an Injun war band prowlin' around that stretch of hills back to the east of us.' He smiled. 'Mr Springer here persuaded them to haul their asses over the ridges.'

'A war band, you say, Mr Culpepper?' Sam said.

Luke nodded. 'Nine of them. Heading north the last sighting we had of them. But bein' Injuns they could have swung this way.'

'I don't think so,' replied Sam. 'My guess is they're still riding north to meet up with Chato and his comancheros at their stronghold somewhere on the Staked Plains.'

'Chato!' said Luke. 'Ain't it a small world, Mr Springer? Why, he's the fella we're tryin' to track down, friend.'

Sam's mouth gaped open in disbelief. 'You're goin' after that murderin' sonuvabitch, Chato? I take it you've got a posse of hard-ridin', fast-shootin' *hombres* comin' in behind you. Then you just might have an odds-on chance of puttin' Chato in his grave. That's if you can find where he holes-up.'

Luke smiled. 'No, I ain't; there's just the two of us. We figure if we're as snaky as a coupla hair-liftin' broncos we'll have a better chance of gettin' close to Chato. Seven hundred yards close is all we need. The big Sharps Mr Springer favours will do the rest.'

'Well, it ain't my business to put a man off what he feels is his duty,' Sam said. He would have liked to know how that duty was come by but it wasn't polite to ask. 'But if I was contemplatin' suicide,' he added, 'I could never pick a surer way.' He gave them both a pitying look. 'And if you don't mind takin' some advice from a stranger, I'd swing further east, towards the Pecos, before headin' north to the Staked Plains, or you'll hit big trouble sooner than you expect. It's open season for shootin' at newcomers ridin' into Lincoln County. Two factions are warrin' up there for some reason or other. Some of them mere kids.'

'We'll take heed of that warnin',' Luke said. 'We don't aim to fight our way up to Chato's front door.'

No, thought Sam, coldly. If you make it to Chato's camp you and your pard will get all the fighting you can handle, and then some. He snapped his fingers as he remembered something. 'There's an *hombre* I know who might be of some help to you in trackin' down Chato. That's if you can persuade a man who is loco to talk to you.'

'As I said, I'll accept anyone's help,' Luke replied, 'if it gets us within shootin' distance of Chato. I take it this loco fella don't hold any good feelings for Chato.'

'I'd put it stronger than that, Mr Culpepper,' Sam said. 'The 'Mole', we call him, seein' as he ain't told us his real name; he don't talk much, but when he does, he heaps curses on Chato's head and shows us the rope burn round his neck. He drifted down here about six, seven months ago, a half-crazy walking dead man, and made camp at Silver Butte, a worked-out old mine three miles north of here, existin' on what he could trap and dig out of the ground. Then he started scratchin' for silver in the mine. The few bits he gets he trades with the agency Apache for what scraps of food they can spare. The Apache use the silver to make fancy geegaws for their squaws.

'Every now and again,' Sam contin- ued, 'me, or my boy, take him some fresh bread or whatever Ma's baked. He tells us he's diggin' for the motherlode.' Sam laughed. 'And I've cash in the bank. I think it's the Mole's way of occupyin' his mind to stop him thinkin' about what happened to him where he came from.'

'It won't do no harm talkin' to this Mole *hombre*,' Luke said. 'Ain't that so, pard?'

Baldy grinned. 'He oughta want to chat with two more crazy men, I reckon.'

Sam watched them ride out, having no doubts in his mind that Mr Culpepper and Mr Springer were living on borrowed time unless they forgot their foolish notion of hunting down Chato. Which would be a pity, he thought, the pair seemed decent, law-abiding gents. He picked up the reins. 'Let's get this ploughin' finished, Earl, Ma will be shoutin' us in for supper soon.'

8

'That must be Silver Butte, Mr Springer,' Luke said nodding towards the dark-faced mass of rock standing on its own away to their left. Straight-faced, he added, 'I'll let you do the talkin', pard; two lonesome drifters oughta see things the same way.'

Baldy replied in a Jethro-like derisive snort.

The trail leading to the mine was overgrown by grass and sage but they could clearly see the deep ruts in the hard-pan ground of the countless wagons loading ore from the mine and carrying supplies in when it was working full blast.

Campbell MacColl twisted and threshed on his bed of dried brush like a man in the grip of a high fever. Sobbing moans racked his body, as once again he was reliving his nightmares, ever since that terrible day on the Staked Plains when what was torturing his mind now, threatening his sanity, had been a fearful reality.

The physical and mental exhaustion of hacking out of the hard rock the strands of silver from the working faces of the mine with old tools left by the former miners somehow kept his night terrors from taking over his daylight hours and pushing him over the edge into the dark despair of total madness.

Campbell came awake, howling like a badly injured dog, hands clapped over his ears to cut out the soul-destroying screams of his dead partner, and saw three men standing in the cave entrance. The fear sweat froze on his body and the scar round his neck burned as though the rope that had caused it was still choking the life out of him. He gave a dry-throated scream of fright as the men hauled him, unresisting, out into the open.

Baldy raised a warning hand. 'The Mole's already got visitors,' he said.

73

'And they don't seem very friendly towards him.'

Luke saw the three men dragging the man who could only be the Mole out of the mine entrance, and not fighting against the rough handling he was receiving. As he rode closer he noticed the Mole was aptly named: long, dirty, straggle-haired, hairy-faced, ragged clothes caked in dry mud from the workings, he made Mr Springer, who wasn't particular in his appearance, look as sharp a dresser as a city tailor's dummy. And he could smell him from here and he was upwind of him. His age was hard to determine, but Luke guessed he could give the Mole a good few years.

'Your diggin' is dirtyin' the crick, you crazy sonuvabitch!' one of the ranch hands said. 'Our boss wants you off this piece of land; pronto like.' The ranch hand laughed as he kicked the helpless Mole in the ribs. 'Do you get the message or do you want me to put it to you stronger?'

Luke's face hardened in anger. He didn't know if the Mole would speak to him and Baldy, and if he did it could put him no closer to killing Chato. It was a chance he had to take. One thing was certain: if he allowed the ranch hands to beat up the Mole he wouldn't be in a fit state to do any talking.

His pistol seemed to jump into his hand, firing off a warning shot over the ranch hands' heads. The Mole dropped face down on to the ground, as the men holding him spun round in alarm, hands clawing for their guns.

'Don't even think of it, pilgrims,' he heard Baldy say. The old trapper had his own pistol out, the long barrel laid steady on his left forearm. 'Or your carcasses will be dirtyin' that crick's water.'

Three gun hands stayed their movement.

'This ain't no business of yours!' the man who had been kicking the Mole snarled back at Baldy. 'This is cattlemen's business, and you better believe it. That stinkin' apology of a man lyin' there is on Circle C land and his scratchin' in the old workings is muddyin' the crick, and that water's the herd's drinkin' water. I've orders to clear the bum outta this mine, the easy way, or the hard way if we have to. Now, old man, to save yourselves a whole heap of trouble, I'd advise you and your pard to keep on passin' through this stretch of territory.'

Baldy's Colt suddenly flamed and boomed and the ranch hand who had been doing the threatening cried out in pain and clutched at his right, blood-dripping arm. The pistol he had been easing out of its holster as he had been talking slid back in again. Face twisted in a mask of pain and anger, he screeched, 'I'll see you hangin' from the nearest cottonwood, you old bastard! There'll be ten guns the next time you see us!'

'Some folk don't hear so clearly, pard,' Baldy said. 'Or too durn foolish to heed sensible advice when kindly given.' Luke cursed under his breath; things had turned sour on them. He kept his gun, unwavering on the trail hands, face pale and angular. Would there have to be more unnecessary bloodshed? He hoped to hell Baldy's single shot had made the ranch hands see reason. Yet he knew from his experience as a peace-officer, a ranch crew was fiercely loyal to each other. A wrong or a hurt, to one was an insult to them all. They would back up a *compadre* in any trouble come hell and high water, even if it meant dying alongside him.

He could only pray that the ranch hands, with guns held on them by men willing to use them, would treat the situation as a Mexican standoff and mount up and ride back to their ranch to tell their boss that his orders to shift the Mole off his land hadn't worked out as planned. He didn't think that likely. His talk with the Mole could now only last as long as he figured it would take for the Circle C boss to round up as many men as he could and ass kick it back here spoilin' for a fight.

'We didn't seek trouble,' Luke said. 'All we wanted was to have a talk with the fella you've been kickin' around. And believe me, we've got strong reasons for doin' so. But what's done had to be done and let it lie at that. So my advice, mister, is to get back to your spread and get that wound seen to. What you feel you oughta do next is your business.' Luke cold-smiled. 'Though I oughta tell you me and my pard will be long gone from here if you opine blood calls for blood. And we ain't easy *hombres* to track.'

Still showing his anger, the wounded man snarled, 'You betcha blood calls for blood. You'd better make your talk with this bum real fast because you're as good as dead! Let's go, boys, and get ourselves a hangin' party rounded-up.' He let loose with a fresh string of curses, as, awkwardly and painfully, he mounted his horse.

'If we're talkin' war here, friend,'

Baldy said, pushing his pistol down the top of his pants and drawing out the Sharps. 'Don't try any skirmishin' till you get the rest of your army. This Sharps can put a man down for keeps at a thousand yards, so don't let me see any of you boys tryin' to Injun back this way figurin' to catch us off guard.'

In return, Baldy got three 'drop dead' looks and a spoken warning, punctuated by more dirty-mouthing, from the man he had winged, that when they returned there would be nothing sneaky about it. They would come in with a rush, and shooting.

Luke watched their fast disappearing trail dust then said, 'Keep an eye on them, Mr Springer, while I have a talk to the Mole.'

He dismounted and walked across to the Mole who was still on the ground but now sitting up. Through the tangled mass of uncombed hair, he saw a pair of eyes glinting wildly at him. Luke had intended, on hearing how the Mole lived, to probe him gently for information about

Chato; he no longer had the time to do that. He didn't know how much time he really had before he heard Baldy yell out that a bunch of riders was fire-balling in. His mission to put paid to Chato wasn't about to be ended here just because he had to plead, humour, cajole, whatever, some half-loco man into talking. Tough, fast questioning was called for.

'Mister,' he grated, 'I don't know who the hell you are or why you've chosen to live no better than some wild critter. I only hope you ain't as crazy as you look and you know what I'm sayin'.' Luke saw no sign in the Mole's unblinking-eyed stare that what he had just said was registering in his brain. He sighed and cast a worried glance at Baldy. He saw the old man give a reassuring shake of his head. Time hadn't run out for them yet. He pressed on with his questioning.

'All I'm interested in is what you know of the comanchero leader, Chato. I've heard you knew of him before you came south to this mine.'

Luke knew he had made a break-through. At the mention of Chato, the Mole flinched as though he had struck him a blow with his fist and saw the staring eyes widen in fear. He gave a grunt of satisfaction. 'I see that you're acquainted with the murderin' sonuv-abitch and it wasn't a joyful meeting. Now I would be obliged if you'd tell me all you know about Chato. M'be give me an idea where the bastard holes up between raids. And make it quick. Those fellas who were roughin' you up will be back with more like-minded gents and this time they'll be that mad they'll see you planted. Now m'be you don't give a hoot whether you live or die, but me and my pard ain't got any death wish. We aim to stay alive and put a bullet in Chato's dirty hide. We're kinda on a blood-for-blood mission.'

Baldy kneed his mount closer to them, though still keeping a watchful eye on the trail. Almost snarling the words out, he said, 'You're beholden to us, mister. We stuck out our necks for you and landed ourselves into trouble we could do without. We could've kept our distance and you would be lyin' there spittin' blood with your ribs caved in — an easy meal for the wolves and wild dogs that must roam around here after dark.' Baldy's voice softened. 'I figure that somehow Chato threw one helluva scare into you,' he said. 'For no white man would live in a hole in the ground like some varmint: unless he was hidin' from someone, or loco.' He took off his hat to show his scalpless head. 'Now the red heathen who did that sure scared the hell outa me, but not enough to stop me from despatchin' him to his happy huntin' grounds, no sir.' Baldy's voice steeled over. 'While you're sittin' there too skeered to even talk about Chato, those ranch hands could be poundin' back along the trail with blood in their eyes. Now that's something to fret over, pilgrim.'

Campbell's mouth gaped open in

horror at the sight of Baldy's horrific scar. Then, looking directly at Luke, gasped, 'Kill Chato? Just the two of you?' He gave a croaking sob of a laugh. 'And you say you haven't got a death wish?'

'Sometimes a man has to risk his life to get even,' Luke replied flat-voiced. 'Call it pride, honour or just plain cussedness, what it is doesn't matter. A man, if he wants to live with himself has to do what he thinks right, what he lives by. And my choice is to see Chato dead. Now tell me about him.'

A flickering spark of anger flared up in Campbell's chest. 'You never had your partner cut to pieces!' he cried. 'Heard every single scream as their knives cut into him until he couldn't scream any more! And I could do damn all to help him!' Campbell glared wildly at Luke. 'I still hear his screams. How do you live with that nightmare, pilgrim?'

Luke and Baldy exchanged significant glances. 'No, I ain't had a partner hacked to death,' Luke said. 'But bein' a US marshal a while back, I had partners killed alongside me. I sure didn't blame myself for their deaths, it was a hazard that came with the badge. What I felt obliged to do was to go out and kill the bastards who shot them.'

Baldy favoured the Mole with a hard-eyed look of contempt. 'The way to get rid of those disturbin' thoughts of yours, mister, is as my pard says: find your backbone and go huntin' for Chato and make him pay for what he did to your pard. Though by the way things have turned out here you've got a fresh load of worry and grief comin' your way.' Baldy jerked Jethro's head round. 'I reckon it's time we were movin' out, Mr Culpepper, this yellow dog ain't gonna tell us anything about Chato. And I sure as hell ain't riskin' my hide to protect him from those boys we ran off when they come hightailin' it back.'

The angry spark inside Campbell suddenly flared red-hot right to his brain. With a strangled cry he sprang to his feet, fists clenching and unclenching with frustrated rage. 'I'm not a coward, you, you old goat!' he yelled. 'If I had a gun in my hand I'd shoot you off that mangey-hide mule you're sitting on!' Then his body sagged, dejectedly, and tears coursed down his cheeks. 'It was my first assignment,' he muttered, all the fire gone from his voice. 'And I let my partner down.'

'Were you peace officers?' Luke asked.

Campbell shook his head. 'No, we were Pinkertons.'

'Pinkertons? Who the hell are those fellas, Mr Culpepper?' a curious Baldy asked.

'They're a bunch of so-called private lawmen run by an Eastern dude called Mr Pinkerton,' replied Luke. 'I didn't know they operated this far west.'

Baldy gave the Mole a pitying look. Eastern dudes trying to track down a gang of wild, killing *hombres*? Baldy thought even city dudes wouldn't be that loco. The kid's partner had been asking to be carved up. And his threat to blow him out of his saddle if he had been fisting a gun had as much chance of succeeding as he and his partner's attempt to capture Chato had. He was shaking like a town drunk seeking his first pull at the bottle of the day. The Mole couldn't hit him even if he was standing nose to nose to Jethro.

But he had needled the Mole into being angry. There was hope yet for him, he thought. If the Mole got angry enough he could lose his fear of Chato.

'If I riled you,' he said, 'I'll apologize, but that's the way me and Mr Culpepper see you. And we can't waste shells on a shoot-out between us, we may need them to beat off those ranch hands we upset when they come ridin' in, if we don't get the hell out of it. Me and my pard ain't hard-assed it all the way north just to exchange lead with some put-out cowboys.'

Luke raised his head and saw the ominous cloud of trail dust of high kicking horses racing in. He bleak-eyed Campbell.

'Are you with us, Mr Pinkerton man?' he said. 'Or are you still a quitter? There ain't no time to enter into a lengthy discussion with yourself to find out what you are. Me and Mr Springer are pullin' out right now. All the fightin' we want to take part in is with Chato.'

Campbell didn't have to do any soul-searching. He looked unwavering-eyed at Luke.

'I'll ride with you, Mr Culpepper,' he said, his voice as steady as his gaze. He knew he was getting the chance to redeem his and the Pinkerton Detective Agency's honour. And somehow he was having the feeling it wouldn't be such a one-sided fight if they did clash with friend Chato and his comancheros. Mr Culpepper and Mr Springer were confident-looking men, capable of giving a good account of themselves whatever the odds.

Luke smiled. 'Good, have you a horse?'

Cambell nodded. 'Yes, it's down by the creek.'

That pleased Luke. He wasn't looking forward to having a man who smelt like a polecat sitting up behind him. He opined even his ex-trapper partner, used to strong smells would balk at having the Pinkerton as a passenger. To boost their new partner's born-again confidence further he said, 'We're right pleased to accept the offer of another gun, isn't that so, Mr Springer?'

'No disagreement from me about that, Mr Culpepper,' Baldy replied. 'You, young pard, gather what bits and pieces you have and get up on your horse, fast. Then you ride out with Mr Culpepper. I'll stay put and try win us some time with the Sharps.'

Baldy's action was sound tactics to Luke. Like himself, the old man had doubts that their new partner, in the state he was in, would be able to stay up on his horse if forced to ride it hard. 'We'll hole-up some place ten, twelve miles north of here, Mr Springer,' he said. 'Where we can get a clear view of our back trail.' He thin-smiled. 'If we can see more than one rider comin' along it, me and the boy will get movin' north again for I'll figure you've either been shot dead, or are swingin' by the neck from some tree.'

'And that would be a durn shame, Mr Culpepper,' Baldy said, ' 'Cos I was lookin' real forward to havin' that sonuvabitch, Chato, framed in the sights of my Sharps, but life ain't always full of good times.'

Luke touched his hat in a salute. 'I look forward to seein' your ugly mug soon, pard,' he said. 'Let's go, kid,' he said, as Campbell rode up from the creek. 'Let the man go about his business.'

* * *

Baldy counted eight riders coming in, hell bent, all bunched up. He raised the back sights of the Sharps, cold-smiling. They wouldn't stay close up for long. He lay prone behind a heap of brush-covered mine spoil. On his right side, standing upright were eight reloads for the Sharps, blunt, ugly pieces of lead. It was open ground in front of him so when he opened up with the Sharps the ranch hands would have to burrow into the dirt like prairie dogs for shelter from his fire.

The Mole not being able to stay the pace if pushed hard, thereby endangering Mr Culpepper's life, hadn't been the only reason for him staying behind. His partner, a plainsman, like himself, would use the won time to hide their tracks for the first few miles out from the old mine to throw their pursuers off the scent if his plan didn't work out in his favour. He brought the Sharps up then eased back the trigger.

The shell passing close by their heads and the aircracking bang of its discharge were clearly heard by the riders, and all reacted to the blood-freezing sounds in the same way. Reins were yanked hard bringing their mounts to an ass-sliding, dust-raising stop that threatened to unseat some of them.

Then came the panic-stricken dash for the hoped for safety of the nearest fold in the ground.

Jeb Carlson, the owner of the Circle C spread, raised his head high enough from the dirt to yell, 'What the hell gun is that, Jake?'

Jake, who had landed heavily on his now bandaged arm, stopped his painful cursing long enough to call back, 'It's the big gun of the old goat who plugged me, boss!'

A shell raising a spout of dust in front of Jeb had the ranch boss eating dirt again, fast. Jesus Christ! he thought wildly, we might as well have come armed with staves for what use our Winchesters are at this range, even if they weren't stuck in their boots on the horses. His body gave a nerve-jangling twitch as another shell thudded into the ground close by him. He kept his head low. Twisting it round he spat out a mouthful of dirt and began shouting out orders. After all he was the boss.

'If any of you boys are close enough

to the horses make a grab for your rifles! Then, by belly-crawlin', you could outflank that sonuvabitch!'

He had hardly got the words out of his mouth when one of the horses gave a snort of pain as a shell creased its left hind leg, and Jeb heard the drumming of hooves as the horses took off to parts unknown. He cursed. The bastard on the ridge must have read his mind; he was playing with them. Soon he would be shooting for real.

He had to accept the craw-choking truth that, armed only with pistols and on foot they weren't going to show the asshole drifter up there on the ridge a taste of cattleman's law. It would take a troop of soldier boys, armed with repeating carbines, to shift the old man off the high ground, and his boys were only ranch hands. He didn't want their blood on his hands. His mind was read again, this time by one of his crew.

'Boss!' he heard one yell. 'I'm pulling outa this mess! You pay me a dollar and three squares a day for tendin' your cows, and m'be throw a scare in any cattle-lifter who comes snoopin' round the herd. Not for me lyin' here pissin' my pants waitin' for that bastard with his artillery piece to blow a big hole in me! I'll pick up what's due to me back at the big house!'

'Hold it, Steve!' Jeb shouted. 'We're all quittin'! We've got to find the horses before it gets dark or it'll take all night and part of the morning to get back to the ranch. And it will just be our goddamned luck to find the herd has wandered clear to the four corners of the range!'

Baldy saw their low-ass wriggling retreat and sent two more shells winging close by them to keep up the speed of their withdrawal. His grin of relief reached his ears; his bluff had worked. If the ranch hands had had the guts to rush he would have had to hightail after his two partners, or end up as the most wanted killer in New Mexico. The Sharps was a hunter's gun, designed to kill buffaloes, bears and other big game. At no time would he have shot at any of the ranch hands. A man hit by one of its shells in the arms or legs, even at the gun's extreme range would suffer a painful mutilating wound that would see him dead as sure as a shot in the head or heart.

★ ★ ★

Between watching the trail for signs of Baldy, Luke gave their new partner a closer assaying look. He now knew his name was Campbell MacColl, an Easterner from Chicago. And a great deal younger than he had first estimated, only twenty-four years old, almost half his age. Luke didn't ask how he came to be captured by Chato and the manner of escape from the comancheros' hands. He could see by the way the boy's fingers kept jerking at the collar of his ragged apology of a shirt, exposing the rope weal, he had a long way to go before he got over his experiences at the comanchero camp to be able to speak about them.

Although MacColl had stated he wanted to ride with him as a partner it would be dangerously foolish to rely on his full backing in a gunfight with the comancheros. And in a tight corner he and Baldy would be too hard pressed saving their own skins to watch over a shattered-nerved greenhorn kid. He would be happy just to have MacColl point him in the direction of Chato's hole-up then he could ride off and scratch for silver or gold in some other old workings.

'Will Mr Springer be OK, Mr Culpepper?' he heard the boy ask. 'He's facing considerable odds.'

'He'll be OK,' he replied. 'You'll see the old goat cock-a-hoop on his ornery mule come riding in soon.' That's if things haven't gone wrong, he added under his breath. 'Things had gone badly wrong for Mr Springer once before and it cost him his hair.' He smiled reassuringly. 'It ain't as if he's tryin' to hold back a posse of men paid blood money by some town marshal, Mr MacColl. They're just hardworkin', poorly paid ranch hands. They'll not have the inclination to put themselves up as targets for a gun that throws .50 calibre shells a quarter of a mile, and hurt real bad if you get one in your hide — if it don't kill you stone dead. I reckon . . . ' Luke suddenly broke off his conversation. 'See!' he said, pointing along the trail. 'Here's our pard ridin' in nice and peaceful. So it looks as though we ain't got the worry of a bunch of angry cow-hands tailin' us.'

Baldy's wide-smiling face as he rode up the grade towards them confirmed Luke's optimistic statement: they were no longer being hunted.

'Any trouble, Mr Springer?' Luke asked.

'Nah!' replied Baldy. Still grinning he tapped the butt of the Sharps. 'One shell from this deadly beauty passin' close by a fella's head quickly gets him to rethink his priorities. Those fellas who came ridin' in to do us harm suddenly found that they had urgent work to be seen to back at their spread. The last I saw of them they were huntin' around for their horses.'

'Are you still willin' to ride with us, Mr MacColl?' Luke said. 'You, more than me and Mr Springer, know what sort of hell we're ridin' into. You're no longer bein' threatened so you can go where you please. You ain't beholden to us, ain't that so, Mr Springer?'

'That's so, pard,' replied Baldy. 'We're only glad we happened to be around to be of some help to you.'

Campbell shot them both hurt, angry-looking glances. 'I gave you my word, Mr Culpepper!' he snapped. 'I'll admit I haven't the appearance of a man who can be trusted, but I'll play my part as a Pinkerton agent when the time comes. You need have no fear on that score, gentlemen.'

Luke grinned. 'We've noticed you've kinda let yourself go somewhat. And that's the first thing we've got to put right now you're a full partner. The next town we ride into you can get yourself spruced up. We don't want the sheriff to throw you in his jail for makin' his town look untidy.' There was, he hoped, the chance to see how the kid shaped up on the trail, see if his nerves had returned to normal, long before their showdown with Chato, though he still thought Mr MacColl's usefulness would be the information he could give them about the location of the comanchero camp. The sooner the boy was willing to do that, the sooner he would be showing he was becoming a man again. 'OK, let's move out,' he said. 'And find you that bath house, Mr MacColl.'

★   ★   ★

It had been three foot-weary, much cursing, hours before all the Circle C had managed to get astride their mounts again and were ready to ride back to the ranch.

'I'm quittin' here and now, boss,' Jake

said. 'I'm goin' to try and pick up the trail of those three *hombres*. No old bastard is gonna put a bullet in me and ride away smilin'. And Kurt's comin' with me.'

'It's your business, Jake,' Jeb growled, bad-temperedly. He was tired and hungry and wasn't about to argue with a grown man about what he ought or ought not to do. He bossed over an outfit of hard men, but Jake, a West Texan, was mean-minded as well. He would pull a gun on a man rather than reason with him in a dispute. In spite of knowing Jake's rep as a stomping man, Jeb was getting a gut-feeling that if Jake and Kurt met up with the *hombre* who had scared them with his fancy shooting with his big gun, and his pard, they would run into deep trouble, Boot Hill-type trouble. Which was a crying shame, he thought, for Kurt, who hadn't much going for him brainwise, or he wouldn't be riding with Jake, was one

hell of a cow-hand. For Kurt's sake
he wished them both good luck, then
said as he dug his heels into his
horse's ribs, 'Let's go boys, and see if
the herd's still in one piece.'

9

Luke, Baldy and Campbell lay soaking in hot tubs. Baldy was still wearing his hat, not wanting to scare off the two Mexican boys who were refilling the tubs with more hot water when needed.

They had ridden into Fort Sumner from the east, by way of the Mexican quarter, a mixture of dry-sprung planked shacks and crumbling adobe buildings. The bath house was next to a sutler's store, opposite was a cantina. Judging by the four Mexican women, showing a great deal of their uncovered bodies, Luke opined the cantina also served as a whorehouse.

Pleasuring Mexican females, long past looking as pretty as prairie roses, was the farthest thought from Luke's mind. It was occupied with how young MacColl was shaping up after four days with them on the trail. The hot bath seemed to have relaxed him somewhat, though he had not yet related his experiences with the comancheros. And that was something Luke thought couldn't be put off much longer. He had a lot of thinking to do. Once the kid had had his bath he would see to it he had some fresh clothes, and a haircut. Then he would start the serious business of questioning him.

Luke got out of the tub first and, as he was towelling himself dry, he said, 'You stay put for a spell, Mr MacColl, until I get you some new gear. Ain't no sense puttin' your old stuff back on.'

Baldy gave a crackling laugh. 'If you stroll out to the stores jaybird naked,' he said, 'those *señoritas* sunnin' themselves out there on the porch will think business is about to pick up.'

Campbell, who had never frequented a lewd house, and had no intention of doing so in the future, blushed embarrassedly; yet was inwardly pleased that his partners had accepted him enough to josh him good-naturedly. He could also mark up another plus: his last night's sleep had been undisturbed by his recurring nightmares. Campbell was well aware that the key test of his found-again confidence and reliability to his partners would come when they finally faced Chato and his killers. And, he also opined, it was time he told Mr Culpepper all he knew about Chato, how he was captured by him, and his escape. Then, he knew, confidently, he would lay the ghost of his butchered partner for ever.

An hour later, he was dressed in the clothes, a store suit and clean shirt, Luke had brought in. Luke gave him a look over. 'I guessed close enough, pard,' he said. 'It ain't as though you're goin' to a fancy reception, is it?'

'They'll do fine, Mr Culpepper,' Campbell replied. 'Now I'll go and get some of this hair off; there's bound to be a barber's further along the street. And I'll take my horse with me and find the livery barn, it's got a shoe loose on one of its back legs.'

'That's OK, pard,' Luke replied. 'Me and Mr Springer will be in the cantina rustlin' us up a meal.' He hard-eyed Campbell. 'Then, while we're eatin', you can tell us all what you learned about Chato. It might give us the chance to get a slight edge over the sonuvabitch, OK?'

'I had every intention of doing that, Mr Culpepper,' Campbell replied, firm-voiced.

Luke's gaze this time was somewhat softer, a more satisfied look. 'I think the three of us are ready to walk the line, Mr MacColl,' he said.

Campbell couldn't hide his good feelings. He smiled, for the first time since his fearful experiences at the comanchero camp. 'I'll be proud and privileged to stand at your sides when that time comes, pards. I'll see you both when I get back.'

* * *

'Well I'll be damned, Kurt!' Jake gasped. 'We've caught up with the sonsuvbitches! That slab-sided mule hitched alongside that big mare is the mount of the old goat who shot me. I knew they would be headin' for Fort Sumner.' He bared his teeth in a wolf-like snarl of a smile. 'Ain't he in for a painful surprise? Get the horses down into that dip; don't make any sense losin' our edge by lettin' them know we're comin'. We'll Indian in on them.'

'What about the other fella, Jake?' Kurt asked. 'The one who caused all the ruckus? His horse don't seem anywhere about.'

'I figure he must be off someplace diggin' another hole in a hillside lookin' for silver,' Jake said. 'But he ain't important: it's the old man I want to be lookin' along my pistol barrel.' He fierce-grinned again. 'I'll tell you this, Kurt, he ain't about to get much older. OK, let's do it. I'll give you time to sneak in by the back door: before I burst in on them at the front.'

Luke and Baldy, standing drinking at

the bar, were caught unawares when Jake stepped into the cantina. They thought he was a man who had come in for a drink, or the services of one of the short time girls sitting at a nearby table, until one of them gave out a sharp cry of alarm. They both spun round, hands scrambling for pistols, and found they were too late to make a fight of it — unless they wanted to die where they stood. Baldy cursed under his breath; the son-of-a-bitch he had winged, smiling fit to bust, had the drop on them. He was definitely losing his touch as a wide-eyed, always on the alert, plainsman. His goddamned mule had a sharper nose for sniffing coming trouble than he had.

The cantina walls vibrated with the sound of a pistol shot, echoed by the frightened screams of the girls. Baldy groaned and fell back against the bar, face paling with pain from the wound in the fleshy part of his left arm.

'That's just to give you a taste of what I felt when you plugged me, old man,' Jake snarled. 'And to stop you from yankin' that pistol you've got stuck down your shirt.'

Luke's face was a hard, expression-less mask as he rapidly calculated if it was possible to draw his gun and shoot the smug-smiling bastard facing him before the ranch hand's killing shot put him down. Jake, guessing his intention, swung his pistol on to him. 'Don't even think about it, mister,' he grated, still showing his stomping man's grin. 'You ain't got a chance to make the draw. Show him he ain't, Kurt.'

A cocky-smiling Kurt leaned across the bar and jabbed his pistol hard into Luke's back. Luke's hopes of a mad-ass shoot-out ended up as a narrow-eyed, drop-dead glare, choking over the bitter acceptance that he and Baldy were as good as dead.

Luke knew they were going to be shot; he could see it in the killing look showing on the wounded ranch hand's face. Maybe not here in the cantina where there were too many witnesses to prove they had been gunned down in cold blood, but at some quiet spot back along the trail apiece. One good thing was coming out of a bad situation, Luke thought: young Mr MacColl hadn't been taken. He hoped the kid wouldn't walk blindly into the cantina and make the ranch hands' day.

His other big hope was that MacColl wouldn't do anything foolish if he discovered the desperate situation he and Baldy were in, such as attempting a rescue mission. MacColl had no chance at all to take on and beat two men to the draw, especially when one of them had the cut of a border ruffian. His crazy notion of tracking down Chato to satisfy his hurt pride was about to get Baldy killed, he didn't want MacColl to throw away his life for a cause he ought to have known had no chance of succeeding.

'Tie them to a coupla chairs, Kurt,' Jake said, then winked at his partner. 'I can smell something cookin'; we might as well eat before we take them in to stand trial for cattle-lifting.' He smiled at the whores. 'You pretty *señoritas* can get on with your own business; there ain't goin' to be any more trouble here.'

Luke's worst fears had been confirmed, he had heard for sure his and Baldy's death sentences. The Mexican owner of the cantina wouldn't put himself out reporting a shooting in his bar if it seemed that two gringo cattle-thieves had been captured by lawmen.

Campbell glanced at himself in the barber-shop's mirror. In spite of looking pale and haggard with his beard shaved off and hair cut short, he had the pleasant, warm feeling of a man who had returned to the land of the living. A dedicated Pinkerton once more, ready, he believed, to face the dangers of his chosen profession, undaunted.

On nearing the cantina, Campbell noticed two horses tethered in a nearby hollow. They could be the mounts of a couple of ranch hands passing through

Fort Sumner. If so why were they partly hidden by the brush in the hollow? And why had he suddenly pulled up his horse without him being aware he had done so? Had he not yet fully regained control of his nerves and it had just been a nervous reaction, or had he unknowingly developed the sixth sense he had been told plainsmen had when danger was close by? Whatever had unsettled him it would be wise to take precautions and prepare for any adverse situation he might walk into when he entered the cantina. As the old saying put it: forewarned is forearmed. He would be both, Campbell thought.

He removed his gunbelt and slung it across his blanket roll, then, digging into one of his saddle-bags, pulled out a much smaller though heavier calibre gun and holster. Campbell smiled thinly; he had never used the gun and its rig before so he hoped if the worst came to the worst the contraption would work. His smile broadened slightly. When he came to think of it he had never fired any of his guns in his service as a Pinkerton. Campbell kneed his horse into a slow walk the rest of the way to the cantina.

Jake dropped his fork with a clatter on his plate and grabbed for his pistol lying on the table close by his hand when Campbell walked into the cantina. He beady-eyed the newcomer, quickly deciding the pasty-faced young dude was just some store clerk taking time off from behind the counter to have his way with one of the Mexican whores. He presented no threat to him and Kurt.

'Take no heed of those characters roped to those chairs, boy,' he grinned. 'They're just a coupla bad-asses wanted for cattle-liftin' from a spread south of the territory. Me and my deputy are takin' them back to stand trial.' He grinned widely. 'Before the cattlemen take them out and string them up.' He lowered his pistol and picked up his fork and began to eat again.

Campbell got the chilling feeling he

had walked into a lion's den. He was getting the chance to prove to his partners he was a man with whom they could safely walk the line, and the line was right in front of him. And so was an early grave. He congratulated himself for preparing for just such a dangerous situation.

More boldly than he was feeling, he favoured Jake with a tight-faced smile and glanced across at the two 'cattle-thieves' as he strode up to the bar. Seeing that Mr Springer had been wounded helped to steel his resolve to do what had to be done. One thing Campbell had painfully learned since riding west of the Pecos, men killed with the gun, knife, rope, without any honour or chivalry. Fair play, codes of civilized combat, were never heard of. Kill any way you could, or be killed was the recognized code in this lawless territory.

Campbell knew he couldn't sink as low, however provoked, as the scum he once had been paid to hunt down, by cold-bloodedly shooting them in the back. Though the only warning the ugly-faced ranch hand would get was the sound of the shot that would put him out of action for a long time.

Luke gave Baldy a despairing look. From some warped sense of loyalty, the kid had come in with some hare-brained idea he could rescue his partners without even being armed. He sure as hell had no chance of sweet-talking the ranch hands into letting them all go; they were worked up for a killing. St Peter himself couldn't persuade them to change their minds.

Luke saw MacColl stop, half turn away from him as he passed between him and Baldy and their captors. Then his ass cleared the seat of his chair, as far as the ropes binding him allowed, with involuntary shock at the ear-splitting crack as MacColl's right hand spouted flame.

The smashing impact of the close range shot of the .45 calibre Derringer flung Jake and his chair hard against the bar, his good arm shattered at the shoulder, to lie there in a crumpled, unmoving heap. Campbell swung the hand-sized pistol on to Kurt, sitting slack-jawed, pop-eyed, at the sudden and dramatic change in his fortunes.

'Mister,' Campbell said, the rope scar on his neck burning like a necklace of fire with nervous tension. Trying to look and sound like a hard-nosed *pistolero* whose gunning down of men was an everyday occurrence, he said, 'There's another load in this pistol, so don't be so foolish as to make me use it. It'll be a killing shot next time,' he lied.

Kurt had never been a fast, deep-thinking man, not until now that is. He glanced fearfully at Jake lying there, moaning low with pain although he was out for the count. Then at the cold-eyed kid and his little, big-killing gun only spitting distance away from him.

Without another second's thought, he knew what he had to do to protect number one. Grinning sickly, he raised both hands high. Dry-throated with fear he said, hoarsely, 'Kid, I ain't hankerin' to have a lump of lead in my hide, I was only backin' up my pard, Jake, and I reckon he'll be in no fit state when he comes round to carry out what we've hard-assed all this way to do. All I intend doin' is to ride back to the spread and ask the boss for my job back.'

'A wise decision, friend,' Campbell said, still keeping the Derringer pointed at Kurt, well aware that over-confidence could get a man an early grave. 'Now, I think it's advisable to get your friend to the local doc before you head back to where you came from.' He leaned forward and with his free hand pulled out the ranch hands's pistol from its holster and dropped it on to the table. Scowling, real *pistolero*-like, he said, 'If we see so much as a glimpse of you snooping along our back trail then there's more than a fair chance you'll never tend cows again.'

Kurt got slowly to his feet, hand still

grabbing air. Casting a lick-lipping, nervous glance at Luke and Baldy, he said, 'You'll never see me again, gents, and that's the gospel truth.' Bending down he hoisted the unconscious Jake across his shoulder, shuddering as he felt the warm stickiness of his partner's blood seeping through his shirt and on to his skin. Bowed-kneed beneath dead weight, he staggered out of the cantina.

Baldy managed a painful twist of a smile. 'We've sure got ourselves one helluva sneaky pard, Mr Culpepper.'

'We have that,' replied Luke, also thinking that Mr MacColl clean shaven, hair cut short, looked too young to be risking his life hunting bandits on the Staked Plains. Then he cursed himself for harbouring such foolish thoughts. The kid had just handled a tricky situation as coolly and expertly as any veteran peace officer, including himself. And, by what he had heard, kids younger than Mr MacColl were raising hell around Fort Sumner.

'You did well, pard,' he said. 'Me and

Mr Springer weren't long for this world, and believe me, that ain't the most joyful of situations. Though it took one helluva risk walkin' in and facing two men with the thoughts of killing in their hearts.'

'It wasn't all that much of a risk, Mr Culpepper,' Campbell said, keeping the pride he was feeling out of his voice. 'I had all the advantages. On seeing the two horses away from the cantina I accepted that they could belong to riders from the Circle C wanting to even things up a little. I couldn't check out the brands on the horses to make certain in case I was being watched from the cantina. I knew if they were Circle C men they would never recognize me as the Mole.' He grinned. 'The Derringer had them fooled. Now let's get you loose of those ropes and see to your wound, Mr Springer. How is it?'

'It hurts like hell, pard,' Baldy said. 'But the shell's gone straight through and it don't seem as though any bones have been broken. I'll live I reckon. I'll clean it with a bottle of that rotgut fire water this place sells for drinkin' man's whiskey. Then, Mr Culpepper, it would be wise for us to get the hell outa Fort Sumner. That fella you put a scare in could be tellin' the town marshal that he and his pard have been set upon on by three border hard-cases. The marshal could take a stroll along this way with a bunch of deputies to rope us in. Sittin' in a town jail ain't gonna help us to bring Chato to his early grave.'

'Makes good sense to me,' replied Luke. 'We've run into enough trouble already and we ain't got within smellin' distance of Chato.' He narrow-eyed Baldy. 'Are you sure you're fit enough to travel, Mr Springer?' Straight-faced, he added, 'Me and Mr MacColl ain't about to act as nursemaids to a sick old man.'

A grinning Baldy took his partner's comment in the manner it was meant. 'Why, it ain't but an inconvenience, Mr Culpepper,' he said. 'Back there in the high country I walked over thirty miles with four Sioux arrow heads stuck in my hide. You get me that whiskey and I'll clean up this scratch.' Baldy's smile changed into a suggestive leer, 'Why, if those purty *señoritas* hadn't just run off and we weren't pressed for time, I would have taken one of them through the back and showed her how half-bear, half-wolf we mountain-men are.'

A smiling Campbell took a quick look round the cantina. 'It seems as though the owner has made himself scarce as well, Mr Culpepper.'

'It figures,' replied Luke. 'Bein' a Mex he don't want to get involved in a gringo shoot-out.' He tossed several coins on to the bar and picked up a nearly full bottle of whiskey. 'While I see to this horn-dog pard of ours, Mr MacColl, I'd be obliged if you could stand watch outside for any *hombres* hurryin' this way. It's a damn shame we've got to leave; I was lookin' forward to a proper sit-down meal. After I've seen to Mr Springer I'll look around the storeroom and pick up what rations we can use on the trail. OK, pard, lets get that coat of yours off so I can do my doctorin'. You can't manage on your own.'

A straight-backed proud Campbell stood on watch on the cantina porch. Not doubting any more that he could stand as an equal alongside his partners, however tough things turned out. He grinned as he heard Mr Springer's shouted curses. The whiskey must be doing its work, he thought.

'There,' Luke said. 'That's stopped the bleedin'.' He had tied a cloth he had found behind the bar round Baldy's wound. He grinned. 'It's made a mess of your fine coat, but it won't stop you from shootin' down Chato.'

Baldy didn't answer him, he was taking a generous pull at the whiskey left in the bottle.

10

Two hours' ride east of Fort Sumner, Luke called a halt and made camp on a rocky, windswept ridge which not only gave them a clear sighting of the Fort Sumner trail but a vast stretch of the arid, treeless territory of the Staked Plains, north and east of them.

'Do we risk a fire, Mr Springer?' Luke asked as they tied up their horses to stout growths of brushwood. 'This is Chato's home ground; the sonuvabitch and his wild boys could be bedded down behind some nearby ridge, nearer than we reckon. It ain't wise from now on in to take chances.'

Baldy's face screwed up in deep concentration for several minutes as he sniffed the air. 'Can't smell any campfire smoke, Mr Culpepper,' he said. 'And Chato's camp, I reckon, will be a big settlement with plenty of cooking fires.' He grinned. 'And there ain't any of our red brethren hereabouts either, Jethro's standin' there as though he ain't got a care in the world. Though as you said, Mr Culpepper, it don't do to take things for granted. I'll light you a fire that'll make no more smoke than a man puttin' a match to his makin's.'

The three partners had eaten well of a meal of bacon, beans and freshly made biscuits, rations Luke had raked together from the cantina kitchen, and now, drinking their coffee, Luke opined it was time their new partner told them what he knew about Chato and how he had ended up as his prisoner, and of his escape from the comanchero camp.

'How did an Eastern private law-enforcing agency get themselves involved in the trackin' down of a bunch of comancheros, Mr MacColl?' he said. 'How come your boss, Mr Pinkerton, thought his men could do better than the lawmen and the soldier boys tryin' to rope Chato in? They know the territory, but the murderin' bastard still runs free.'

'We were hired by Mr Charles B. Nicholson, a New York businessman,' Campbell replied. 'His son and several of his friends were here in New Mexico on a guided hunting trip. Unfortunately, they were ambushed by Chato and his gang. Only one of their party escaped with his life, one of the guides. Though badly wounded he staggered into Portales, a small township east of here, and raised the alarm. All the rescue party found was the ransacked camp, and the bodies of the Eastern hunting party, stripped of their clothes and . . . ' Campbell s voice broke — 'and mutilated.

'Not satisfied with the seeming lack of progress by the estate's efforts to bring Chato to book, Mr Nicholson, a wartime friend of Mr Pinkerton, asked the agency to help in tracking down his son's killers.' Campbell smiled wanly at Luke and Baldy. 'And here I am. Not a very good showing for yours truly and the Pinkerton Detective Agency, Mr Culpepper, is it? One agent, Mr Parker butchered, me well on my way to being mad, if you hadn't given me the chance to come to my senses.'

'Jesus H. Christ,' Baldy said. 'What did your boss expect, sendin' two men, Eastern dudes at that, after the most bloodthirsty sonuvabitch in the whole of New Mexico?' He spat in the fire in disgust.

'There's only three of us, Mr Springer,' Luke said. 'And one of us is an Easterner.'

'Yeah that's true, pard,' replied Baldy. 'But we know what we're up against. Some big shot of a detective sittin' in an office back East ain't sent us here.' Baldy grinned. 'And besides, we're loco.'

'Mr Pinkerton didn't expect Mr Parker and me to capture Chato, Mr Springer,' Campbell said. 'By listening and asking discreet questions we could maybe get a line on where Chato's camp was, then notify the nearest army post of our findings. Mr Pinkerton thought that being just two of us we wouldn't attract unwelcome attention to ourselves. Being Easterners we wouldn't be suspected as lawmen.'

'And this quiet snoopin' around, Mr MacColl,' Luke said, 'didn't pan out as planned?'

Campbell's face hardened into deep bitter lines. 'No, it didn't, Mr Culpepper.' His voice was low and toneless. 'Portales was as good a place as any to begin our searching for intelligence regarding Chato's whereabouts. Portales is an isolated township in the middle of what is ideal territory for comancheros' encampments, or any other outlaws' camps. Mr Parker figured it was more than likely there would be men there who had contact with Chato, possibly to warn him if any army cavalry patrols were in the area.'

Campbell's head dropped dejectedly on to his chest and he gazed unseeing into the fire for several moments before raising his head and resuming his story once more.

'We were right, Mr Culpepper,' he

began. 'Chato had his agents in Portales. They must have heard of us asking questions about Chato; we hadn't been discreet enough. One night, as we were returning to our rooms four men attacked us, knocked us out cold before we could draw our pistols. When we came to, we were roped across the backs of our horses and being led, fast, in a northerly direction. The reason we had not been killed out of hand and dumped in some side alley in Portales, we found out later, was that Chato wanted to question us, to find out what type of lawmen we were and whether we were on our own, or part of a posse coming into the territory to hunt him down.'

'So you got to see the sonuvabitch, Chato, then, Mr MacColl?' Luke said. Then, impatiently, he asked, 'Could you find your way back to the camp?'

'Oh, we saw Chato all right,' replied Campbell. 'He's a man of Mr Springer's build but with a face and eyes that would throw a scare in the Devil himself.' The haunting, faraway look came into his eyes again as he touched his neck. 'It was Chato who marked me for life. As for finding his camp, well, as I said, it was dark and what with being pistol-whipped and the hard riding, I was in no fit state to do much observing. Later, when it was daytime and I was lying on a ledge on the face of a butte, I do remember seeing some features, a peculiar shaped ridge, twin rocky peaks, I would recognize again if I saw them.'

Luke raised a questioning eyebrow. 'How did you come to be perched on a cliff face, Mr MacColl?'

'Chato has some unpleasant ways of extracting information from people, Mr Culpepper,' Campbell said. 'As unpleasant as mine was, I lived through it. Though not by any change on Chato's part, I might add.' Campbell shuddered. 'Mr Parker had no such luck at all. Still hearing his screams as he was being cut to pieces was the reason I ended up at the old mine, working like a slave. Didn't give a damn if the roof caved in on me.' He looked Luke full in the eyes. 'I wanted to die, but I hadn't the guts to put a bullet through my head,' he sobbed.

Regaining control of his emotions, voice firm, he said, 'You and Mr Springer gave me a reason for wanting to live and I thank you both for that. Now I'll tell you why I came to be clinging to the face of a butte, Mr Culpepper.

'On reaching the camp,' Campbell continued, 'we were thrown into a hut, hands and feet still bound.' He gave a wry grin. 'I suppose Chato didn't like his sleep disturbed unless it was a real emergency. Come daylight we were dragged out of the hut to face the man we had been charged to bring to justice. Chato. As I have said, a fearful-looking man, hawk-faced and of mixed blood, every drop of it bad. He lashed us both with his quirt a few times, then he really got down to the business of making us talk.'

Then Campbell told his partners how Parker had been taken away, stripped naked, and pegged out on the ground. He'd had a noose placed around his neck, then, Chato, up on his horse, began hauling him around the camp. 'My bonds had been removed, Mr Culpepper,' he said. 'Chato didn't want me to choke to death before finding out how much a threat Mr Parker and I were to him.' Campbell paused, reliving the fearful events again.

Luke reached out a comforting hand, and gripped Campbell by the shoulder. 'There ain't no need to tell us any more, son,' he said, soft-voiced. 'Recollectin' bad memories ain't the most joyful of pastimes.'

'It's OK, Mr Culpepper,' replied Campbell. 'They're no longer nightmares. I feel the need to talk about them to prove that.'

A stone-faced Luke and Baldy listened to Campbell explain how the lie of the camp had saved his life.

'The encampment was sited in a

large grassy hollow on a flat-topped butte, hedged on one side by high ridges,' Campbell said. 'The second time Chato dragged me round the camp, I managed to get some leeway on the rope and slipped the noose off my neck. Still on my stomach I rolled over several times and was over the lip of the butte. It wasn't that I was contemplating suicide, Mr Culpepper. I had the mad idea I could survive a fall down a cliff face and somehow make my escape. If I didn't make it then at least it would be a faster and a damned less painful death than Chato had in store for me.' Campbell looked appealingly at Luke. 'It meant leaving my partner, but what could I do to help him? I guess I was in a blind frightened panic.'

'There ain't nothin' to be ashamed about, Mr MacColl,' Baldy said. 'Your pard was as good as dead. In that situation a man has to look out for himself. Foolishly sacrificin' your life to the enemy is plumb loco. Tryin' to keep yourself alive to get back at the sonuvabitch who's puttin' you through hell is all you should have been thinkin' about. You've proved yourself right: you've won your chance to kill Chato.'

'I guess that is so,' Campbell replied. 'Though lying on that ledge listening to Mr Parker's screams I just couldn't convince myself of that.' Again Campbell's mind drifted away for a while before continuing with his story. 'Where I had gone over the edge of the butte wasn't a clear straight drop but rather a steep slope so I just kept on rolling until I was stopped abruptly by a clump of bush growing out of a fissure in the cliff face thirty or so feet down. The impact of hitting the brush flung me into the narrow slash in the rock. I lay there unseen by anyone looking down from the rim, half-mad, half-dead with pain, fearfully listening to Mr Parker's dying tortured screams as the murderous scum cut at him with their knives. Then I blacked out, coming to again in fading daylight.'

Campbell sighed deeply like a man

who had had a heavy load taken from his shoulders. He raised his head and looked across the fire at Luke and Baldy. 'What happened next is only a vague recollection. I had to have a horse, water, and maybe a gun, in that order or die slowly of thirst on that ledge. And all those essentials to me staying alive were in the comanchero camp. Somehow I must have scrambled up the slope, and with the luck I never expected, I managed to get hold of a saddled horse, a canteen of water, but not wanting to stretch my luck by searching among the sleeping comancheros for a rifle or a pistol, I rein-walked the horse out of the silent camp. Then, mounted up and rode fast and wild like a man escaping from hell, as I surely was, Mr Culpepper.

'Existing on handouts from kind-hearted farmers and ranchers I finally made it to where you found me. That must have been nine months ago. Mr Pinkerton must think we are both dead, because I never contacted the agency of the failure of our assignment. Most of the time I was at the mine, I believed I was dead, spiritually, at least, Mr Culpepper.' He favoured Luke with a quizzical look. 'Is your reason for wanting to see Chato dead as pressing as mine, Mr Culpepper?'

'I'd like to think so, Mr MacColl,' replied Luke. 'One of Chato's wild boys put two arrows in me, and I ended by nearly drownin' in the Pecos. Though that ain't the main reason.' He told Campbell about the wagon-train massacre and how he felt obligated to hunt down Chato. 'It's the least I can do for lettin' those poor folks down.'

Campbell glanced across at Baldy. 'And your reason, Mr Springer,' he said, 'was it of account of your . . . ?'

'Because of my Injun haircut, Mr MacColl?' Baldy cut in. He grinned. 'Naw, that was just the doin' of an everyday bad-ass Injun. I kinda tagged along with Mr Culpepper after he got me out of a tight scrape with a bunch of cattle-lifters. I had nothing else particular to do in mind. Now we've bared our souls to each other, Mr Culpepper, and all of us agree that the world will be a better place if Chato was in Hell just how we gonna send him there? I figure it's time we come up with some sort of a plan.'

Luke gave him a lopsided grin. 'I've already thought of one, Mr Springer,' he said. 'I'll admit it ain't a humdinger of a plan, but I reckon it's the only option we've got. And it all depends on the co-operation of our young pard here.' Serious-faced, he looked at Campbell. 'Do you want to hear it, Mr MacColl? I won't be offended if you tell me you won't go along with it.'

'There's too much at stake for pards to get offended with each other, Mr Culpepper,' Campbell said. 'Tell me about your plan and what my role will be in it.'

'We make for Portales,' Luke began. 'And if it's OK with you, Mr MacColl, I'd like you to act as bait for the drawin' out in the open Chato's 'eyes' in the town. Ask nosy questions again, as you did with your late pard. You might not need to ask around if the same fellas who jumped you are in Portales, they'll recognize you. This time it will be your pards who will be doin' the cold-cockin'.' He grinned wolfishly. 'And I figure Mr Springer will know of some Injun way to persuade them to tell us where Chato's stronghold is.'

Baldy matched Luke's grin with a mirthless grimace of his own. 'A whole damn bagful of them, Mr Culpepper. If I really tried I would have an *hombre* tell me tales he wouldn't confess to a priest on his death bed.'

'It's a high risk I'm askin' you to take,' Luke said, turning to face Campbell again. 'I'm askin' you to put your life in the hands of a coupla old farts. But it's the only scheme I can come up with. I'm open to any other suggestions.'

Campbell felt a flicker of fear run through his body and hoped it hadn't shown in his face. He didn't want his partners to think he had weakened in his resolve to ride and fight alongside them, lost his self-respect and courage. He guessed he was still somewhat apprehensive about how he would bear up when his moment of truth finally came. He looked at his partners with a steady-eyed gaze. Although he had only known them for a few days they were tough men, men who would try their damnedest to protect him.

'I have to walk the line with you both sometime,' he said. 'Portales seems to be the obvious place to do it.' He smiled. 'This time I'll also have the Derringer handy.'

Both Luke and Baldy smiled. 'Good,' said Luke. 'Portales it is then. We ride in separate, from different directions, me and Baldy first. We'll all book in at the same roomin'-house then we've got you covered the twenty-four hours.' He got to his feet. 'Let's move out, pronto; I'm gettin' kinda uneasy bein' this close to Fort Sumner. It seems quiet enough now hereabouts but by what me and Mr Springer have been told there's a small war takin' place here. And wars, however small are trouble we want to stay well clear of. While we're in Portales you can go and see the town's doc, get that wound of yours checked over. Me and Mr MacColl ain't strong enough to stand the kick of that heavy gun of yours. And I'm bankin' on the Sharps bein' put to good use, blowing Chato all the way to Hell.'

Luke heard Baldy grunt; whether it was a grunt saying he was going to the doc, or not, he couldn't tell. Then he wondered why the hell he was talking to a man who had only stayed alive most of his life by being smarter than the wild redmen whose land he lived in. The old goat, Luke knew, would do what he thought he should do. He didn't need a nursemaid.

As the trio hit the trail to Portales, Campbell began to do some wondering of his own, wondering if Mr Culpepper and Mr Springer really meant to use their knives on any comanchero they managed to capture to make him talk.

Or were his partners joshing him? Campbell's blood chilled slightly. He didn't think so. Smiling or not, Mr Springer would try out his bag of Indian tricks, as he put it.

Then his blood pumped warm again when he thought of the fearful agony that Mr Parker had suffered, not forgetting the pain and mental trauma Chato had put him through. The war against Chato had to be fought by comanchero rules, no holds barred, or it was lost before they had fired the first shot. By thunder, Campbell thought, angrily, he would like to use the knife himself. Then he put all fanciful thoughts out of his mind and tried not to think too much of what could go wrong for them in Portales. Mr Culpepper had said it was a mad-ass plan. It was a sober-faced Campbell who rode the rest of the way to Portales.

11

From the porch of the rooming-house, Luke watched Mr MacColl walk into the High Plains bar. The kid hadn't had a change of heart, lost his nerve; he was doing what had been asked of him. Now it was was up to him and Baldy to look out for the Pinkerton, or, like the German farmers and his former partner, Mr MacColl would end up dead.

Luke had ridden into Portales first, booking in at what Mr MacColl had told him was the only rooming-house in town. He had then come outside to sit on the porch to wait for his two *compadres* to show up.

Half an hour later, as the saloon lights were being lit, he saw Baldy coming out of the livery barn and make his way towards him, carrying his Sharps. Luke grinned, force of habit, he thought. Mr Springer's normal rooming-house would be anywhere beneath the big skies of Montana and Wyoming where a rifle was essential to a man sleeping peaceful as a fire and a blanket were. He had left his Winchester in the safe keeping of the livery-barn owner.

A while later, Baldy came out of the rooming-house, gave him a curt nod and strode across to the High Plains bar. Not long after, Campbell came into Portales. As he passed him on the porch, Luke said softly, 'Mr Springer's already across at the bar. We're ready when you are.'

Campbell quickly unpacked and was back outside on the porch within ten minutes. He managed to raise a confident smile at Luke. Now it was up to him. Knowing that his partners had every confidence in him helped to allay his fears somewhat. He stepped off the porch and walked boldly across to the bar.

Luke waited five or so minutes after the bar doors had swung closed behind

Campbell before getting on to his feet. It was time for the hunt for Chato to be started in earnest. He eased his pistol in its holster; trouble could come fast and he wanted to meet it and come through on the winning side. He followed two trail-hands into the bar.

The bar was crowded with drinkers and card players, but he managed to find a seat at a table near the door and began to take in the scenery. From where he was sitting, Luke could see both of his partners, standing at the opposite ends of the long bar. Between them they had Mr MacColl well covered in the event of anyone making any hostile move against him.

Luke tensed up suddenly on noticing MacColl casting sidelong glances at three men playing cards at a table close by him. Two of the players were swarthy, hatchet-faced men, mixed-blood *hombres*, Luke thought; the third, a big barn of a gringo, though he was as mean-faced as his *compadres*. Lying on the table was a long-barrelled shotgun, whose working parts were protected by a fringe-worked hide sleeve.

Campbell turned away from the bar and nodded in the direction of the three men. He couldn't see either of his partners but he knew they would be watching him. He wanted to let them know he believed he had spotted three comancheros, or at least men who traded with them.

Luke close-eyed the men. He noticed Baldy had changed his stance and was also looking at them. Had Campbell recognized them as comancheros? They looked vicious enough to be three of Chato's band of killers, but so did half the drinkers in the bar, including Mr Springer. Yet something about them had alerted Mr MacColl. It was time he got the kid out of the bar before the hard-cases cottoned on to the fact they were under surveillance, or recognized him as the Pinkerton agent who, they thought, had fallen to his death over the edge of a butte.

Luke stood up and, waiting until Mr MacColl had picked him out, did some head wagging of his own, jerking it in the direction of the door. Satisfied both of his partners had got the message he walked out of the saloon. He stood at the far end of the porch until Baldy, closely followed by Mr MacColl came out into the open, then stepped down into the side alley.

'Mr Culpepper,' Campbell said, as he came up to Luke, eager to tell him who he thought the three men were.

Luke raised a warning hand. 'Hold it a second, Mr MacColl,' he said. 'I want to make sure those *hombres* you were interested in ain't got likewise feelin's towards you. Both of you get further along the alley. I'll join you if everything's OK.' Baldy and Campbell waiting in the deeper darkness of the alley, pistols fisted, heard Luke say as he came along the alley, 'It's OK. I reckon I was worryin' like some old maid. But it's better than bein' careless. We all know what grief and pain carelessness can bring on a man. Now, Mr MacColl, why were you so interested in those three hard-cases?'

'It was the gun lying on their table that first drew my attention, Mr Culpepper,' Campbell said.

'I saw it,' Baldy said. 'And a mighty fine piece it was.'

'Exactly, Mr Springer!' Campbell said excitedly. 'It was a Purdy, made by Purdy's of London, England, one of the finest gunsmiths in the world, a gun no ranch hand could afford to own. Even if he had the cash to buy one he would have to travel east as far as Chicago, m'be right back to New York to find a gun store that sold Purdys.'

'And you think that fine English gun was taken by the comancheros when they looted the camp of those Eastern dudes they massacred?' interrupted Luke.

'There's no other way, Mr Culpepper,' replied Campbell, 'that gun could have showed up here in Portales in the hands of those men.'

144

'I think we oughta have words with those *hombres*,' Baldy said. 'The white-eye will be the more loose-mouthed under pressure. His two buddies have Injun blood in them. They'll take it as honour not to tell us anything no matter how uncomfortable we make it for them.'

Campbell suddenly felt a sickly feeling at the pit of his stomach. Torturing a man had suddenly lost its earlier appeal. As much as he wanted to see Chato dead, he could never take an active part in torturing a comanchero to have the satisfaction of avenging Mr Carter's death.

'It's a mite too soon to go out on the warpath, Mr Springer,' Luke said. 'Every bad-ass in the territory ain't a comanchero though their possession of that English gun needs explainin'.' Luke smiled icily. 'We won't find that out unless we step right up to the guys and accuse them outright of being comancheros.' Luke looked at Baldy. 'If they are, Mr Springer, we'll have to down those two Mexicans; we can't handle three prisoners.'

Campbell gulped hard, and got the chills again. Mr Culpepper was talking about cold-bloodedly killing men as though he was discussing the price of corn with Mr Springer. 'Is . . . isn't that acting as judge, jury and executioner, Mr Culpepper?' he said weakly.

'Out here, Mr MacColl,' Baldy said. 'Sometimes a man has to act like God, make up his own rules and act pretty damn quick on them if he wants to stay alive. If they are comancheros, then they're long past due for payin' the price for all their thievin' and killin'. Or would you let them live so they could sneak up on us along our back-trail? And remember, the sonsuvbitches gave you no choice whether you lived or died.'

What Mr Springer had said was correct, Campbell knew, but still the action seemed drastic. Though he didn't openly say so to his partners.

Luke, sensing Campbell's uneasiness,

146

said, 'Mr Springer's right, boy, we've got a whole passel of trouble some-where ahead of us, we sure as hell don't want any comin' up behind us. I know some of our rough Western ways don't settle too easy on an Easterner's stomach, but that's the way things are played out here. And you've had to swallow some rough treatment.'

Luke smiled fatherly at Campbell. 'It ain't as though I'm goin' to back-shoot the pair. I'm givin' them the chance to draw. More than they gave the fellas they faced, I reckon.'

'Won't that be risky, Mr Culpepper?' Campbell asked in alarm. Though, he thought Mr Culpepper seemed to shrug off trouble with the ease a dog shakes water from its coat.

'Don't you fret none, Mr MacColl,' Luke replied. 'Mr Springer will be my back-up if things go wrong. And to tell you the truth, the chance those two fellas think they've got ain't no chance at all. They'll be sittin' there thinkin' thay can beat me to the draw when I'm standin' in front of them, bold-assed enough to still have my pistol holstered. What I — '

A smile of realization flooded across Campbell's face as he interrupted Luke. 'But you'll have my Derringer, won't you, Mr Culpepper?'

Luke beamed back at him. 'That I will, Mr MacColl, that I will. Now I'd be obliged if you'd hand me that sneaky piece. I don't want its rig. Then me and Mr Springer can get back into the bar and keep a watchful eye on those three. You go and collect our gear from the rooming-house, saddle up our horses. Bring them here. Let me know when you come back, then I'll start the ball, OK?'

'OK, pard,' replied Campbell. He pulled up the sleeve of his jacket and slipped the Derringer out of its spring clip and handed it over to Luke. 'It's got two loads in and the safety's off, it's ready for instant use.'

Luke hefted the small gun in his hand. 'Two loads will be all I need, Mr

MacColl. I'm not aimin' to start a shoot-out in a crowded saloon.' Luke turned and faced Baldy. 'It don't look as though you'll get to see the doc, Mr Springer. But I reckon a piddlin' little bullet hole won't put out an *hombre* who, stuck full of arrows, and carryin' his mule, walked sixty miles across rough country.'

'Yeah, you're right, Mr Culpepper,' Baldy said, equally straight-faced. 'We Big Horn country boys ain't noted for our delicate constitutions. As that fella I'm going to bend my Sharps' barrel over his head will soon find out.'

* * *

Luke was bellied up to the bar, trying not to make his eyeing of the three men too obvious. They would be natural suspicious-minded men, trigger-fingered, ready to leap to their feet and cut loose at all and everyone if they suspected they were being watched. Or quit playing cards and head outside to

149

do some eyeing of their own. And for him to try and follow them would be asking to be shot down as soon as he stepped out of the bar.

Baldy was much closer to the table, keen, Luke opined, to put down the beefy gringo. He hoped the old goat wouldn't get carried away in the excitement and lay the man out grave cold. He gave Baldy a get ready nod: he had seen Campbell come into the bar. The boy caught his eye then turned and walked back through the door. Luke smiled to himself. The boy wanted to be his back-up as well as Baldy when he confronted the three hard-cases, not to stay out in the street looking after the horses.

'The sounds of gunfire could spook them, Mr MacColl,' he had told him. 'While I'm only reckonin' that the Derringer's two loads will give me the upper hand things don't always pan out the way you hope. It could turn into a real shoot-out and scare the horses. And we'll not have the time to chase after them, or unhitch them from a post if we have to cut and run for it.' He didn't tell Campbell that if things didn't go right, he and Baldy would more than likely not make it alive to the door, let alone to their mounts. He hoped that situation wouldn't happen for then the kid would have to make a hard choice, stay and fight or hightail it out of Portales. Though Luke thought, knowing Mr MacColl's pride and loyalty to his partners, he would opt for standing his ground and making a fight of it. Luke cursed softly. Even when he was dead he could be responsible for someone's untimely death. Face set in hard, grim lines, he strode across the bar to the three men.

Baxter, the full-white, scowled up at Luke. Luke gazed at bleary, red-rimmed eyes. He had been hitting the bottle hard, he thought, which would be in their favour. A drunk would be easier to handle.

'What the hell are you standin' there for, mister?' Baxter mouthed, drunkenly.

Luke ignored him. Baldy would put

paid to him when the time came. He kept his eyes on the expressionless-faced 'breeds, the men he had to kill when they made their play. He began to act out his bluff, all the while watching the 'breeds' shoulders for the giveaway twitching when they grabbed for their guns. He wouldn't be able to read their intentions in the dead-eyed faces.

'That fine gun lyin' there, *amigos*,' he said, 'once belonged to some dude hunters who got themselves massacred by a bunch of comancheros led by the renegade, Chato, not a coupla stones' throws away from here. I think you boys, and your fat-gutted gringo *compadre*, rode with those no-good killers and I'm takin' you in.'

Luke drew back his lips in a fierce grimace as he saw the warning movement of the 'breeds' shoulders. The bastards had fallen for his bluff, the killing time was here. Yet he waited that split-second until the 'breeds' guns were almost clear of the edge of the table before swinging the Derringer into view. He had to show clearly to any interested parties the 'breeds had drawn first.

The two shots showered ceiling dust on the alarmed drinkers flinging themselves to the floor or behind upturned tables and chairs for safety. The two 'breeds bounced up against the backs of their chairs then flopped forwards across the table, each with a weeping red eye in their foreheads. Luke caught a glimpse of Baldy bringing down the Sharps hard on the third man's head, wincing at the sickening sound of steel striking against flesh and bone. Baldy's victim's expression changed from one of surprised shock at seeing his *compadres* gunned down to a fixed mask of pain as he slid from his chair, out to the wide, to hit the floor with a heavy thud.

'It's all over, folks!' Luke called out, turning away from the killing scene. 'I'm a US Marshal, and that gent with the rifle is my deputy!' he lied. 'These fellas we've had trouble with we believe they are comancheros, part of Chato's gang. I only wanted to ask them some questions but the 'breeds took it in their heads to make a fight of it!'

A beefy, longhorn-moustached man heaved himself up from beind a table and came across to Luke. Suspicious-eyed, he growled, 'A marshal, you say? I ain't seen you in the territory before and I reckon I'm acquainted with most of 'em. I'm Sheriff Hogan. I keep peace in this town and don't take kindly to any *hombre*, badge-totin' or not, havin' shoot-outs in a crowded bar.'

'I understand that, Sheriff,' replied Luke. 'But as I've said I only wanted to question these fellas and the next thing I knew the sonsuvbitches were pullin' guns on me.'

'Yeah, I saw that,' Sheriff Hogan said. 'They thought they had the edge on you.' He hard-eyed Luke. 'It was kinda fortunate you just happened to be carryin' a hideaway gun, ain't it, Marshal?'

'Fortune had nothin' to do with it,

154

Sheriff,' replied Luke. 'Ours is a hazardous profession, and it don't do not to take precautions for any upset. I got careless once, cost some folks their lives. My deputy relaxed his guard one time, Sheriff. Show them, Mr Springer.'

A smiling Baldy removed his hat. Luke heard one of the saloon girls give a muffled scream and a gasped, 'Holy Mother of God!' from the sheriff.

'I take your point, Marshal,' the sheriff said, though still out of sorts at having his poker game interrupted, especially when he was on a winning streak — and the loss of dignity to his calling by hiding like a scared kid behind a table with one of the girls. 'But,' he said, to regain his standing as the town's peace officer, 'it would have been only right and proper for you comin' into my town to make an arrest, to pay a call on me. Let me know what you're about. I could've let you have a coupla shotgun deputies; those 'breeds wouldn't have drawn on you then. Would've saved you havin' to kill them.'

155

'I didn't know they were in town, Sheriff,' Luke lied again. 'Me and my deputy only came into Portales for supplies. We walked into the bar for a drink, then I happened to see that gun there lyin' on the table and I knew the three must be comancheros, or have close links with them.'

Sheriff Hogan glanced down at the Purdy then favoured Luke with a puzzled look. 'It's only a shot-gun to me, a fancy one I'll admit, but what's it got to do with them bein' comancheros?'

'That 'fancy' gun belonged to a party of Easterners out hereabouts on a huntin' trip,' Luke said. 'Chato and his comancheros massacred them, looted their camp. I wanted to ask them how the gun came to be in their possession, but the 'breeds weren't in the mood for talkin'. You saw the rest.'

'That's right, Sheriff,' Campbell said, as he came up to the pair. He had heard the two shots then silence. He knew it had been the Derringer that had been fired but he would be damned if he was going to stand out in the street holding horses' reins like some stable boy and wait until Mr Culpepper and Mr Springer came out of the bar and told him how things had gone down. He had loose-hitched the ropes round the post and stepped up on to the boardwalk and entered the bar.

'Who the hell's he?' Sheriff Hogan barked out. 'Another one of your deputies? He ain't gonna give the ladies a fright if he takes his hat off, is he?'

'I'm a Pinkerton agent, Sheriff,' Campbell said, stiffly. 'I take it you've heard of the agency.'

'Yeah, yeah, I've heard of them,' the sheriff replied, irritably. 'The whole territory was crawlin' with them a while back after the killin' of the dudes the marshal here spoke of. I heard two Pinkertons were killed by this Chato. Then a Mr Charles B. Nicholson, a well-heeled New Yorker, into steel and railroads, showed up, kickin' ass, army and lawmen, for not tryin' hard enough to rope in Señor Chato, the killer of his boy.' The sheriff looked down at the unconscious man. 'If he's a suspect comanchero I'd better put him behind bars until he comes round.' He grinned at Luke. 'If he's one of the bastards who killed that big-shot's boy I might get me a medal.'

Campbell shot a glance at his two partners. They hadn't risked their lives to get a prisoner who could be their lead to Chato's stronghold, only to see him thrown in jail by a fat slob of a sheriff so he could get himself a piece of glory. He began to embellish the truth somewhat.

'The agency's motto, Sheriff, is, 'We never sleep'. Agents are still active in the territory working on the massacre case. I'm working closely with Marshal Culpepper. The marshal has been appointed specially by the Governor of New Mexico, who, incidentally, is a personal friend of Mr Charles B. Nicholson, to make every effort to track down Chato, the scourge of the state.

We intended taking our prisoner to Fort Sumner where he will be interrogated by Mr Alan Pinkerton, the head of the agency, himself. That's how important that man is to us. Naturally, when I write my report, I'll mention that the Sheriff of Portales gave us every assistance regarding the apprehension of our suspect.'

Sheriff Hogan thought for a minute or two. Anything for a quiet life, he thought. He didn't want Pinkertons, Eastern big-shots or specially appointed state marshals descending on Portales. He couldn't cope with all the hassle. He would have to kiss good-bye to his regular poker game. The dude kid promised he would get a mention in his despatches. That ought to get him re-elected sheriff for another term.

'You can take that fella back to Fort Sumner, Mr Pinkerton man,' he said. 'Hang the murderin' asshole when you've done talkin' to him.' He raised his voice and shouted, 'Billy Joe, Clancy, haul these two dead *hombres* along to the mortician's. One of you barkeeps clear away this table and bring out another, there's blood on this one! If you and your deputies are stayin' the night in town, Marshal,' the sheriff said to Luke, 'I'll lodge that fella you cold-cocked in a cell for the night. Kinda take him off your hands if you want a drink,' he grinned. 'Or female companionship.' The sheriff eyed the shot-gun longingly. 'M'be I oughta take charge of that gun as sort of evidence.'

'You do that, Sheriff,' replied Luke. The comancheros had had the gun once, if things went wrong for them he didn't want the sons-of-bitches to get their hands on it again. 'And thanks for the offer, but we're ready to ride out. There could be other comancheros in town who might try to effect a rescue of our prisoner, or silence him. He's the only lead to Chato we've got, I can't afford to take the chance of losin' him.'

'You could be right there, Marshal,' the sheriff admitted. 'That bastard Chato always seems one jump ahead of any posse tryin' to hunt him down. Bein' this is cattle country strangers regularly pass through Portales, some of them could be Chato's 'eyes'.'

Luke's smile held no warmth in it at all. 'If that *hombre* on the floor sings sweet and loud we'll be waiting at the spot Chato's aimin' to jump to.' He turned and faced Baldy. 'We'll tie him up good and tight and sling him on the back of my horse, Mr Springer, then we'll head for Fort Sumner.'

Their ride to Fort Sumner was for the sheriff's benefit. Once clear of Portales they would head north where, Luke believed, Chato's stronghold lay. Then, at some lonely spot on the trail, Baldy would do his Indian tricks on their prisoner to find out exactly where Chato's camp was.

'Give me a hand, pards,' he said, and bending down, grabbed the inert comanchero by the shoulders.

12

At first light, Luke started the serious business of making their prisoner believe he would suffer the tortures of a hell on earth if he didn't show them the way to the comancheros' hold-out.

They had made camp in a hollow sheltered by a stand of close-growing cottonwoods, well clear of the main trail running between Portales and Fort Sumner. The campfire was low burning, Luke well aware there were all kinds of killing men prowling around the territory, Chato and his butchers, the factions in the so-called Lincoln County war, and the war band they had frightened off back along the trail. They were seen riding north and could be sitting around their own fire hereabouts.

Luke didn't want to face shooting trouble now. There was a good chance they would be able to sneak up on Chato's stronghold. Though sneaking up on the sonuvabitch's camp, Luke thought soberly, was a long ways from getting close enough to kill the comanchero chief, it was a move in the right direction. It was up to Baldy and his knife to get them in closer.

'It's time we woke up that fella from his beauty sleep, Mr Springer,' he said. 'It looks as though you're ready to perform. You sure scare the hell outa me, and I reckon, Mr MacColl as well.

Baldy had stripped to his waist and removed his hat. His torso was as coppery as an Indian's, pock-marked with the white scars of old wounds, which made Luke think, what with being scalped and all, the old goat had suffered some painful experiences in his life. His story about walking all those miles in the high country stuck full of Sioux arrows could be almost true.

Baldy grinned. 'I'll do the wakin', Mr Culpepper,' he said. 'I ain't a purty sight, the sonuvabitch will think Judgement Day has arrived, scare him real good straight off.' He spat on the blade of the Bowie he held in his right hand, heard it sizzle and evaporate instantly in a slight puff of steam. His grin became demonic.

Campbell shuddered, hearing Mr Carter's agonizing screams again. Mr Culpepper was right, Mr Springer's appearance frightened him. With that fearful head scar and body wound marks, he would not look out of place standing alongside that archfiend, Chato. Though he told himself that Mr Springer was only play-acting, Campbell gave both his partners a long, searching look and came up with the uneasy feeling neither of them *were* acting. In fact, Mr Springer seemed eager to use his knife on their prisoner. He asked himself the question of does the means justify the end? And found he couldn't answer it. One thing he did know for certain, he was too queasy inside to stay and watch what was about to be done to the comanchero. He prayed it was only play-acting.

'I'll check on the horses, Mr Culpepper,' he said. 'That's if you don't need me here.'

'You do that, Mr MacColl,' Luke replied. 'That *hombre* won't be no problem to me and Mr Springer.' He guessed why the kid couldn't stay and didn't blame him. Baldy could be forced to draw some of his blood, painfully, to give him the impression he was in the hands of killing men as merciless as any comanchero. Like Mr MacColl, Luke wasn't anxious for that to happen, but his mind went back to the sight of the rough wooden markers on the graves along the Pecos and he convinced himself that drastic measures had to be taken to prevent similar such-like massacres of innocent folk.

Baxter groaned loudly and came alive, slowly and painfully. His head was still pounding from the vicious blow he had taken and his right cheek stiff with caked blood from the wound. And he discovered he was bound hand and foot and tied to a tree. At least the bastards who had taken him hadn't shot him like they had Felix and Jose and he wondered why. They couldn't be lawmen, or he would have been behind bars not feeling all cramped to hell with being roped to a tree for most of the night. Who his captors were had him worried.

Then, through pain-blurred eyes, he saw a bald-headed old man dressed only in buckskin pants, a knife glinting ominously in his hand, coming towards him and he really began to worry. Baxter blurted out a stream of panic-stricken curses. Since being knocked out in the bar by white men, Indians had somehow got their hands on him. What they intended doing to him almost made him lose control of his bladder. Felix and Jose had been the lucky ones, he thought, wildly.

As the knife-wielding bronco came closer, Baxter gasped in surprise. He was a white man and he wasn't bald but had been scalped. But the ugly, mad-eyed face belonged to an Indian worked up into the killing lust. Baxter lost the battle with his bladder.

It might not be such a blood-letting job after all, Luke thought, the comanchero hadn't wet his pants with joy. He gazed down at him. 'Mister,' he grated, 'we know you and the two 'breeds I shot back there in Portales rode with Chato and his gang, that shot-gun told us that. Now I ain't bothered if you were in the murderous bunch who killed the Eastern hunters and stole their fancy guns and gear, all I want to know is where Chato's hole-up is. Give me that information, pronto-like, and you'll be free to go. But only in the direction I point you in.' Luke grinned an all-tooth grim smile. 'I can't have you asskickin' it back to your boss and telling him that some *hombres* are comin' in to kill him.'

A nerve-twitching-faced Baxter looked up at his captor. He saw nothing in the tall, horse-faced son-of-a-bitch's frozen-eyed gaze that gave him any comfort. 'You can't let that old man use his knife on me, mister!' he pleaded, throat dry with fear. 'It . . . it ain't Christian for a white man to carve up another white man!'

Baldy laughed. 'Do you hear that, Mr Culpepper? He's talkin' there about Christians. And I bet the murderin' sonuvabitch has bein' doin' the Devil's work since he could cock a pistol. He sure ain't been handing the Bibles out when he rode with the comancheros.' He knelt down and ripped open their prisoner's shirt and laid the knife close to his chest. Scowling, he snarled, 'Now quit stallin' and tell my pard what he wants to know, or so help me I'll start cuttin'!'

Baxter's eyes widened with terror. He gave a deep hiss of pain and drew back hard against the tree as he felt the heat of the blade and smelt the acrid stench of his singed chest hair. Yet, stubbornly, he refused to talk. He was hanging on to the desperate hope his captors were bluffing against the sure certainty that Chato would see he died real hard and painful if he found out he had betrayed him.

Baldy raised the stakes in the bluffing game by slashing the knife across the comanchero's chest, a trickling red line following the point of the blade.

Campbell, making himself busy at the horse lines, heard the shrill scream. He listened, nerves twanging painfully, but heard no more tortured cries. He prayed it wasn't because Mr Springer had been too heavy-handed with his knife and killed their prisoner. There and then he decided, if he was alive after all this was over, and still a Pinkerton agent, he would cry off taking any assignment west of the Mississippi. The brutal, cold-blooded way justice was administered out here, west of the Pecos, turned his stomach; he wanted no part of it.

Baxter broke. 'I'll talk, I'll talk!' the words bubbling out as hysterically as his scream. 'Just don't let that white-Injun work on me with his knife any more!'

Luke breathed a silent gasp of relief. Baldy's playacting — he hoped it was just that — had scared the wits out of their prisoner.

'There, Mr Springer,' he said. 'I know you'll be a mite disappointed at not sheddin' any more of this *hombre*'s blood but I told you he would soon see reason when he knew we meant business and tell us what we want to know.' Luke cold-smiled down at their captive. 'But don't put your big knife away just yet in case this *hombre* is tryin' to play us along. If he is, you can show him what real pain is.'

Baldy stood up, still wearing his mad-eyed scowl. 'If the sonuvabitch is stallin', Mr Culpepper, then you won't be able to stop me from slicin' him up. I've kinda worked myself up for some blood-lettin'. Ain't done any since I left the high plains.'

Baxter looked up in horror at Baldy.

He knew the painful manner of death Chato would give him if he found out he had betrayed him, but that possible death was forty miles away. An equally agonizing death was only inches from his nose, in the hands of a man as blood-mad as Chato.

'Chato's camp is forty miles north-west of here,' he said. 'Cut through those mountains you can see, until you come across a crick. Follow it due east until you come across two pointed peaks and you'll be almost at the camp.' Baxter didn't tell his captor that Chato had double guards posted on four lookout posts, day and night, on the last half-mile of the trail into the camp. The three bastards would be dead a long ways before they reached the camp.

Luke saw the light of that hopeful thought in the comanchero's eyes. He grinned. 'We ain't so foolish as to ride right up to the stronghold's front door. When we go in we'll go in Injun-style, quietly and quickly. Isn't that so, Mr Springer?' Baldy beamed at Baxter.

Which to the comanchero, losing his last ray of hope that his pain and the killing of Felix and Jose would be avenged, seemed as frightening as the old bastard's scowl.

'Is Chato at the camp now?' Luke asked. Baldy waved his knife in front of Baxter's face and made to go down on his knees alongside him. 'Take it easy, Mr Springer,' Luke said. 'Give the *hombre* time to answer. He's been co-operative up till now. He knows how painful it will be if he turns awkward.'

'Yeah, he's there,' Baxter said. And to show how co-operative he was being, he added, 'Though he'll be ridin' out tomorrow, south, to the Rio Grande to meet up with a Comanche chief. And that's all I can tell you!'

'OK, OK,' Luke said. 'I believe you. Now that just leaves us with the problem of what to do with you, friend.'

'But you promised I'd go free if I told you what you wanted!' Baxter cried. 'I had nothin' to do with the killing of those dude hunters! The two Mexes you shot in Portales were in on the raid, that's how they came by that shotgun!'

Before he could answer the comanchero, Luke heard Baldy gasp, 'Where the hell did they come from!' He turned and saw five riders picking their way through the trees.

'Not by the way we come into the timber,' replied Luke, eyes narrowing in concern. 'But it's too late to do anything about it. They ain't some of Chato's bunch, or they would have come in shootin', but if they favour one side or the other in the Lincoln County trouble it would be advisable not to go for our guns, or they could take it that we support the opposite faction. I only hope Mr MacColl is OK.'

'They're only kids, Mr Culpepper,' Baldy said in surprise.

'That may be true,' Luke said. 'But they're armed up and as tetchy-lookin' as growed-up *pistoleros*. We'll have to try and sweet-talk our way out of any trouble those kids are bringin' in with them, Mr Springer.'

Campbell saw the riders enter the timber and dropped flat to the ground, trusting that the horses' legs would shield him from the riders who rode past the horse line and right up to the camp. He had just decided to go back to the camp to see how the prisoner was faring. Mr Culpepper and Mr Springer's attitudes to law-enforcing could never be his way, but they were his partners and he had to stand by them. And that standing by them was here right now; his partners could be in danger. He put aside all his worrying thoughts about how law and order issues were dealt with west of the Pecos and reached up and drew out Mr Springer's shotgun from the pack on Jethro's saddle and began belly-crawling towards the camp.

Baxter's face lit up in a hopeful smile when he saw the riders. 'Billy!' he yelled. 'These bastards have took me prisoner! They're workin' on me with a knife like some heathen Injuns!'

Billy the Kid leaned forward in his

174

saddle, elbows resting on the saddle horn and cast a curious glance at the two 'white' Indians. He wasn't someone who was easily rattled but the two men unsettled him somewhat. They were men who wouldn't be intimidated by his reputation in the territory, if they knew who he was. Press them into a corner, Billy thought, and the old man with the Indian haircut would leap at him and slice him open with that big pig-sticker he was toting, even if he emptied his Colt into him. As for his pard, he had the unwavering, all-seeing look of Marshal Pat Garrett. The tall man was a lawman, or at one time wore a peace-officer's badge. Prod him and he would get trouble.

Marshal Garrett was the reason he and his boys were making for the dog-dirt town of Portales. Garrett and his shoot-on-sight posse were making things too hot for him across at Fort Sumner, pressing him hard enough to force them to stay clear of the main trail to Portales and skulk along dry washes and gullies like hunted game. Otherwise they wouldn't have spotted the camp and came to see who was at the fire. And here they were, Billy opined, out of Pat Garrett's skillet and into two hard-faced *hombres'* fire — if he pushed the bastards to a showdown. The flames of that fire suddenly licked around Billy's ass as he heard the ominous clicks of the hammers of a shotgun being drawn back. Billy cursed softly and stayed resting forward on his saddle.

'We're not seeking any trouble, mister,' Campbell said, voice hard and steadier than he was feeling. 'I take it you men are actively engaged in the war we have heard is going on in the county. Well, we have no part in that conflict. Our war is with Chato and his comancheros. But if you think otherwise I'll tell you this, though it goes against my principles; if you make a hostile move against my partners, I'll backshoot with this shotgun. And at this range at least three of you will cease worrying how things are going for your side in the war.'

Billy laughed and straightened up in his saddle. 'You're makin' war against Chato? Do you hear that, Charlie?' he said to the rider alongside him. 'We've rode into the camp of three loco *hombres*. Goin' up against Chato without a company of blue-belly horse soldiers to back you up is one of the fastest ways I know for a *hombre* to get himself dead. I hope you gents don't take it unkindly me tellin' you that. You with the scattergun at my back, you'll get no trouble from me and my boys. You and your pards' plates are heaped with it already, though it ain't hit you yet. Are you lawmen?' a curious Billy asked.

'Vigilantes, you could say, Billy,' Luke said. 'The three of us all have damn good reasons for seeing Chato dead. Kinda blood-for-blood situation.' He fish-eyed Billy. 'It sure upsets me to hear that gringos are killin' each other hereabouts for what reason I don't know, or care about while Chato and his renegades are runnin' free, butcherin' New Mexican women and children. It seems that the so-called *hombres* in the territory ain't got any pressin' intention of tryin' to rope in Chato.'

'Or ain't got the balls, Mr Culpepper,' Baldy said, fierce-eyeing the riders.

'Me and my boys have balls, old man!' Billy said angrily. 'But we've prices on our heads and when lawmen like Marshall Pat Garrett are trailin' us, we need all the time we've got to look out for ourselves. And besides, Chato and his bunch are hard *hombres* to track down. We don't even know where the sonuvabitch rests up!'

'We know where that is, Billy,' Luke said. He jerked a thumb at his prisoner. 'That feller is a comanchero. My pard kinda persuaded him to tell us where Chato's camp is.'

'Comanchero, eh?' Billy said. The look he gave Baxter told the comanchero his plea for help had fallen on deaf ears, and chilled his blood. Billy the Kid had given him the killing look. 'So you know where Chato's camp is,' the Kid continued. He favoured Luke with a mocking buck-toothed grin. 'What are you gonna do, surround it?'

'What we're after,' Luke said calmly, holding on to his temper, 'is to get near enough to the stronghold for Mr Springer to draw a bead on Chato. We know what the bastard looks like. Mr MacColl, who's the gent holdin' the shotgun on you, was Chato's prisoner once. We ain't contemplatin' a stand-up fight with Chato's outfit; all we want is a few seconds of good luck that places Chato, in the back sights of Mr Springer's Sharps, then we hightail it out of there.'

Luke was wishing Billy would do likewise out of their camp. Though Billy had said he wasn't about to cause trouble, wild kids with prices on their heads were unstable characters. And Billy, Luke figured, was a youth of wildly swinging moods: laughing and joking with you one minute then still grinning his toothy smile, capable of gunning you down.

'You can come round front, Mr MacColl,' he said. 'We'll take Billy at his word that he's payin' us a friendly call.' Billy didn't think much of Mr Culpepper's plan to put paid to Chato, less so when Mr MacColl came into view and joined his partners. MacColl had spoken like some high-faluting Yankee lawyer and, when he saw him, Billy knew for certain he was an Eastern dude, not much older than he was. Billy thought he could be lookin' at his grandpappy, pa and elder brother. Mr Culpepper spoke of a few minutes of good luck. In his considered opinion, the three loco *hombres* would need a year's good luck to get anywhere near Chato unseen, let alone kill him.

He told Luke about some of his misgivings about his plan. 'You might not be able to make a run for it, Mr Culpepper,' he said. 'Those comancheros will know their own backyard real well. They'll jump you before you get clear.'

'Chato bein' dead could kinda throw the rest of the comancheros off balance,' Luke said. 'They could want to elect a new leader before doin' anything about the killin' of their old one, like the Injuns do. I grant you it ain't much of a plan, in fact it ain't no plan at all. But we've got ourselves a long ways closer to Chato than when we first started out and if our luck stays with us there's nothin' to stop us from finishin' things in our favour.'

Billy grunted. Crazy or not he had to admire men who were about to ride calmly along a suicide trail. He thought it must be one big hate the trio held against Chato, to want to carry out such a mad-assed plan.

Then Billy had a disturbed feeling: was it because he was upset at being called ball-less? Or was he having pangs of jealousy knowing how high the three *hombres*' rep would be if they succeeded in killing Chato? Out-shining his and his boys standing in the territory; the kids who were running Marshal Pat T. Garrett ragged; who came and went when they pleased, shooting their way out of trouble. Why, the Mexicans sang songs in their cantinas about the wild exploits of Billy the Kid. Even Governor Lew Wallace had offered him a free pardon if he gave himself up peacefully.

Then, surprising himself, he said, 'Boys, what say you if we tag along with these three gents, and if things seem favourable, help them to kill Chato? It'll be a mite more excitin' than sittin' on our asses in some stinkin' bordello in Portales all screwed up in case Garrett and his deputies come poundin' along Main Street to shoot us down like mad dogs.' Billy grinned. 'That's if Mr Culpepper and his pards don't mind ridin' alongside a bunch of desperadoes wanted by the law.'

Charlie Bowdrie, Billy's right-hand man, knew it would be a waste of time trying to talk Billy out of what he thought was the most hare-brained caper the Kid had ever come up with, because he didn't like his schemes criticised. Though this time he felt worried enough, and bold enough, to state his doubts about Billy's suggestion.

'There's a helluva lot more of them comancheros than us, Billy,' he said. 'And if we're lucky to kill Chato, I can't see Marshal Pat Garrett handin' us the reward money. The only thing that long streak of misery will dish out to us is a magazine-load of Winchester shells.'

Billy laughed. 'You worry too much, Charlie. As I said, if we don't like the situation when we get to Chato's hole-up why we just swing round and head for Portales. It ain't like we're soldier boys, and Mr Culpepper ain't our capt'n, orderin' us to do this and that.' He looked at Luke. 'Are you willin' to allow me and my boys to ride with you, Mr Culpepper?'

Luke had already thought he was willing to accept the Devil's help, if the

Devil carried a gun, to kill Chato. While Old Nick had not yet volunteered his services, he was being offered help from men who, he had a gut-feeling, would be meeting up with the Devil before they got much older.

'I have no problem with that, Billy,' he said. 'Neither will my pards. As I said, killin' Chato is all we're interested in. Though I ain't a blue-belly capt'n, I must insist from now on in, Mr Springer will tell us how we ought to do things. We're within forty miles of Chato's stronghold and we don't want to ride there like a bunch of war-time Missouri brush boys raidin' some Kansas free-stater's holdin'. We go in Injun-style, a style Mr Springer has picked up by livin' among the Sioux and the Crow way up in Montana.'

Billy almost told Mr Culpepper that his old pard couldn't have been much of an Indian fighter to allow an Indian to sneak up on him and lift his hair, but to keep friendly with his new partners, he said, 'Me and my boys can move

184

around sneaky-like, Mr Culpepper.' Then looking at the prisoner, he said, 'What about him? He's a comanchero, isn't he, a woman and child killer?' Billy's hand blurred in movement and the Colt it held barked and flamed. Baxter slumped in his bonds, a red stain spreading across his shirt front. The pistol was slipped deftly back into its holster and a smile was back on Billy's face. 'That's one less comanchero we've got to kill, Mr Culpepper. Now we're ready to ride out on your sayso.'

The shooting had happened so fast and unexpectedly that Luke had had no time to explain to Billy he was going to let the comanchero free for being forthcoming with the whereabouts of Chato's camp. And his early reading of Billy riding along the turnpike to Hell had been proved justified. Then, he thought, coldly, siccing killers on to killers seemed good tactics.

The cold-blooded killing had only confirmed Campbell's strongly held belief that God had no part in creating some of the men west of the Pecos.

Though Baldy saw the stark logic of Billy's action, that of never leaving a live enemy behind you, he made a mental note to keep a watchful eye on the young killer. He had seen by the look on Billy's face he was of a rare breed, someone who enjoyed killing. He could get the urge to kill his three new partners.

'We'll break camp right away, Billy,' Luke said. 'We need to check out the approaches to Chato's camp before dark. Then we've got all night to try and come up with some sort of a war plan. I'd be obliged if you ride point, Mr Springer, warn us if we're makin' dust, we don't want to make a hash of it now. Does that sit with you OK, Billy?'

'It's your show, Mr Culpepper,' Billy replied. His kid's grin lit up his face again. 'I'll tell you when it ain't. Now, if you allow my boys to step down we'll finish off that coffee you've got heatin' on the fire while you get packed up.'

13

Baldy hadn't let them down, Luke thought. He had led them to the hills unseen, as far as could make out, and fast. Knowing that Chato was riding south tomorrow, time wasn't on their side. He noticed that even Billy was impressed by the old mountain-man's skill on the trail.

When they reached the creek their prisoner had told them to follow, Baldy suddenly drew up Jethro and began gazing hard at the high ridges ahead of them.

'Mr Culpepper,' he said sharply, 'I think it's advisable to go to ground in yonder rockfall.'

'The old man ain't gettin' nervous, is he, Mr Culpepper?' Billy said. 'Now we're gettin' close to Chato's stronghold? I reckon what with bein' tailed by lawman and bounty hunters, I've got me a fine instinct for sensin' trouble comin' my way and it ain't sendin' me any alarm signals right now.'

Luke grinned. 'Me neither, Billy. But Jethro, Mr Springer's mule can smell comancheros, or the part-Injuns who run with Chato, hereabouts. See the mule's ears stickin' up? That's a warnin' sign.'

Billy's eyes widened in disbelief. 'You're ribbin' me, ain't you, Mr Culpepper?'

'Billy,' Luke said, as he swung down from his mount, 'if you want to stay alive you'd better believe it. That mule don't kid. Make for those rocks as Mr Springer says.'

'OK, boys,' Billy said, albeit reluctantly, still doubting Luke's word. 'Do the old man's biddin'. But if any one of you tells any *hombre* we took orders from a dumb-ass mule, so help me I'll plug him.'

Once sheltered by the rocks, Baldy explained to Luke what his next moves were. 'I'll scout ahead on foot,' he said.

He grinned at Billy. 'As Jethro's told us, there's comancheros close by. That prisoner of ours didn't tell us Chato had lookouts posted in these canyons; he was hopin' we'd walk slap bang into them.'

When Baldy was ready to move out, he was stripped to the waist and had marked his face, Indian-style, with moistened dirt and was only armed with his Bowie. With a curt nod to Luke, he slipped out between the rocks and was gone from their view in a matter of minutes.

'He's more Injun than a real bronco,' Billy said. 'I don't scare easily, but I wouldn't care to meet up with the old goat in the dark, especially when he's heftin' that big-bladed knife.'

'That's what he's doin', Billy,' replied Luke. 'Actin' like an Injun. If he's unlucky enough to get captured or killed by the comancheros, what with bein' scalped and all, they'll take him for a lone crazy white man. Not one of a band of men comin' in to raid them.'

Luke was having second thoughts about taking Billy and his gang as allies. His plan for seeing Chato dead was for Baldy to be perched on some rock high above the camp, with MacColl, using his army glasses to point Chato out to Baldy. Then it was all up to the old man and his Sharps. Afterwards they'd pull out fast. Billy, he opined wouldn't want to sit on his ass when lead was flying around; he'd want to take part in the action. And they weren't strong enough to have a shoot-out with a whole gang of killers, and pull through.

★   ★   ★

Luke began to worry; Baldy had been out almost three hours and it was coming on dark. He had heard no sounds of gunfire so unless Baldy had been killed silently, he assumed he was still alive. He heard Jethro whinny and stamp his feet. Luke smiled his relief: Baldy was on his way in.

Billy was half asleep up against a

rock, wishing he had taken his boys to Portales after all; this waiting was boring the pants off him. Suddenly, in front of his nose a dirt-painted face appeared as from out of nowhere. Billy jerked upright. 'Jesus!' he gasped 'You almost scared the crap outa me, old man!'

Baldy grinned. 'If I'd been a real bronco, Billy, I would have had your hair hangin' on my belt. Which would have been a shame because you and your boys are goin' to get all the shootin' you can handle. Come across with me to Mr Culpepper and I'll explain how I think we could not only put paid to Chato, but most of his murderous bunch.'

The killing ground was a bluff overlooking the comancheros' camp, Baldy told them. Loose soil and shale for the first hundred feet or so, then levelling off halfway up into a rocky and brush-covered strip of ground, then climbing again to the ridge peak. 'I'll be up on the top ridge,' Baldy said. 'And start needlin' the sonsuvbitches with the Sharps. When they see it's only one man with a single-shot rifle who's puttin' them down for good they'll come up that bluff seekin' my blood. They'll have to use both hands to haul themselves up that first stretch of the bluff so they'll not have their guns drawn.' Baldy favoured them all with a fierce bronco-grin. 'When they make it to the ledge, you gents, hunkered down in the brush, will be able to shoot them down as slick as the Sioux wiped out Custer's command way up there on the Rosebud. Then I reckon eight Winchesters, rapid firin', should send the comancheros left down below in the camp harin' for safer holes.'

It seemed a better plan than his, Luke thought, though he did raise a point. 'What about Chato?' he asked Baldy. 'Do you want Mr MacColl up there with you on the ridge to point him out?'

'Naw,' Baldy replied. 'I'm firin' at buffalo-gun range. Mr MacColl will serve our cause better by being with you bushwhackers.'

The plan seemed mad-assed enough to please Billy. He was always willing to take a chance if it was exciting enough, and if shooting came into it. Though he did ask Baldy how he knew so much about the lie of the land at the stronghold. Good-naturedly he said, 'Did you walk bold-assed right into the camp, Mr Springer? And ask them where the best spot was for a fella to shoot down on them?'

'Something like that, Billy,' Baldy said, matching Billy's humour. 'Why, one of them offered me some coffee and beans, but I had to decline, tellin' him I had to get back and put some youngsters to bed. And that will be only for a coupla hours 'til the moon gets up. Then you're all goin' to sweat your balls off doin' some hard climbin'.'

14

Chato was in a good mood. He was sitting in a battered old hide armchair at one of the campfires, drawing contentedly on a fine gringo cigar. Felix, one of his lieutenants, had sent word back from Portales that the army patrols searching the territory for him were now far west of Fort Sumner. That information meant he would have a clear run south to the border with his band for a rendezvous with the Comanche chief, White Eagle.

It would be a good trade, Chato opined. He had much to offer White Eagle, guns, ammunition, whiskey and white women. Chato's lips curled in the shadow of what passed for a smile on the all-bone face. Maybe not virgins, he had seen to that, but strongly built women, able to work hard for the chief and provide enjoyment for him at night

194

on his blanket. White Eagle would trade horses and cattle in exchange. Felix and Jose, and the gringo, Baxter, were due back before noon and as soon as they rode in he would give the order to ride for the Rio Grande.

A sour-faced Howling Wolf, wrapped up in his blanket, at a nearby fire, gazed angrily into the flames. He wished he had the 'breed, Chato, dangling on the end of a rope over them, savouring the pleasure of his screams as his flesh began to roast. His grand dreams of riding out of Chato's camp with twenty or so Winchester repeating rifles and belts of shells, enabling him to double the strength of his band, had come to naught. The guns Chato had traded with him for the Mexican gold were old, single-shot rifles, some with worn-out barrels and broken stocks. The 'breed had made him lose face as a chief in front of his warriors. 'Warriors'. Howling Wolf spat in the fire. He had allowed his men to have several bottles of whiskey so they could forget their disappointment at not being the proud owners of repeating rifles. Now they were sprawled out in a drunken stupor, the unblooded boys lying in their own vomit.

The hatred he felt for Chato burned like a flaming brand in Howling Wolf's chest. Somehow, he promised himself, he would have to kill the comanchero dog or he would never get any peace of mind in this life or the life he was destined to live when his time came to pass through the gateway of death.

Luke, crouched low in the brush, alongside Campbell and Charlie Bowdrie, waited impatiently for Baldy to start the small war. He opined the old man was waiting for the last of the night mist to clear away from the camp before he opened up with the Sharps. The camp was waking up, men relieving themselves, women building up the fires ready for cooking meals. Luke wanted to catch the comancheros still half asleep, with their pants more or less down. It had been a hazardous trail from the lonely graves on the Pecos, and now his moment of truth was only the sound of a rifle shot away. Luke thought that Billy and the rest of his boys, in the brush on the other side of the track the comancheros would have to follow to get to Baldy, were feeling just as edgy.

Billy also wanted the action to start, to make someone pay for his aching feet. The old man had led them up hills, down into canyons and draws until he didn't know if he was still in New Mexico or the Texas Panhandle. He wasn't quite sure whether Mr Springer had Indian blood in him but he was certain he was part goat. He had brought them down into the brush without pausing for a rest or to wonder in which direction he should head, then hauled himself back up the ridge they had just come down from. Billy hoped the old goat hadn't tired himself out and fallen asleep up there, or by hell he'd stroll down into that camp and start the war himself.

Baldy laid the Sharps' sights on a comanchero standing at one of the fires. He had seen no signs of a man wearing a fancy-looking Mexican officer's tunic that young MacColl told him Chato rigged himself out in. Once he started the killing, the sly murdering son-of-a-bitch whould soon show himself; then by hell, Baldy thought, he would be dead. He pulled the trigger and the Sharps kicked and barked flame and smoke.

Howling Wolf saw a comanchero flung backwards from a fire, arms grabbing wildly at the air, and fall to the ground, dead as any man he had seen killed. Then he heard the resounding crack of the gun that had fired the deadly shot. It was the gun that killed from great distances, the weapon of the old white-eye who had warned him with the same gun not to attack him and his *compadre*. The two white-eyes, he thought must hold great hatred for Chato and have the fearless courage of Cheyenne dog soldiers to attack so many of their enemies.

Howling Wolf sprang to his feet as another comanchero fell victim to the long gun, and began poking his men in the ribs with his rifle to rouse them out of their drunken sleep. It was time they rode out of the camp before they got shot. He owed no loyalty to Chato to fight alongside him, and he was beholden to the old white-eye for not killing him on their first meeting. And while the comancheros were busy fighting their battle he would help himself to some of the repeating rifles that were in crates on a wagon near where their horses were tethered.

It was as though he was shooting into a herd of buffalo to Baldy, targets that he couldn't miss. Methodically, every five or six seconds he sent a comanchero on his road to hell. Turning the once quiet camp into an uproar of shouting and cursing men, running every which way to seek shelter from the deadly fire. Added to the noise, were the screams and cries of the terrified women and children.

Chato brought some order into the chaos raging all around him. The sound of the first shot had him leaping out of his chair, his cigar dropping from a mouth open wide in alarm. He dived for cover behind the nearest wagon and began, frantically, to take stock of the situation that had suddenly burst upon him. It wasn't long before he realized it wasn't a full-scale attack on the camp by US cavalry. He started dirty-mouthing. one lone gunman was killing his men. He stood up and ran across to the nearest bunch of his men who were firing their rifles at the sniper on the ridge behind a barricade of crates.

'You loco bastards!' he screamed, waving his pistol at them. 'The sonuvabitch is out of range! We've got to go up there and take him! And take him alive so we can kill him slowly!'

By curses and threats to shoot them if they didn't follow him, Chato rallied about a dozen of his men, then they set off in a crouching low, zigzag run for the bluff. Baldy hadn't intended on firing on them, his whole plan was to draw the comancheros on to him, and into the ambush until he saw one of the leading comancheros wore an officer's tunic. Baldy smiled. He didn't think God answered old sinners' prayers. He thumbed a load into the Sharps and drew a bead on the comanchero chief.

A comanchero slightly ahead of Chato slipped sideways on a patch of loose shale and caught the shot that was meant for Chato. His head blew apart in a bloody mess of bone and brains. His body fell against Chato's, knocking him to his knees. He fell flat on his face and slid down to the bottom of the bluff.

Which suited Chato well. It had not been a good idea being up front with his men wearing his *federale* officer's tunic. He knew the shot had been meant for him and the sniper wasn't going to have another chance to shoot off his head. Bruised and bleeding, Chato began belly crawling along the foot of the bluff, seeking a hole to lie up in until his men brought down the sniper, every few yards casting a fearful glance upwards to make sure he was out of sight of the killing gun.

Baldy swore. He had had Chato in his sights and missed the son-of-a-bitch. He took a quick glance down but got no sighting of him so he looked for a new target.

'Get ready, Mr MacColl,' Luke said softly. 'They're here!'

Campbell saw a ragged line of comancheros come into view then bunch up to make it through the brush. Several of them began to unsling their rifles from their shoulders, or draw their pistols. It was Billy who opened up the killing time, firing non-stop from the hip with his rifle. Then a deadly hail of Winchester shells from both clumps of brush swept the comancheros off their feet as though blown down by a high wind. Some lay where they fell, others tumbled back down the bluff setting the whole of the loose face moving. The few comancheros who had been following them turned and took off in a sliding, jumping run to escape the wall of rocks thundering down on them, and kept on running once they had reached the flat in the desperate haste of men who knew they had lost the day.

A Rebel-yelling Billy came out of the brush, his smile reaching his ears when he saw the comancheros fleeing for the horse lines. When Luke and the rest of the bushwhackers joined him, he said, excitedly, 'We whupped them, Mr Culpepper. We whupped them good!'

'That we did, Billy,' replied Luke. 'You can put your guns down, *amigos*, we've done enough killin' this day. We'll go down now and tell the womenfolk the fight's over and they can tend to their wounded. Mr MacColl can check over the bodies to see if Chato's body's among them. Is that OK, boy?'

'OK, Mr Culpepper,' Campbell replied. Though he didn't relish turning over dead bodies to see if one of them was Chato's. He had read about massacres in his history books at school, but never in his wildest dreams had he thought he would be taking an active part in one. He felt blood drained.

The sudden burst of rifle fire changed Howling Wolf's plans of getting hold of the new rifles. It was a good killing-day for the old white-eye and his *compadres*; he didn't want himself and his band added to that total. While the old man may have saved his life, he could expect no mercy from the men with the rifles. All Indians off the agency were shot down like mad dogs. He shouted at his men to pick up the rifles of the dead comancheros, but to be quick if they wanted to live.

Then the Great Spirit smiled on Howling Wolf, or so he thought, when he saw Chato hiding behind a close-by hut. Chato only realized the danger he was in when he felt a split-second of blinding pain as Howling Wolf's rifle butt struck him hard on the head, then everything went black for him. Part-carrying, part-dragging, Howling Wolf got the unconscious Chato to the horses and slung him across the back of a saddled beast. Leaping on to his own pony he led his warriors out of the camp in a dust-raising gallop.

Baldy had joined them when Campbell came back to report to Luke that Chato's body wasn't among the dead or wounded, news which set the disappointed Luke cursing. The Devil, he thought bitterly, looked out for its own. Baldy also did some cursing.

'And I had the sonuvabitch in my sights, and missed him!' He shrugged. 'Still we've done ourselves proud here.'

'You and your boys better move out, Billy,' Luke said. 'All the firin' could be drawin' men here you'll not be overjoyed to meet up with. And thanks for your help. Without it we couldn't have wiped out this sidewinder's nest.'

Billy grinned. 'It helped to pass the time for us, Mr Culpepper. Better than sittin' on our asses drinkin' in some bar. And it's been a pleasure to have made your acquaintance.' He winked at Baldy. 'We'll get those cows and horses that're wanderin' about round-up and drive them towards Fort Sumner. It'll give Pat Garrett something to do; other than chase after us, he can sort out who they belong to.'

'Billy,' Luke said poker-faced. 'Far be it from me to try and lead youngsters off the straight and narrow, but if I was you I'd drive those critters across into Texas. The money you get for them will pay for the shells you've used and tide you over for chow, or whatever, for the next few weeks. Count it as the reward the state owes you but you ain't in a position to get.'

'Why didn't you think of that, Billy?' Charlie Bowdrie said, wide-smiling. 'You reckon to be boss of this outfit.'

Billy pushed back his hat and scratched his head. 'I dunno, Charlie,' he said. 'M'be it's because I'm a river-baptized Christian and such sinful thoughts like cattle-liftin' ain't entered my head. It's sure got me puzzled.'

Baldy burst out into a cackling laugh. 'And m'be the hair will grow back on my head! Now go about your thievin' business before we all get religion!'

15

It was still a downcast and silent Luke who rode alongside his two *compadres*, keeping his own counsel on the trail to Fort Sumner. Baldy, seeing how disappointed Luke was at not having paid his beholden debt in full by killing Chato, tried to lift up his spirits.

'We did better than we could have honestly expected, Mr Culpepper,' he said. 'Did better than all those soldier boys who've been chasin' their asses all this time tryin' to hunt down Chato. We've cleared Chato outa his stronghold for good. Though the sonuvabitch slipped through our fingers, his raidin' days are over for a long spell, if not for good, bein' we wiped out most of his men.'

'Yeah, you're right, Mr Springer,' replied Luke shaking off his gloomy feelings. He thin-grinned. 'We didn't do too bad for three loco *hombres*. And young Billy and his boys were happy at the outcome. They're only a bunch of kids, but I ain't seen anyone enjoy killing as much as they did.'

Billy and his young *pistoleros* had left them back along the trail, whooping and joking, to drive the sixty or so longhorns and horses east across into Texas for a quick, no-questions-asked sale.

'You boys take care of yourselves now,' Luke had told them when they were ready to move out. 'And thanks again for your help, we couldn't have pulled it off without your guns.' He grinned at Billy. 'If we meet the law on our way to Fort Sumner and they ask us if we know of your whereabouts, I'll tell them I ain't even heard of a *pistolero* called Billy the Kid.'

'I'd take kindly to that, Mr Culpepper,' Billy replied. 'I don't hanker having that long streak of a lawman Pat Garrett and his hangin' posse catch up with us herdin' these cows to the border.' Billy then stood up in his stirrups and yelled, 'Get these critters moving, boys!'

The three of them watched their former allies until all they could see of them was the trail dust of the cattle.

'I must have Injun blood in me, Mr Culpepper,' Baldy said. 'But I can smell death hangin' over those kids' heads.'

'They are takin' part in a war, Mr Springer,' Luke said. 'And men get killed in such-like activities. And we'd better keep a sharp eye out for any trouble on the trail, or we could end up bein' casualities in a war we know damn all about.'

'Mr Culpepper,' Campbell said, 'I'm disappointed as you we didn't send Chato to Hell, but we did our best. And an Eastern dude thanks you both for giving him back his self-respect — his very life for that matter.'

'You paid your debt back, Mr MacColl,' Luke said. 'By savin' two stupid old farts' necks with that sneaky pistol of yours. You're a good man to have walked the line with, Mr MacColl. Now ain't that so, Mr Springer?'

'I ain't the most sociable of characters, Mr MacColl,' Baldy said. Pick and choose who I ride with.' He grinned. 'There ain't no good reason for you to stay here in New Mexico; Chato will be pushin' his horse across the Rio Grande by now to hole-up in Mexico someplace but if you're loco enough to step this side of the Pecos again and you want a pard, well, providin' me and Jethro are still movin' around, I'll ride with you.'

Campbell's face hardened suddenly. 'I'll have to make it east of the Pecos first, Mr Springer. And we've just picked up some company who could have a say in that. See!' He pointed behind his partners' shoulders.

Luke and Baldy twisted ass in their saddles and saw the line of hostiles. Luke swore. 'Well, I'll be damned! That's the same bunch who tried to hurrah us way back along the trail to Silver Butte to have words with you, Mr Springer.'

'And I sent that chief a message, a Sharps' slug close to his head, tellin' him not to mess about with us.' Baldy said. 'It seems he didn't read it right.' He drew out the Sharps. 'It looks that now they're all armed up with long guns they mean business this time.'

'And here's one of the red devils comin' at us!' Luke growled, pulling out his own rifle. 'It could be a young blood wantin' to prove his manhood. That big gun of yours, Mr Springer, must still have them worried, the rest of them're keepin' their distance. What do we do, stand and fight here, or make a run for it? You're the Injun expert.'

For several seconds, Baldy keen-eyed the rider coming in at a walking pace before, he thought grimly, the son-of-a-bitch chose the moment to ribkick his pony into a suicidal dash to claim a white-eye's scalp. Baldy sighed; he had tried hard not to have a war with the warband. He swung the Sharps up to his shoulder, only to quickly lower it again as a smile creased his face.

'It just goes to show, Mr Culpepper,' he said. 'It ain't wise to judge a fella too hastily. That ain't a young buck comin' in with blood in his eyes; though I ain't seen him before I reckon it's Mr Chato up on that horse. Is that so, Mr MacColl?'

'Good Lord!' Campbell gasped. 'You could be right, Mr Springer. Though I'll know for certain when I can get a closer look at his face.' He looked enquiringly at Baldy. 'But why? Why did the chief send Chato to us?'

'You're seein' an Injun honourin' his debt, Mr MacColl,' replied Baldy. 'Many of us white-eyes would find a way out of paying our debts; some have been known to kill rather than settle their dues. That chief is givin' us Chato's life for me allowin' him to keep his. He reasoned we must want Chato badly, or why would we attack his stronghold with so few men. You go out and bring him in, Mr MacColl, before the murderin' bastard falls off his horse. He don't look too steady in the saddle.'

213

Baldy raised the Sharps above his head, the peace gesture, then let out a bubbling Sioux victory call. Howling Wolf blinked his eyes in surprise. Who was this old white-eye, he thought, who knew the ways of the Indian? It was good they had not fought. He had the 'breed Chato's scalp, both his and the old white-eye's honour had been satisfied. He cupped his hands to his mouth.

Baldy grinned and lowered the Sharps as he heard the barking, wolf-like call. He saw the chief raise his own rifle above his head, then the war band turned away from them in a flurry of hoof-raising dust and rode south. He would liked to have passed the time of day with the chief, Baldy thought.

'Mr Culpepper,' he said. 'A half-crazy Eastern dude, a bunch of wild-ass kids, an Injun chief and an old man who oughta be sittin' in a rockin' chair on some front stoop, ain't much of an army, but it proved good enough for you to pay back what you felt you owed those poor Germans lyin' in those graves back there along the Pecos.'

'How the hell could we not pull it off, pard,' Luke said, smiling, 'when I had a mule taggin' along that could smell trouble as far away as the next county?' Face serious, he added, 'I'd like the kid to take Chato in, if it's OK with you?'

'It's OK by me,' replied Baldy. 'It'll buck him up no end, give him back his pride, if he ain't got it back already. And, as you said, if it hadn't been for the kid's quick thinkin', me and you wouldn't be havin' this conversation.'

'Mr Culpepper! Mr Springer!' they both heard Campbell yell out as he reined-led Chato's horse towards them. 'Chato's been scalped!'

A shock faced Campbell drew up alongside them. 'It's Chato all right,' he said. 'He's hardly alive. Only being tied to his saddle has kept him on his horse.'

Luke and Baldy gazed impassively at the slouch-backed figure of Chato, and his bloodstained gargoyle's mask of a head.

'Yeah, I guess he's feelin' sorry for himself right now,' Baldy said. 'M'be reflectin' on his evil ways and all the grief and pain he's inflicted on folk in the state. Well, the rope round his neck at Fort Sumner will put an end to his pain this side of Hell.' He kneed his horse nearer to Chato's mount to take a closer look at the comanchero chief. 'Don't fret none, Mr MacColl,' he said. 'The sonuvabitch won't turn his toes up on us, he'll live to dance on air at Fort Sumner.'

★   ★   ★

They had been three days at Fort Sumner and seen Chato quickly paying for all his years of killing and robbing, the whole town turning out to see him hang. A wide-smiling Campbell told Luke and Baldy he'd had a Western Union wire from Alan Pinkerton offering him the post as field director at the new office the agency was opening at Fort Worth, Texas.

216

'I did promise myself,' he said, 'I'd never come west again if I remained a Pinkerton, but director is a position I can't turn down. I only hope I can hold the job down, Mr Culpepper.'

'Mr MacColl,' Luke replied, fatherly, 'you'll do just fine. In fact you have proved to me and Mr Springer you're capable of commanding a company of Texas Rangers, and they come no tougher and more ornery than those *hombres*. You take the job with your ex-pards' blessin's.'

Campbell said his farewells to them then left to ride north to Sante Fe there to catch an east-bound train to Texas and his new post.

'I'm heading Texas way myself, Mr Springer, Big Springs,' Luke said. 'My old pa owned a piece of land there. I reckon it's more than a mite run down by now, but it's big enough to run several hundred head of cattle on it. You're welcome to make the trip with me, Mr Springer. You mountain men are expert cabin builders.' He grinned.

"'Course, tendin' cows might be too quiet and peaceful for an old hell-raiser.'

'Mr Culpepper,' Baldy said, 'me and Jethro crave peace and quietness. We've been seekin' that since we drifted into New Mexico. Some men have a lustin' for women, some crave hard liquor, me — and I've never told this to anyone but Jethro before — I have a great longin' to be able to rest peacefully in a real bed, boots and clothes off, before I die. I'm too old for cold camps and tryin' to sleep on hard ground. And I reckon Jethro wouldn't curl up his lip at sleepin' in a barn. Mr Culpepper, I'll build you a fine cabin, tend woollies if I have to, my wanderin' days are over.'

'I'm pleased to hear that, Mr Springer,' Luke said. 'You're my first hirin'. Now let's get some supplies for the trail, pard, and get the hell outa Lincoln County in case we get dragged into young Billy's goddamned war.' He grinned at Baldy. 'We ain't got the Mole ridin' with us to pull us outa the crick if we get into deep water. We two old has-beens will have to fend for ourselves from now on in.'

THE END

We do hope that you have enjoyed reading this large print book.

Did you know that all of our titles are available for purchase?

We publish a wide range of high quality large print books including:
Romances, Mysteries, Classics
General Fiction
Non Fiction and Westerns

Special interest titles available in large print are:
The Little Oxford Dictionary
Music Book, Song Book
Hymn Book, Service Book

Also available from us courtesy of Oxford University Press:
Young Readers' Dictionary
(large print edition)
Young Readers' Thesaurus
(large print edition)

For further information or a free brochure, please contact us at:
Ulverscroft Large Print Books Ltd.,
The Green, Bradgate Road, Anstey,
Leicester, LE7 7FU, England.
Tel: (00 44) **0116 236 4325**
Fax: (00 44) **0116 234 0205**

BRAZOS STATION

Clayton Nash

Caleb Brett liked his job as deputy sheriff and being betrothed to the sheriff's daughter, Rose. What he didn't like was the thought of the sheriff moving in with them once they were married. But capturing the infamous outlaw Gil Bannerman offered a way out because there was plenty of reward money. Then came Brett's big mistake — he lost Bannerman and was framed. Now everything he treasured was lost. Did he have a chance in hell of fighting his way back?

DEAD IS FOR EVER

Amy Sadler

After rescuing Hope Bennett from the clutches of two trailbums, Sam Carver made a serious mistake. He killed one of the outlaws, and reckoned on collecting the bounty on Lew Daggett. But catching Sam off-guard, Daggett made off with the girl, leaving Sam for dead. However, he was only grazed and once he came to, he set out in search of Hope. When he eventually found her, he was forced into a dramatic showdown with his life on the line.

SMOKING STAR

B. J. Holmes

In the one-horse town of Medicine Bluff two men were dead. Sheriff Jack Starr didn't need the badge on his chest to spur him into tracking the killer. He had his own reason for seeking justice, a reason no-one knew. It drove him to take a journey into the past where he was to discover something else that was to add even greater urgency to the situation — to stop Montana's rivers running red with blood.

BLACK RIVER

Adam Wright

John Dyer has come to the insignificant little town of Black River to destroy the last living reminder of his dark past. He has come to kill. Jack Hart is determined to stop him. Only he knows the terrible truth that has driven Dyer here, and he knows that only he can beat Dyer in a gunfight. Ex-lawman Brad Harris is after Dyer too — to avenge his family. The stage is set for madness, death and vengeance.